The Great Snap

a novel

Christine M. Alward

BookLocker
Trenton, Georgia

Print ISBN: 978-1-64719-946-3
Ebook ISBN: 978-1-64719-947-0

Published by BookLocker.com, Inc., Trenton, Georgia.

Printed on acid-free paper.

The characters and events in this book are fictitious. Any similarity to real persons, living or dead, is coincidental and not intended by the author.

BookLocker.com, Inc.
2022

First Edition

Library of Congress Cataloguing in Publication Data
Alward, Christine M.
The Great Snap by Christine M. Alward
Library of Congress Control Number: 2022902600

To my late mother, Rose.

Thank you to my children. You're my everything.

Special thanks to Michael Patrick Shiels and Jennifer Christiansen.

Aaron Christopher Sizemore. I'll miss you until I take my last breath. I couldn't have done this without you. "My soul loves you."

Chapter One

2016
"Looking at You"
by MC5

"Am I about to get fucked, Jack? Just give it to me straight. I know it can't be good." said Nicolina Carlson-Pratt, looking lovely in a black Jessica Simpson sundress. She was already in such a state, that she had begun to lose her manners and class when speaking to her late father's best friend and lawyer.

Nicolina, "Lina" as most called her, was impeccably made up, with every blonde hair in place, and sporting a fresh manicure. Her closest friend, Ricky, had advised that the dress brand was perfect, as most noted that Lina herself resembled a trim Jessica Simpson, with Liz Taylor's violet eye color. She had decided if she was going to be broken on the inside, she should at least look fabulous on the outside.

June's humidity had made its first seasonal appearance in suburban Detroit that week, and the air conditioning at Anson's funeral home struggled to keep the conference room cool. Lina's skin clung to her dress as she shifted anxiously in her seat. She was running on empty in so many ways, and the lack of sleep and nourishment for the last several weeks had amplified her discontent. Terror had set in at the realization that Lina's stepmother was probably controlling her father's assets the same way that she manipulated his life. Everything had happened so fast, and now Lina was sitting across from a man she had known her entire life, at Bill's last big event.

Jack studied the face of Bill's daughter. At forty years old, Lina was just as stunning as she had been in her youth. As pretty as she was, when she opened her mouth and spoke, it was the same direct, no-nonsense words and attitude of his newly-departed old buddy. The Carlson's certainly never minced words.

William "Bill" Carlson, father of Lina, had died just four days earlier. His family had lived in Rochester, Michigan for over eighty years. Bill's father before him, Bill Senior, had started a lumber company in town several decades before. Carlson's Lumber had put Nicolina's grandparents at the top of Rochester society back in the 1940s. They were still considered pillars of their affluent suburban city and of Greater Detroit as a whole. Jack Nelson, Brad Bates, and George Anson all came from original Rochester families and were lifelong friends of her father's. At age sixty-five, the four men, including Bill, had still been shooting skeet together several times a week, and all belonged to the Oakland Creek Country Club, located just north of town.

Jack cleared his throat and spoke calmly, unable to disguise the grief in his voice.

"Now, it's customary to have this meeting after all of the funeral proceedings have ended. But since the guys and I are leaving tomorrow to honor your dad's wishes, I thought we would talk now."

"You're taking his ashes to Lake Superior tomorrow? Already?" asked Lina, incredulously, as her jaw slightly dropped.

Jack was shuffling folders and paperwork around as he answered absentmindedly, "Yes, everyone has the time to do it this weekend. And the weather will be perfect."

I'm completely left out again, she thought.

Lina had moved to Southern California in 1994, after high school graduation, to attend San Diego State University. In her twenty-two-year absence, it was as if everyone had forgotten she existed or that she was Bill's only child.

I should be the one taking his ashes to Lake Superior and making all the decisions, she thought. *Nobody even asked me.*

All of this was simply adding fuel to the fire that had already begun to burn through Lina's peace of mind.

"Are George and Brad going with you? Oh, and by the way...why is George kissing Carol's ass?" asked Lina, becoming more emotional by the second.

"George is not kissing Carol's ass. He owns the funeral home, and she is a client," Jack managed to say before being cut off.

"Am I about to get fucked, Jack?" Lina repeated. She had never sworn in front of her dad's best friend before this day. She was usually very proper and polite around certain company, including her dad's conservative friends. Lina's grief and frustration, along with all the other challenges in her life, had come to a head.

Jack let out a long, apologetic sigh. His face softened into a sympathetic half smile as he sat and looked into Lina's unique eyes. Jack didn't know Lina very well anymore, but he had fond memories of her as a child, and loved his best friend's feisty little girl. He remembered how charming little Lina had been at dinner parties as a child. Like an old soul, laughing at adult jokes and sneaking sips of champagne. But Jack had practiced law for over thirty-five years and knew that legally there wasn't much he was going to be able to do for her.

"You aren't going to be *fucked*, Lina," said Jack in a calm, gentle voice. "Your father left you two life insurance policies and a few of his belongings. He left you his Corvette…"

"What about the house? My *MOTHER'S* house?" interrupted Lina.

Jack took a careful breath before speaking. He had paperwork he was placing in front of her.

"This is the prenup that your dad and Carol signed."

Tears were filling her eyes, causing the words on the page to appear blurry.

Jack spoke again. "While you are the legal owner of the house, Carol is allowed to stay in the home as long as she pleases. As long as she follows the conditions in the prenup."

Lina felt her world crumbling with Jack's words. She was sick to her stomach.

How could my dad do this to me? she thought.

Lina dug deep to control her emotions before speaking again. "What are the conditions?" she asked.

Jack looked at the prenuptial document he had drawn up with Bill before his wedding to Carol. Jack didn't like Carol, but Bill had been a grown man and was free to make his own choices. Jack was just there to legally protect him from his choices.

"She has to pay the mortgage and taxes and keep up on any and all repairs to the property," answered Jack.

One of Lina's tears had escaped down her face. Grabbing a Kleenex from the box on the funeral home desk, she dabbed under her eyes.

Lina spoke again in desperation. "What about everything that is in the house? What about all my mother's things? How is there even a mortgage? This doesn't make any sense!" she said, shaking her head as she spoke. "Jack, I went over there the other night…the night that my dad *died*. I had to beg to be let in the house!"

"My partner will go over the details. Your Dad had clever ways of writing off taxes. The mortgage is relatively new." said Jack, trying to fit a word in.

"How long does she get to stay there? Forever? Is there a deadline? When do I get to occupy the house I own, Jack?"

"There's no deadline, Lina. As long as she follows the conditions, she can live out her days there." said Jack, looking down.

"Jack...her mother just died last year at age one-hundred! My parents died at thirty-five and sixty-five...that bitch is going to outlive me! I don't believe this!" she cried.

Jack understood Lina's emotions. He didn't blame her. "Lina, I did everything I could do when we created the prenup. At least I got him to keep the house legally in your name. Your dad didn't even think he'd need a prenup! I stepped in and had him do it this way. I'll talk to her about the house contents, but unfortunately, Carol was upset with your dad about the prenup. She threatened to call off the ceremony at city hall, so your dad hastily crossed things off the document, to make her happy. Poor guy. He had just thrown her that elaborate engagement party. He didn't want to look like a fool."

Each word that escaped Jack's lips were like loose embers meeting with volcanic ash, that already resided within her. Lina felt her skin flush as there was nowhere for the eruption to escape. Her eye released another tear, but the steam had already traveled to her mind, causing her newly-broken soul to simmer. She felt intense, bottled-up anger towards her father and he was gone.

Lina had only been ten when her mother, Fara Mancini-Carlson, had succumbed to a heart condition. Fara's father, Frank Mancini, had comforted young Lina through her grief. But Grandpa Mancini was gone now too, and Lina had never felt more alone.

"What about my mom's will and trust!?" she countered desperately.

Jack answered her question with a balanced, firm tone. "Your dad became the executor of the trust when your mom passed. He had the legal right to change it."

Lina stared at Jack blankly before speaking.

"This woman was married to him for one year," she said with increasing frustration. "One fucking year! She is the new character that joined the cast, the last ten minutes of my dad's movie…and she is taking half of my money??? The money my mom had made sure was put away for ME? And now Carol is allowed to legally stay in my mother's house that I own?! And I'm just supposed to be cool with it? What the FUCK?!"

In an effort to distract Lina and calm her down, Jack stood calmly and lifted a large box off the counter that had been sitting there the whole time. Lina was so upset, she hadn't noticed it.

"Here is a box containing all of your parents' legal documents. Deeds to properties, copies of birth certificates, passports. Oh…and he left the apartment building downtown to you. Carol gets the place in Cabo. Rest assured, the house at Crystalline Lake is still owned by the Carlson family, of course. You, your Aunt Isobel, and Cousin Miles."

Jack's words became babble to Lina's ears. He may as well have been an adult in the Peanut's cartoons. "*Womp, womp*" was all she heard anymore. There was so much coming at her and she was already struggling in so many ways. Her cheating husband, raising young twins, and readjusting to life in Michigan were already taking a toll. She had hoped to move back into her childhood home, while she contemplated the future of her marriage. Now that plan seemed off the table and her list of responsibilities had grown. She was now landlord of an aging building that would constantly need repairs, and faced the heavy task of pulling off her dad's final construction project for the family business. She felt overwhelmed as the weight of the world seemed to shift and rest on her shoulders.

She looked at the large cardboard box. It had "Carlson" written with a black Sharpie marker in large letters. This box would come to be known as her "orphan box." It contained all of her parents' hopes and dreams. Paperwork they had excitedly signed when buying a new home, documents they had notarized while grieving their own parents, everything that would be important for Lina to have one day. Their whole lives condensed into a neat, brown box to be given to Lina at one of her darkest hours. The box that would aid their only child, as she took over the reins of life for the Carlson family one day.

She had known and buried all of her grandparents. Now, her parents' generation was gone. She could feel her own mortality moving up to the front of the death line.

"Well, my parents are both dead. That means I'm next! I'm a forty-year-old orphan! That generation is gone! I'm next!" exclaimed Lina, now acting and sounding like a crazy woman. Like the homeless people she had seen shout at nobody in the streets of San Diego.

Jack tried to break in. "Lina, you're only fort…"

She cut him off. "FUCK THAT BITCH! FUCK THAT FUCKING WHORE!" She screamed through tears as she rose to leave. A couple of guests who were standing outside the conference room door looked both ways before walking away uncomfortably. An older woman took their place to try to listen. Lina couldn't bear this. She needed some nicotine. Jack spoke, very aware that this woman was breaking before his eyes.

"Lina, try to calm down. Look, I have another trip booked right after I return from Lake Superior. My partner at the firm will handle everything for you in my absence. Just call the office for anything you need. Again, he will go over more details with you about the mortgage and estate."

Lina didn't mean to be rude to Jack. None of this was his fault, but she had lost control of her emotions. Something her father would have criticized her for. The way he had criticized her at her mother's funeral for crying in front of guests at age ten. For appearing weak. For being an outwardly-emotional Italian like her mother. Lina took a deep breath.

"Fine," she said, carefully dabbing her tears as she approached the door. She felt too upset to leave the room and face all those people, but knew she had no choice. Visitation had been in intervals starting the day before, and the final morning service was to be followed by that evening's big banquet, which was scheduled to begin in half an hour. Jack stood to help her with the door.

"I'll have someone bring the box to your house," he said softly. "I'll see you shortly in the banquet hall."

Nicolina Carlson-Pratt simply nodded at Jack and emerged from that conference room a changed woman. An angry woman. A woman who was tired of being nice. A woman who seemed to be losing her cherished childhood home, her husband, and her youth. A woman who no longer had any shits left to give. This was the moment that Lina had snapped.

The thumb had met the middle finger to form the snap a year before, when Lina had first met her father's new wife. Her dad's terminal illness and death had moved the thumb along the middle finger, and the news that her late father's closest friend just delivered had created the official sound. Lina would remain in full snap for the next six months, as her best friend, Ricky, would relay to future generations.

She entered the main parlor. She had to walk through all those people in order to exit the building and get to her car, where her vape pen awaited her. She had quit smoking cigarettes ages before, but had started vaping upon learning her father was terminally ill. She was on a mission. *Must get to vape pen,* she thought. *I need some nicotine before I fucking kill someone.*

Brad Bates stood by the door with a short glass in his hand. Brad was her father's other close friend who would be joining Jack on the ashes trip. As she began to pass him, he leaned into Lina.

"I think this water could use some whiskey," said Brad, already visibly drunk.

Since George Anson was the owner, all the old friends from school had already been permitted to enter the bar area and return to the visitation center with drinks. George himself was grieving and tipping the bottle, so all normal rules went out the window.

Lina flashed some semblance of a smile and kept walking, when she saw a circle of three visibly-intoxicated men. She realized the loudest one, who was joking and laughing with the other two in a yamaka, was her father's dentist, Dr. Stein. The other men were Harvey Glickman and his son, Seth, whom Lina had grown up with.

"Hello, Gentlemen," said Lina politely, while trying to brush past without stopping to chat. Dr. Stein's arm fell around her shoulders.

"I'm so sorry about your father," slurred her dad's dentist. "He was a great guy."

"Thank you," managed Lina, while noting the alcohol on his breath.

As she broke from his drunken embrace, she felt his hand move to her bottom and make a quick squeeze. She ignored the advance and kept heading to the doors. *Dr. Stein did not just grab my ass at my father's funeral. Seriously?!* she thought, craving nicotine more than ever now.

She spotted her Aunt Isobel, arriving fashionably late to her younger brother's visitation.

"Darling," said Aunt Isobel, coming in for a light hug and air kiss. Lina could smell the scotch whiskey on her breath.

"How nice of you to join us. Several of the elders from town have been asking for you," Lina said with polite annoyance.

"Well, I wasn't able to get the proper jewelry from the safe without assistance, my dear. I spent the *entire* day here yesterday and wanted to look my best for the party. You *do* understand, darling," said Aunt Isobel in her high class American/British accent, like someone from the 1950s. Lina had used this form of speaking quite regularly in her own life too. By watching Aunt Isobel, she learned that you can say the bitchiest thing to someone, but if done using an old movie accent and vocabulary, you could get away with it. After all, no one can be angry with a person from the 1950s.

As Aunt Isobel turned away to greet a guest who had just arrived, Lina started working her way toward the door again.

"Lina!" said a familiar female voice. When the woman grabbed Lina's arm, she realized it was Mitzy Hamilton, a bitch she had known in school. Mitzy's father owned the local insurance agency that her family had used for generations, which gave Mitzy a valid reason to attend this event. Mitzy's mother was the librarian at the local public library. Lina hadn't seen Mitzy in years, but knew full well that Mitzy was only there to collect gossip.

"Mitzy! Good to see you. I have to go," said Lina, barely pausing to make eye contact.

Mitzy gently held onto Lina's arm to keep her in place for a moment. "Lina, I am so sorry for your loss." Her face arranged itself in a fake look of deep concern. "I don't know what the inheritance situation is," she said in almost a whisper, while moving her hands in front of her chest as if performing a magic trick with cups, "but we will need to discuss all of that. So be sure to call the office for an appointment!"

Lina had already freed herself from Mitzy's grasp and was walking again. She was a woman on a mission for the sweet relief of nicotine.

"Lina, honey. What did Jack have to say?" asked another female voice. This time it was Denise, the mother of her best friend Ricky. Her wife, Greta Goldman, was standing beside her. Denise was Ricky's biological mother, and Greta had been there since Denise was pregnant. The two women owned the famous *Motown Mood Café* on Main Street and had proudly raised Ricky together. They were also like mothers to Lina.

"Can we discuss it later? I just really have to get out of here," said Lina with a quick peck to Denise's cheek.

The women stood watching with concern as Lina hastily walked away. Greta put a comforting arm around Denise.

An older woman whom Lina recognized as a friend of her father's family was moving towards Lina.

"Nicolina, don't worry! Your father is still alive in Heaven," stated Mrs. Howell, while smiling brightly at Lina.

"Nope! I saw him. He was definitely dead!" Said Lina, as she began to walk away. "Dead as a fucking door nail," Lina said quietly to herself, although everyone in earshot heard her, as she passed through the nosey crowd.

She needed to get to her car immediately. She wanted that vape pen to calm her nerves. She knew she was growing bitchier and more emotional by the second, and nicotine withdrawal wasn't helping.

She reached her white Ford Flex, jumped inside, locked the doors, and took a long, deep puff. *Alone, safe and secure*, she thought. Feeling calmer now, she looked past her windshield at the bustling downtown area. For other people in the world, this was just another day of work and cooking dinner. She noticed that the parking lot was filling quickly with guests for her father's memorial banquet, and she slumped in her seat as she exhaled her vape down low, so nobody would see. After a few minutes, she knew she had to go back inside, and the vapors escaped into the humid breeze as she opened her vehicle door. She struggled to find her footing to go back inside, as going in and out of air-conditioning on an empty stomach was making her dizzy.

All the funeral guests were now funneling into the banquet center behind the parlor. The Anson's had expanded over the years, and they now owned several funeral parlors with adjoining banquet halls all over Metro Detroit. They were known for upscale accommodations in their clients' times of need. Lina and Carol had met with Kyle, the son of George Anson, three days before to make meal and drink selections. Carol Lipschitz, Bill's dark-haired, pale-skinned, underweight new wife, had wanted to have a cash bar and a buffet. Carol had suggested that they save money by catering the event with her own catering business, a food truck, but luckily that was not permitted by Anson's.

Lina had already experienced a sampling of Carol's food from the "*Carol's Creations*" truck and wondered how she managed to stay in business. "*Never trust a skinny chef,*" Lina's father used to say, until Carol and those little blue pills had entered his life, making him forget all about that funny tip he always used to give. Carol could do no wrong in Bill's desperate eyes. He had been alone for a very long time and had money, which made Bill an unsuspecting target for gold diggers. There had been other ladies, such as Bill's maid, who had been happy to spend the night and help out, along with several other "friends" that Bill would entertain over the years. But Bill had never allowed anything to become serious and by the time he had reached his sixties, there had been far less options and loneliness had set in. Carol had obviously sensed this when she met Bill just over a year ago, and seemed to be a quick study. It had become apparent to Lina that Carol had manipulated her way into matrimony and just three months after their visit to the court house, Bill learned he had terminal cancer.

Lina had been horrified at the thought of Carol's tacky food truck supplying the food for her father's banquet. She even heard a rumor that a cockroach had been seen scurrying away from the truck one day. Even though Ricky believed that had been a different food truck, Lina was adamant that it was *definitely* Carol's food truck and that Ricky should never correct her while she told the story.

Lina had also been raised to believe that a cash bar was wrong and that a buffet was only acceptable for small affairs.

"*Aunt Isobel would be mortified!"* she had said before having a fit at the meal selection meeting. "*You wouldn't invite someone to a party at your house and ask them to pay for a drink! How could you even suggest we go cheap on my father? The whole city, hundreds, if not a thousand, will be in attendance and you want to have a cash bar and a fucking buffet?"*

Carol had been infuriated that Lina wanted her to spend so much of her new money on this. *Spoiled little bitch. Go back to California*, she had thought as she conceded to Lina's demands. *You'll be the one picking up the tab for all this*, decided Carol, silently.

Between the effects of the outdoor heat and everything unfolding with her stepmother, Lina felt as though she might faint as she entered the banquet hall. Brad, already on the microphone at the front of the crowd, was giving an impromptu eulogy with slightly-slurred speech. Brad, known for his charm, had the room full of laughter as he spoke. The ballroom looked lovely with all the floral arrangements brought in from the visitation room and the marble floors that gleamed in the lighting as she made her way up front.

Lina took a seat at the reserved table near where Brad was speaking. Her children and husband were already seated with

Ricky, Denise, and Greta. In usual fashion, her husband Luke barely glanced her way and didn't greet her. He was a quiet man who gambled, cheated, lied, and ignored his wife. Nobody thought he deserved to be with Lina. Most guys who knew her assumed that he must make a lot of money in order to have snagged her. Unfortunately for Lina, that wasn't the case. Lina had married Luke because he seemed quiet and safe. His gambling problem hadn't surfaced during their short courtship, and he had seemed like a good guy on paper. Not only was Luke employed, but he had never been married and had no kids. And most importantly, he actually *wanted* to settle down, which had been hard to find in Southern California. After reaching the age of thirty, her father would ask when she was going to settle down on every phone call home. She had wanted to have a family and didn't want to wait too long. Luke had seemed like a Godsend just ten years prior.

Lina picked up one of the two cocktails that Ricky had waiting for her. He knew she would need it. As she finished the first vodka and cranberry, she noticed a plate of loose Oreo cookies sitting on the table. A quick glance around the room revealed that they were on every table.

"What the fuck is this?" asked Lina with an annoyed whisper in the direction of Denise, Greta, and Ricky.

Ricky shrugged.

"Carol said your dad liked Oreos and put them out." answered Denise.

"Where *is* Carol?" asked Lina, as civilized as she could. Her anger and annoyance were mounting at Carol's tacky gesture.

"I don't know, hon. Last I saw her she was outside, speaking to a gentleman I didn't recognize." answered Greta in a whisper, before adding, "Hey, I ordered some Kabbalah information from Amazon for you and Ricky to get started. You guys are forty now, and I really think it could help you with your grief, Lina."

The room erupted in applause and drunken whistles as Brad finished giving his eulogy speech. Now very buzzed, having not eaten that day and just downing her second drink, Lina decided it was time for her speech.

Lina rose and approached the microphone, giving Brad a kiss of thanks on the cheek as he left the podium to take a seat. She saw Aunt Isobel enter like a debutante, as she was ushered to their table.

Lina smiled brightly at the large audience of family, old friends, colleagues, and even enemies of her late father's.

"I just wanted to say I am humbled by the outpouring of love and concern from everyone at this trying time," she said. She smiled, making eye contact with people throughout the room before continuing. "You know, when Carol first suggested we have a buffet and cash bar for this event," said Lina, talking like a motivational speaker to disguise her irritation, "I just knew we had to do better."

A couple of wealthy wives of Bill's friends grinned and nodded knowingly that a cash bar just wouldn't do for this occasion.

Still sporting a big, superficial smile, Lina continued. "This party isn't just to celebrate my father's life, it's to celebrate all of *you* for being such an important part of it. You are all the threads that created who my father was, and the backbones of this fine community. I thank you all for taking the time out of your day to provide comfort to my family and me," said Lina as she blew a theatrical kiss out to the crowd.

Before leaving the podium, Lina leaned back into the microphone. "Oh, and a proper dessert will be served after the meal. Not just cheap Oreos that have been left out in the elements for people to sneeze on," she stated in a chipper tone, smiling big with her mouth only.

Aunt Isobel kept her same pleasant expression as she began to applaud, having no clue what was going on, as she had been drinking scotch all day. As the equally-buzzed audience clapped, Lina leaned over to her husband and whispered quickly that she *had* to go and she would see him at home. He nodded.

Tipsy Lina exited the banquet hall and was back in the lobby of the funeral parlor. George Anson, the owner and close friend of her father's, stepped out from his office with a portrait of Bill.

"Nicolina, where would you like us to put this?" George asked, speaking low and sympathetically as he held the large, framed photo in his hands.

Lina didn't even slow her pace. She was angry that George had seemed to be catering to Carol more than to her in this process.

"How about up Carol's ass, George?" called Lina, still walking. She had never addressed Mr. Anson as "George" in her entire life.

Surprised and confused, George Anson watched as Lina walked off. Just then, Carol exited the women's powder room, where George was standing.

"Ah, uh, Carol?" said George, nervously offering the portrait to her.

Ricky had pulled up his getaway car out front and was now standing in the lobby looking fabulous in a trendy, form-fitting suit with his Afro pulled neatly into a bun. He had been there long enough to witness the interaction that Lina had just had with Mr. Anson. Kermit Karnes, the most flamboyant gay in town and former love interest of Ricky's, walked over to join Ricky near the doors, while sipping his cocktail from the banquet.

Lina was still walking, as a young male assistant began to hold out a vase of flowers for Lina to take. Without stopping, she grabbed the flowers by the heads and threw them in the garbage can just ahead of her. The assistant was still holding the vase and looked shocked, before Lina paused for a moment, remembering her manners and turned her head to explain.

"Allergies," she said, with a polite smile and nod, before springing back into motion. Her expression quickly turned to a look of desperation, as she faced Ricky and Kermit again and headed for the exit.

Just as Lina was nearing the doors that lead to the getaway car, Kyle Anson, the son in charge of the banquet hall, stopped Lina.

"Mrs. Pratt, I see you are leaving. Here is the bill for the banquet portion of the event." Lina glanced quickly at the bill Kyle held in his hands. It was for $33,800.

"My father's wife will be handling the bill. She's right over there," said Lina, pointing in Carol's direction. George and Carol were still off in the distance, talking about the portrait.

Lina spun on the balls of her open toe, sling back stilettos and was opening the door to freedom. At that, Kermit Karnes turned to Ricky. "Best funeral *ev-er*!" exclaimed Kermit, as he sipped from the straw of his drink excitedly and walked away.

Ricky joined Lina outside, and both were finally seated in the car, alone at last. Ricky took a breath, then smiled and looked at Lina. "That was straight up *gangsta*!" whispered Ricky, smiling with admiration. His inner excitement and laughter were now mounting within him. "Did you really just fuckin' do that? Oh, my God!" Ricky covered his mouth and began to bounce with laughter. He did his best imitation of Lina, "My father's wife will be handling the bill. She's right over there."

"GO! Come on, drive!" urged Lina

"That was some *Dynasty* shit! That was awesome!" said Ricky, still laughing hysterically while pulling away from the curb and into traffic.

Lina also began to laugh. Ricky had a knack for finding humor in everything, and it was one of the many reasons she loved him.

"STRAIGHT UP GANGSTA!" Ricky exclaimed as he tapped the top of his steering wheel with his fist, still laughing.

CHAPTER TWO

1987-The Great Joining of Forces

"We're Going to be Friends."
by The White Stripes

Eleven-year-old Nicolina Carlson was at her family home, Fairview, where her father had lived as a child. Aunt Isobel sat in a casual blouse and slacks, while sipping tea at the dining room table, as the book slid off Lina's head and into her arms.

"Try it again!" coached Aunt Isobel, "You're doing well, Darling, you just need to keep practicing. You will thank me one day! Trust me." she said, looking pleased at Lina's progress so far.

"I've been walking with a book on my head for like, an hour though," complained Lina.

"Okay," conceded Aunt Isobel, "come take a seat and have some tea."

"I don't like tea."

"It's something you must acquire a taste for. You'll be in the company of many fine people who enjoy tea when you're older. Our cousins in England would go absolutely mad without it," said Aunt Isobel in a very British way.

She and her third husband, Winston, had taken up permanent residency at Isobel's late parents' home, something Isobel had always done when in-between husbands. She had been living there for three years when her mother, Victoria, passed away, and had never left. The home had been inherited by both Bill and Isobel, but Bill had a home, so it made sense for Isobel to live there, even after her marriage to Winston.

Lina had never known Aunt Isobel to stay in Michigan during the winters. Her aunt usually left to stay with cousins in England during the cold weather. The trio would then travel together to warm, exotic places from there, while Lina's father, Bill, took care of Fairview. He kept the bills paid and the driveway plowed, and he made sure the pipes didn't explode in the winter cold. Bill had people to do that, of course, and secretly looked forward to his older sister's departure each winter.

Isobel could be very overbearing and opinionated when it came to Lina, especially since the death of Lina's mother, Fara, the previous year. She had never approved of Lina's Italian Catholic mother for Bill, and had made life quite unpleasant for Lina's late mother at times. Isobel had decided that it was her place to ensure that Nicolina grew into a proper Carlson, as she was the only descendent to carry that name. Isobel had even taken it upon herself to purchase Lina's mother a dress for a social event that she'd be attending with the family for fear that Fara would embarrass her by wearing something drab. Isobel had even declined the invitation to Lina's first communion. "I can't be seen entering a Catholic church. You *do* understand, darling." Isobel had said to Fara.

Lina put the book down and began to move towards the dining room table, before she noticed the large photograph of Lina's other aunt, Sophie. There was also a framed picture of her father as a teenager in a new, red sports convertible. He was smiling from the driver's seat with his arm around his older sister, Sophie, who donned a neatly-tied scarf around her blonde hair.

"How old was your sister when she died, Aunt Isobel?" Lina asked, as Isobel's maid, Olga, brought Lina a fresh cup of tea. Surprised by the question, Isobel took a sip of tea, and thought about her slightly younger sister, Sophie, who had tragically taken her own life.

"She was twenty-eight," said Isobel, taking another sip, "she did it just to get attention." Her mood suddenly irritable.

Olga had a pained look of irritation as Isobel's words entered young Lina's ears. The drunken voice of Winston, Isobel's third husband, was then heard from the den.

"Oh, bullshit!" he yelled in response to what he had heard Isobel say about her late sister.

With that, Isobel rose from her seat, teacup in hand, and walked to the wet bar, just outside of the den. She added some whiskey to her cup as she yelled back,

"How the hell would you know?"

Winston was seventy-six and thirty years older than Isobel. He had made his money in the boating industry, which had been very lucrative in the Metro Detroit area. Many residents who lived in the more affluent suburban areas, had summer homes in Northern Michigan. Lina's Grandpa Carlson had purchased several boats from Winston over the years, for their home on Crystalline Lake, which was a summer playground for the Michigan elite. As a teenager, Isobel had met Winston when he delivered a customized, twenty-five-foot boat to her father at the lake house. Isobel had married twice since their first encounter, and after her second divorce, Winston happened to be newly-widowed. In his grief, he had come calling to Fairview, as Sophie's beautiful face had been etched in Winston's mind for all those years. Isobel had been there to give him the awful news.

"She killed herself because she couldn't escape you or your damned mouth!" yelled Winston from the den.

Winston was wheelchair-dependent now, but had no problem bending his elbow to drink or chain smoke. He mostly sat in the den and did just that. He was also anxiously awaiting Isobel's departure. It had been clear to Winston after only one month of marriage that it had been a mistake, so he dealt with it the only way he could.

"My sister killed herself because she wanted to stay young and beautiful forever, while I aged, so she would always be remembered as the most beautiful one!" she said, turning and giving Sophie's portrait the finger.

Isobel was forty-six years old and still gorgeous. She had maintained her figure and looked to be around thirty-five. She had been spoiled by her parents, as all three of the Carlson children had, and was known for public fits of rage when things didn't go her way. Everyone in town knew to steer clear if Isobel seemed to be in a bad mood, which was happening more often due to hormonal changes and her only child, Miles, leaving for college. But at one time, Sophie and Isobel had been known as the most beautiful sisters in town, and men had fallen all over themselves to win their attention. Now the younger generation of men in town fell all over themselves, trying not to piss Isobel off. Winston hadn't been the only victim of Isobel's depression and hormones.

"Isn't Lina's grandfather coming?" interrupted Olga, in an effort to nip an awful fight in the bud.

"Yes. Lina, he'll be here any minute, dear," said Isobel, composing herself with a quick touch to her hair.

Lina's maternal grandfather, Frank Mancini, lived in town above the old movie theatre on Main Street. He moved in after the death of his wife, Ninfa, three years before. Frank was an Italian immigrant who had come with his parents to Detroit when he was a child. He had six children with his late wife, and all but Fara had moved far away from town. Two of Fara's sisters were even living in Sicily now. Poor Frank had only his beloved granddaughter near, and took great pleasure in helping Bill out, after Fara's death. It takes a village, and Lina's village consisted of Frank, Aunt Isobel, and the occasional appearance by her father, Bill.

"I'll wait outside!" said Lina, as she dashed out to sit on the grand, front steps of Fairview.

It was a beautiful spring day, and everything seemed to be coming back to life as the snow melted. Lina studied the concrete steps where she sat, as she touched and ran her fingers along a few small cracks. She thought about the different people whose shoes had touched those steps over the years, beginning with her late grandparents.

Bill Senior, "Grandpa Carlson," had built Fairview in 1940, just before Isobel, the oldest, had been born. His wife, Victoria, an immigrant from England, had given birth to Sophie three years later. Then in 1951, Bill Jr. joined the family. He had been unexpected, and many joked that he had been a cocktail party afterthought. Nonetheless, Bill Sr. had been ecstatic and was pleased to have a son that could take over Carlson's one day.

Lina heard a loud, noisy vehicle coming near. She couldn't see it yet, down the narrow, hidden driveway, but she knew it was Grandpa Mancini and smiled knowing he was there. The noisy truck was now in view and Lina rose to greet her grandfather. She ran out to meet the yellow truck, opened the passenger side door and climbed in. She was proud that she could now do that herself, without assistance.

"Hiya, doll," said Grandpa as she loaded herself into the truck, "How was today?"

"Boring. I'm glad you came to get me."

Frank grinned in appreciation of his granddaughter's blatant honesty and shifted the old vehicle into gear. As they began to drive onto the main road, Lina could hear the extra-loud muffler, which was barely clinging to grandpa's truck with a coat hanger.

"It's so loud, Grandpa!" exclaimed Lina with excitement. "Everyone is looking at us. This is so cool!"

Frank turned and glanced at his precious granddaughter with a loving smile. She looked so much like his late daughter that he adored and missed. She had his daughter's lovely dark-blue eyes, that sometimes appeared violet. Frank's late daughter, Fara, had been a dark-haired, Italian beauty. Lina had light brown hair and mostly resembled the Carlson family, but her mannerisms, her eyes, and even her changing body were so much like Fara's. Sometimes when he looked at Nicolina, he had to hold back his tears. She was growing up so fast, and he wished his Fara were there to see it.

Frank's thoughts were interrupted by a sudden, loud THUD, and the truck's noise was immediately amplified. The muffler had fallen onto the road as the truck rambled on.

Lina's eyes grew big and as she bounced in her seat with excitement, "Wow! Now it's SUPER loud, Grandpa!"

Frank wasn't sharing her enthusiasm with the situation, but he smiled at Lina with endearment.

"Well, we're on our way to enrich my social security, so I can get the thing fixed," stated Grandpa, as he reached over and touched Lina's hair with a smile.

"Are we going to the gambling house?!"

"We are going to go hang out with family for a little while…at the gambling house," said Grandpa.

It had been explained to Lina before about how Sal Perillo was a third cousin to her grandpa. All Sicilians from the metro Detroit area seemed to be familiar with Sal's place, also known as "The Gambling House," located on the east side in Macomb county. Grandpa tended to "enrich" his social security payments this way, or so he always said. Lina didn't mind their visits to the gambling house, as everyone was so loving and welcoming towards her. And anything was better than staying at Aunt Isobel's.

Grandpa turned up the tune on the truck radio to drown out the noisy muffler. The song, "I've Got a Gal in Kalamazoo" by Glen Miller played, and Grandpa whistled along as they made their way to the east side of the Metro Detroit area. Lina enjoyed Grandpa's big band music too, as she watched the scenery whiz by. Spring had finally sprung, and all the motorists on the road seemed to be enjoying the effects, as different tunes escaped from various car windows.

As they reached their destination, Grandpa lowered the volume and pulled onto the secluded, gravel driveway, which led to another secluded parking area. It had been said that the property had originally belonged to "Tony the Terminator" back in prohibition days, which included an underground tunnel that led to a second home on the same land where the Perillo "Gambling House" was now stationed and had been for decades. Grandpa had only recently begun to bring Lina with him, and nobody minded her as she was a quiet, well-mannered child.

The two were now parked and standing at the side door of Sal's place, where Lina knew the secret password would be given through a small window on the door. Sal obviously already knew his cousin, Frank, but it was fun for Lina to say the password, so he followed the procedure for people Sal didn't know whenever he brought her.

"Okay, ready to say the password?" asked Grandpa, smiling.

Frank tapped on the door, then lifted Lina so her head was level with the door window, which had its own tiny door.

"Pistachio pudding!" She called into the window.

The door opened, and there was Sal Perillo, "Heyyy, Frankie!" he said, as he gave Grandpa a peck on the cheek and winked at Lina.

This always struck Lina as odd, since you would never see two men kissing on the Carlson side of the family. The cousins were now speaking Sicilian, which Lina didn't understand. She followed them into the underground tunnel, which she had always found fascinating. These days, the tunnel was fully lit with electricity, but she imagined how dark and scary it must have been, back in the old days. It had been constructed with different-colored rocks and cement, which she found beautiful. She could feel the aged and shifted cobblestones through her pink Chuck Taylors, as natural light slowly became visible.

The three had reached the end of the tunnel and were now entering the gambling house, far back on the property and hidden nicely in the woods. As they stepped in, they were greeted by the usual cast of Sicilian characters and Lina took a seat at the bar, in anticipation of being given a lollipop. This was a treat which Lina had become accustomed, and looked forward to, as they were the large kind, with white swirls. She didn't particularly care for the taste, but they were super fun to eat.

After about an hour and what seemed to be a winning streak for Grandpa, the two said their good-byes and before she knew it, they were back on the road.

"Are we going home now?" asked Lina, still nursing the last of her pink lollipop.

"I'm taking you to your dad's jobsite, then I'm heading home. I have dinner plans," said Frank, as he touched his granddaughter's sweet face.

Bill Carlson and the other men at the work site barely glanced at the loud noise approaching them as Frank and Lina pulled up. They could see Bill and the other guys were busy, talking about something. The body language of the men seemed tense, so Frank instinctively knew that they should wait in the truck with the windows down, until it seemed appropriate to join Bill.

The spring breeze sifting through the truck windows felt chilly, as the day turned to early evening. She noticed there were still a few patches of snow clinging to life just inside the trees, that they were actively chopping down to build houses. The pair sat silently, as Frank listened carefully, in an effort to hear what Bill was discussing with the men. Lina moved her focus from the trees, and she wondered who might move into some of those homes that her dad was building in her neighborhood. She had daydreamed that a girl her age would move in and they would become best friends. They would share secrets and giggle together, the way the other girls at school did. The sad truth was, Lina didn't have any friends. She had no mother, no friends, and a mostly absent father.

Six months before, Aunt Isobel had advised her younger brother, Bill, that Lina was in need of proper undergarments to accommodate her developing body. In response, Bill had given Lina a store credit card for use at Mitzelfeld's department store on Main Street. She had walked to the store by herself and shyly purchased a bra, with the help of the kind saleslady who had known her father's family for years. She felt sad, thinking about how much she missed her mother since her untimely death a year prior, and had wished more than anything that she could at least make a friend to confide in. Just as she felt the tears begin to form in her eyes, the men's voices became louder.

"Vaffanculo!" she heard one of the men yell towards her father, after he had turned his back to walk away. She heard other familiar Italian cuss words exit the mouths of some of the other men too. Lina and Frank watched in silence as Bill turned around to face the Italian workers, whom he had contracted to build the new homes downtown. Italian/Sicilian was Frank's first language, so he knew what the men were saying. They were words he used himself all the time, causing them to be familiar to Lina.

Bill's six-foot-two inch frame stood tall as he walked back to face the men.

"Guys, I was married to an Italian and I know what you're saying!" he said firmly and with authority, "I will not accept this language. If you don't want this job, you can leave! If you are staying, you will get your FUCKING heads out of your

FUCKING ass holes and do the FUCKING job right or get the FUCK off my job site! Do we have an understanding???"

The men said nothing and immediately went back to work constructing a brick wall and keeping it up to code, as instructed. Bill did not want any trouble from the city building inspector and especially did not want to waste time and money having to have them start over again, if it failed inspection.

Feeling satisfied, but full of angry adrenaline, Lina's father turned and began to walk towards the truck.

Lina asked softly, "Grandpa, why was my dad being so mean? Like a bully?"

Frank was quiet, before speaking with his faint, Italian accent, "He wasn't being mean, Nicolina. When it comes to business, a good leader must make sure his workers do the job right. Otherwise, there *is* no business."

Lina thought about this as she and Frank exited the vehicle. Bill shook her grandfather's hand before resting his palm on Lina's shoulder.

"Hi, Frank. Thanks for picking Lina up."

"I see some of my language helped you out there," said Frank, grinning, "You need me to talk to anyone before I go?" offered Frank.

"No, but I have you on speed dial!" Bill said with a chuckle and wink.

Lina gave Frank a good-bye kiss on the cheek, before he started up his noisy truck and left the job site.

"Jesus! Why doesn't he get that fixed? Does he need money?" asked Bill, feeling slightly guilty. Frank did so much for Lina, but lately Bill had become oblivious to things.

"I think he has the money now," said Lina, remembering the gambling house winnings.

Bill loaded Lina into his truck, and the two stopped at McDonald's before heading home for the evening.

###

Lina woke up the next day with a slight bellyache. After her morning relief ritual, she noticed blood when she wiped. She froze. *Why am I bleeding*? she thought. She wiped again, and there was more. It wasn't drying up like a scab would when she scraped her knee. She wadded up a bunch of toilet paper and stuck it in her underwear. *Maybe I have a bad cut and it will heal*, she thought.

She finished getting dressed and walked out into the kitchen. Bill was already on the phone discussing business. She knew better than to interrupt him and decided to slip out. *What should I do today*? she thought. She decided to retrieve her bike from the garage and take a Saturday ride through town to see if anything exciting was happening.

Lina rode her powder-blue, ten-speed bicycle through Downtown Rochester. The breeze filled her hair as she rode past the glistening Paint Creek towards Grandpa's apartment on Main Street. As she cut through a condo complex, practicing riding hands free, she heard the voice of a boy yelling "stop it!" along with obnoxious giggling from other voices of boys her age. She slowly circled back and stopped behind some garbage dumpsters. She saw Seth Glickman, Lawson Jones, and Patrick "Fitz" Fitzpatrick throwing rocks and anything they could find at a black boy she had never seen before. Lawson was yelling to the stranger while laughing and picking up broken glass to toss his way

"New kids aren't allowed back here! Especially sissies!"

Lina and most every kid in town who encountered these boys, was harassed by them. All three lived in Lina's neighborhood. They called her things like "nerd" and "weirdo" and made fun of her because her mom died. "Ha-ha, your Mom is dead. Why don't you go cry?" they'd say as they balled their hands into fists and moved them over their eyes as if wiping tears. Lina hated these boys, even though she knew Fitz and Seth were only following what Lawson did to be cool. When Lawson wasn't around, both boys were actually quite nice, and Seth's family were Lina's neighbors at the Carlson cottage located in Northern Michigan.

"Hey, losers," called Lina to the three boys she knew.

The new kid turned and looked at her with both surprise and relief.

She turned her attention to Lawson. "Nice new braces, metal mouth," she said with an obnoxious laugh to match theirs.

Seth called back to her in Lawson's defense. "Shut up, stupid bitch!"

Lina rode her bike down closer to the scene. She met eyes with all three. "Leave him alone! What did he do to you?" she called.

"None of your business you ugly, stupid nerd." yelled Fitz, laughing as he looked to the other boys for approval.

"Stupid nerd. Interesting." said Lina, now standing right in front of the assailants. Her comment was lost on them.

"How about this?" asked Lina. "We have a contest to see who is smarter. If I win, you leave him alone forever. If you win," she hesitated, thinking of what they might want most.

At school, they were always making comments about girls' boobs, teachers' boobs, and the boobs of celebrities.

"If you win," she started again and swallowed, "I'll lift my shirt and show you my bra."

She knew they would either laugh and tease her about the offer or accept it. She nervously waited for their response. The three looked at each other.

"Deal!" yelled Lawson without consent from his peers.

Fitz had sat next to Lina in class the year before and had reservations about accepting this challenge. He knew Lina was actually really smart.

"Okay," Lina began, feeling relieved at their acceptance of the agreement. "Who was the third president of the United States?"

The truth was, Lina had read her parents' encyclopedias and memorized random facts, specifically for situations like this. The three bullies looked at each other, clueless as to what the correct answer was. She waited a few seconds before making the "ehhh" noise to replicate the sound of the red X from TV's *Family Feud*, which sounded and appeared when a contestant answered with something not on the board.

"You lose!" she called, sneaking a quick glance at the stranger, who had a look of relief on his face.

Lawson's face turned red with anger. "WAIT! We get to ask a question too."

Shoot she thought. *What if I don't know it?* After taking a deep breath, she stood extra tall, then said, "Fine. Go ahead. I'm ready!"

Seth Glickman, looking very confident, smiled at the other two boys as if to say *I've got this*. Then he said, "Name all five Great Lakes."

Lawson gave Seth an irritated shove and Fitz moaned. Of course, she was going to know the answer. They lived in Michigan.

Lina exhaled. It was a piece of cake. When her grandmother was still alive, her grandparents had taken her to each Great Lake in their Fifth Wheel camper over the course of five summers. She held her head high as she proudly named all five Great Lakes correctly. "Superior, Huron, Michigan, Ontario, and Erie!"

Fitz and Lawson called Glickman a moron, and he waved his hand dismissively at the boys as they continued to give him a hard time. With defeat, the bullies got on their bikes and left.

She approached the stranger. "Hi, I'm Lina. Are you okay?"

The boy looked relieved and smiled for the first time. "Yeah, I'm Ricky. You seem pretty smart. Thanks, you saved my life."

"It's nothing," said Lina, feeling triumphant. "Those boys are mean to everyone. Don't pay any attention to them."

Ricky was bleeding from his arm. "Want to come to my house?" he asked, shyly.

"I was headed to my grandpa's apartment on Main Street," she said. "Where do you live?"

They rode their bikes together to Ricky's new "house." It was the old movie theatre on Main Street. They were moving into the other, larger apartment across the hall from her grandfather, above the theatre. As they walked in the front door of the old theatre, they were immediately met with a loud gasp, before a white woman, resembling VH-1 host Rosie O'Donnell, came running to Ricky.

"Oh my God, what happened!?" exclaimed Ricky's mother, Denise Levine-Goldman.

Ricky told her about the boys. Then he continued by describing how Lina had saved his life and how smart she was.

Denise looked down at young Lina with adoration. "Well, Lina. It is very nice to meet you." She took the hands of both children in hers and walked them further into the building. "While I get Ricky bandaged up, why don't you sit down? Enjoy a pop, and we will tell you all about our new 'Motown Mood Café' that will be opening here soon."

Lina noticed her grandfather standing outside. "Thank you, but I was on my way here to see my grandpa. He lives in the other apartment in this building."

Denise looked over at her long-time life partner, Greta Goldman, who had been watching and listening from behind an old concession stand that would soon be remodeled into the café bar, and the two women shared a smile. Frank Mancini was their new tenant, as they had purchased the entire building.

Frank noticed Lina and entered into the café doorway. "I see you met the new landlords!" said Frank, greeting Ricky's mothers, whom he had just recently met.

"Yes, and this is Ricky! exclaimed Lina, "My new friend," she said, suddenly feeling shy. What if this new kid didn't consider Lina to be his friend?

"*Best* friend," corrected Ricky, smiling. "She saved my life."

At that, Denise held back grateful tears of joy. She and Greta had hoped for nothing more than for their son, Ricky, to make friends. Denise and her life partner, Greta Goldman, had set the script for a very unusual life for Ricky.

In 1976, twenty-year-old Denise Levine had been a community college student living in her hometown of Long Island, New York. Her mother was an Irish Catholic woman, and her father was a Jewish accountant. She had attended a live music event at a local bar with friends one night. Thanks to her fake I.D. and several drinks accompanied by countless shots, Denise had been wasted drunk. When the band finished playing, the sax player came over to talk to Denise.

He was a black man who said his name was Jerry Porter and that he was a signed musician with Motown Records in Detroit. He had explained to Denise, who was struggling not to fall out of her chair, that he was just in Long Island to help out a friend, but was about to be a big name in the music business. He also told a young, gullible Denise that he had been looking for someone like her to settle down and start a family with. Denise went back to his motel room that night and left with Ricky in her womb.

After several failed attempts to track this man down locally, a terrified and newly-pregnant Denise had purchased a bus ticket to Detroit to find her baby's father. She knew her parents would disown her when they found out, so she figured she had nothing to lose. While the details of the evening that Ricky was conceived were fuzzy at best, she remembered that Jerry had said he wanted a family. *Maybe he'll be happy?* she had hoped.

Unbeknownst to Denise, Motown Records had moved their operations to Los Angeles in 1972, four years prior. When she had arrived at the old Motown Records site on West Grand Boulevard in Detroit, there was a sign which read "Closed", hanging on the front door. As her eyes began to well, she felt her morning sickness kick in, and ran to the side of the building to vomit. When she looked up, thirty-year-old Greta Goldman, former Motown recording artist, was standing nearby.

"Are you okay, Sweetheart?" asked Greta with a grin, assuming the young girl had overindulged in alcohol.

Although Motown headquarters had moved, many of their most popular artists had stayed behind in Detroit, since it was where they were from and where their families lived. Greta had decided to stay behind, by request of Barry Gordy, to work with the artists who remained. While Greta had started as a back-up singer in the early sixties, she soon found herself recording a solo album, which had produced a top forty hit, "Sunshine through the Snow," in 1965. Greta's success was short-lived when she permanently damaged her vocal cords, and had started working as a songwriter and vocal coach for upcoming talent in Detroit. She was also a lesbian who had longed for that special someone, that person she could somehow start a family with. She had wanted a child so badly that she had even considered marrying a man. She was working in the old studio alone, when she saw somebody through the side window, and came rushing out to investigate. She was relieved to see it was just a young girl who was feeling ill.

"I'm okay!" said Denise, startled. "I'm looking for Jerry Porter. Do you know where I can find him?"

When Denise looked up and her brown eyes met Greta's blue eyes, both felt an inexplicable spark. One that they would speak about many times over the years, with a sentimental glow. Greta had never heard of any sax player by that name in all her years in the business. So Denise found herself alone in Detroit with no money or desire to return to New York. Greta extended an invitation to stay with her, and soon after, the two fell in love. Denise had felt attracted to girls in the past but had always suppressed those feelings in an effort to avoid disgracing her family. Thirty-year-old Greta, who strongly resembled Barbara Streisand, was exactly what twenty-year-old Denise needed and wanted. For the first time, she had felt true happiness.

Greta had joyously purchased a crib and other items needed for the baby. She had never been happier and was especially pleased that her child was going to be a quarter Jewish, biologically. Greta had only recently become more active in her religion and had hoped for a Jewish partner. Although half-Jewish Denise had been raised Catholic by her mother, she was excited and more than willing to become a practicing Jew and raise their baby in the Jewish religion. Everything had gone as planned. Denise gave birth to an eight-pound baby boy who they named Richard "Ricky" Goldman.

Ricky was now eleven and their Detroit neighborhood, which had been fine when he was little, had become increasingly violent and they were looking for a safer area to raise him. Their first choice had been West Bloomfield, as that was the location of the world-renowned Jewish Community Center, but they were also looking to fulfill Greta's dream of opening a musical café in a downtown setting. They hadn't found a good fit in West Bloomfield or Bloomfield Hills, so they decided to look at a commercial space that was for sale on Main Street in Downtown Rochester.

The site of the old movie theatre had sat vacant since going out of business two years earlier, but it would be a perfect fit for Greta's vision and livelihood. She wanted Denise to remain a stay-at-home mom and had decided that this would be a great way to invest her savings. There were also two apartments in the building - one would add extra income for them and the other would provide a safe residence for the family. This building would soon be known as the popular “Motown Mood Café” and would become an important fixture in the Rochester community for decades to come. Denise and Greta were now smiling down at their most precious commodity, Ricky, with a new friend.

Grandpa Mancini, also feeling pleased with the new friendship, looked at the two and smiled. It had always broken his heart that his beautiful, sweet, good-hearted granddaughter couldn’t seem to make any friends.

“Say, Nicolina, why don’t you show Ricky around the neighborhood?" offered Frank.

His granddaughter was eleven and a half now, and he thought bonding with this friend, even if he was a boy, could be good for her. Lina looked at Ricky’s excited eyes, then the two of them looked at his two mothers.

“Go ahead! Go!" said Greta with a big smile, making a shooing motion to the kids. She wanted to put her arm around her wife, but Frank was there, so they had to act like roommates.

The new friends went outside and sat on the sidewalk next to their bikes. Lina picked up a twig and Ricky a small stone, which they each scraped against the pavement, unsure of what to do.

“So, what is your new place going to be, again?" asked Lina.

“It’s going to be a place where there’s live music. Coffee during the day, grown-up drinks at night, food. It’s a Motown music theme, but all kinds of music will be played there," informed Ricky with pride.

“I love Motown music, of course. All music.”

“I like your ten speed," said Ricky.

“Thanks, I got it for Christmas.”

"You're lucky. I'm Jewish. We don't do Christmas."

"Oh. Yeah, my Dad said that all the Jews are starting to bleed over into Rochester because there's no room left in Bloomfield, so that makes sense," said Lina.

Still trying to think of something fun they could do, Lina remembered Mr. O'Malley's record and assorted junk store, just a few doors down from where they sat. Shopping there had always been an experience, so she decided to take Ricky inside.

"I have an idea of something exciting we can do," offered Lina.

With a sneaky smile, Lina motioned for Ricky to follow her. The new friends walked down Main Street until they reached a small, dark hole-in-the-wall with an old, faded sign that read "ROCHESTER RECORDS" on the door.

"Okay, I want you to go in and ask the guy at the counter if he has any Madonna CD's." instructed Lina.

Ricky looked confused. "Why?" he asked.

"Just do it," said Lina.

Ricky agreed and the two entered the store. The stench of cat urine and feces flooded their senses as they walked in. Ricky spotted the man behind the counter. He was an obese man with long, stringy grey hair, wearing a stained t-shirt and sweatpants. He was seated, staring into an old television on the counter with tinfoil wrapped on the antenna, while drinking a "Milwaukee's Best" beer.

The man's name was Ian O'Malley, and he had owned that store for several years. Ricky hesitantly approached the counter while Lina hung back, watching him carefully with a coy smile on her lips. When Ricky reached the counter, he cleared his throat.

"Do you have any Madonna records?"

Mr. O'Malley looked up at Ricky from his seated position. He slowly stood as his calm face suddenly turned red and angry.

"NO!!! I don't carry that WHORE in here! I don't care if this is her hometown, she encourages GAYS! You keep listening to her and you'll find yourself gay too, my boy!" yelled mean Mr. O'Malley. "This is a Christian establishment!" He added, before lifting his beer from the Hustler magazine that had been serving as a coaster.

Lina was laughing at this point. She knew that would happen because it happened to everyone that asked Mr. O'Malley for Madonna, Prince, Wham, and any other artist O'Malley deemed queer or untalented. Almost in hysterics, Lina ran up to Ricky, who was standing before Mr. O'Malley in shock. She grabbed his arm and laughed as she guided him quickly from the store. After exiting, the pair kept running until they reached the new Motown Mood Café. Lina was still laughing when they stopped running and sat on the sidewalk.

Ricky, still in shock, asked, "What just happened?!" before his shock turned to laughter.

"That guy is crazy!" exclaimed Lina while laughing and bending at the waist to catch her breath. "He called me and my Grandpa stupid dego waps one day…then my grandpa swore at him in Italian! It was awesome!" she said gleefully.

An encounter with Mr. O'Malley was the most excitement available in 1987 Rochester, and the pair would eventually refer to Mr. O'Malley as "Fuck Face O'Malley". It was a bonding experience that the two would never forget.

Denise saw the two kids appear in front of the café again, laughing together. She smiled through the window at Lina with love and admiration. That little girl had stood up for Ricky, a stranger, and protected him. Now this girl was giving her son friendship, something she had wanted so badly for him. Denise, still smiling, walked out to greet the two eleven-year-olds. As Lina stood up, a large bloodstain on her butt caught Denise's eye.

"Lina! Hello! Why don't you come with me, dear?"

Denise brought Lina upstairs to her bathroom and mothered Lina in a way she needed so badly. From that day on, Lina was as much a daughter to her as Ricky was her son.

After Denise helped Lina, giving her some pads to take with her, Lina said goodbye to a confused Ricky and headed home to change clothes. As she coasted her way home through the lush, suburban landscape, she felt overwhelmed by what was happening to her changing body, but she also felt very fortunate that she had met Denise. As she turned onto her street, she spotted two unfamiliar boys tossing a football near her yard. When she came closer and rode up her driveway, she decided that one looked to be about thirteen years old.

She was putting her kickstand down with her foot when a ball flew down and hit her bike, causing it to fall over. Startled and annoyed, she bent down to lift up her bike and noticed the reflector had broken off in the hit and fall. Lina tried to put it back into place, but it didn't stay. Realizing she'd have to ask her dad for a new reflector, she felt a flash of anger before noticing one of the boys was standing before her.

"I threw it so hard that it knocked the reflector off?" asked the boy, enthusiastically.

"I'm your new neighbor."

Before she could respond, the brown-haired boy bent down and snatched the reflector from her hands.

"Hey! What do you think you're doing?! Give it back!" she said, angrily.

The stranger was suddenly taken aback as Lina looked directly at him. He wasn't expecting this younger girl to be so cute. A smile came over his face, and he shoved the reflector into his pants.

"You want it? Come and get it," he teased with a flirty grin.

Before Lina could respond to this very strange and different situation, a female voice called out. "Kirk! K i r k!!!" yelled the woman's voice. "Dinner!"

With that, the attractive stranger flashed Lina a devilish grin, before running off with her reflector to one of the new houses on her street.

I will have to tell Dad, so he can go tell that boy's parents, she thought before walking into the house to clean herself up. She was very happy that the older boy didn't seem to notice the red spot on her pants. Denise had given Lina her personal copy of *Are You There, God? It's Me, Margaret* by Judy Blume. After taking a bath and putting on fresh clothes, she was happy to get comfortable on her bed and read.

The day had turned to night, and Lina was thoroughly enjoying the book. As she turned a page, there was a tapping sound. After it happened again, Lina followed the sound to her bedroom window. She pulled up the shade and didn't see anything.

Until…

"Hey," said the thirteen-year-old boy from earlier, as he stood up from under her windowsill.

"Oh, my God! What are you doing?! If my dad hears you, we will both be dead," she informed him. She looked toward her closed bedroom door and back at him.

"I'm sorry I broke your reflector," he said. Then he produced a brand new one, just like hers, from his pants pocket. "I wasn't trying to be a jerk or anything. I'm Kirk."

"Thanks," she said, pleased that the new one would be easy to slip back on with the backing intact. "I'm Nicolina, but people call me Lina for short. How am I going to get the reflector from you, though? My window screen is in the way."

Kirk looked at Lina and her stomach fluttered. She hadn't noticed how cute he was before. He had light-brown eyes and tiny freckles along his perfectly sculpted face. She noticed he had broad shoulders and was about a head taller than her. His sandy-brown hair pulled his entire package together, even though it was clear he was the type of older boy that liked to tease. Kirk broke his gaze from Lina's violet eyes before tearing a hole in the bottom corner of her window screen. He pushed the new reflector through. She pulled it from the other side and into her hand. He was so handsome, that she wasn't even thinking about how angry her dad would be at the torn screen.

"I gotta go," he said reluctantly, looking back towards his new house. "I'll see you around, Lina."

CHAPTER THREE

2016-Back to The Snap
"Still the Same"
by Bob Seger

It was two weeks after the funeral of Lina's father, Bill. Her husband, Luke, had taken their son, Marty, and daughter, Frankie, camping at Torch Lake in Northern Michigan. This was a much-needed break for her, as she could barely take care of herself. It wasn't so much the grieving of her father, the two had never been close, it was all the drama and responsibility that had fallen on her shoulders.

Lina had been having trouble sleeping at night and had resorted to taking over-the-counter sleeping pills. The pills didn't keep away her nightmares or anxiety though. She still found herself awake during the night, screaming and crying into her pillow. As much as she didn't want to leave her bed, she had decided that she needed to take advantage of the alone time and get her life back under control. She needed to pay her bills, check on when football and cheer registration for the twins would be, and most of all, check to see if she even had any money in her bank account. Luke had been running the show at their home the last few weeks while Lina mourned, and she knew the camping trip would be an added expense.

She made herself a cup of coffee and logged into her bank account from her laptop in bed. Luckily, she had prepared herself for what the account information would reveal, so she was able to keep her anger at bay. They had exactly $126 in their checking account. There were no groceries, and a quick glance at her calendar showed that the children's fall sports registration would be the following day. Lina would need to provide a check for six-hundred-dollars in order to register the children. She felt the most authentic form of depression and desperation as she stared blankly at the computer screen. *What am I going to do?* she wondered.

Lina began to think about that beautiful portrait of Aunt Sophie that hung on the wall of Fairview. They had never met, as she had taken her life at only twenty-eight-years of age. Lately, Lina had become envious of her aunt. There had been many nights where she lay awake, wishing she had the courage to just end it all. There would be no more watching Carol dangle her mother's house and belongings in front of her face as she lied to the town, telling everyone that Bill loved her so much that he left everything to her. Carol had been actively using this facade to illustrate to everyone that Lina had been an awful daughter and that Bill had cut her off. This infuriated Lina, since from the outside, Carol's claims would appear to be true. Lina then thought about the sheer devastation it would cause her seven-year-old twins and pushed those thoughts from her mind. She couldn't, and never would, do that to them.

Her mind began to drift to Grandpa Mancini. She remembered how she used to enjoy going to church with him. How he had told her that it was an hour each week to reflect on your life and to seek guidance from God during the darkest hours. There hadn't been a day that went by that Lina hadn't missed her grandfather.

Frank Mancini had passed away two months after Lina moved to San Diego for college. His heart had suddenly stopped while resting in his favorite recliner and watching the Detroit Lions game. While Lina had been grateful that her grandpa hadn't suffered, the sudden loss had blindsided the then eighteen-year-old.

She remembered the call from Denise and the news that there would not be a funeral to attend for him. Frank had died a poor man, and Bill had refused to foot the bill for Frank's funeral. Bill had felt that one of Frank's three living children should be responsible for paying and arranging a service. Bill could afford to pay for the funeral of his former father-in-law but felt it was the principle of the matter. This had always angered Lina, and Bill's recent death was bringing old grievances to the surface. Lina looked up church times on her laptop before closing it shut, taking a shower, and getting ready for the day.

As she was still a complete wreck on the inside, she followed her philosophy from the funeral and made sure she looked as good as possible on the outside. She dressed herself in a skirt and sleeveless, summer-knit sweater and slid her polished toes into her heeled sandals. She was pleased that she had forced herself to be outside by the pool while in her altered state, as she studied her reflection in the mirror. Her tan was even deeper than it had been at the funeral, and a quick step on the scale revealed that she had lost five pounds. She grabbed her purse and drove her white Ford Flex towards town.

Lina pulled into the St. Hubert's Catholic Church parking lot and sat for a moment, collecting her thoughts. For some reason, she felt nervous about going inside, even though a flood of positive memories and feelings swept over her. She took a hit from her vape pen, checked her reflection in the visor mirror, and exited her vehicle.

Although the church was open, there was no mass being held, as it was a Monday. A few older parishioners knelt, praying with rosaries. There was a priest inside, wearing a long white robe with a sash, who had just exited the confessional booth. He seemed to give Lina a double take as she crossed herself and knelt to pray.

Tom Kowalski had been a new clergy member at the church when Lina was in high school. He remembered seeing her enter the church with her grandfather all of those years ago, and had asked Frank about her after she left. Lina didn't know, but Tom had even performed a small memorial in church for him after he passed.

Lina tried to remember all of the prayers from her childhood as she continued to kneel with her palms together. Lina's mother had taken her to all of her religious catechism classes after school and helped her to achieve each of her sacraments. After Fara passed, the religious education part had ceased, but Frank still took Lina to mass with him every Sunday. It was due to this fact that Lina couldn't remember various roles in the church and didn't have a complete understanding of Catholicism. But this was the only church she would feel comfortable in as she struggled to keep her sanity after her initial snap two weeks prior.

As Lina silently recited the "Hail Mary" in her head, she felt the presence of a man scooting in next to her.

"Miss Mancini?" inquired Tom Kowalski, timidly.

Lina was taken completely off guard as this was the maiden name of her mother and name of her grandfather, but not hers.

Tom, suddenly sensing that he might have the wrong person, began to speak again, nervously. "I'm sorry, I thought you were the granddaughter of Frank Mancini. I must be mistaken."

"No, I am," explained Lina, still surprised. "But it's Nicolina Carlson, actually. Pratt now." She smiled politely.

"Oh, yes. Sorry Mrs. Pratt. Carlson, yes, I remember now," explained Tom nervously. "I remember seeing you at mass with your grandfather…years ago. I was new at the church before you left."

Lina blushed at the fact that he remembered her from all those years ago and suddenly felt uncomfortable. She slid back up into a seated position on the pew next to him.

"So, you are married then, I presume?" asked Tom.

Lina began to remember that she was there for strength and guidance. She suddenly, and possibly inappropriately, began to expel the truth about her troubled marriage in desperation.

"Yes, technically, I am," she stated, sadly.

She didn't want to reveal her marital problems too much to Ricky or the Moms yet, since she wasn't sure what she was going to do. If she decided to stay married, then they would all hate him. She needed to talk to somebody though, and her marriage was only the start of it. Her stepmother coming into her life right before her father died and continuing to reside in her mother's house, which she owned, was a whole other heap to unload. It was out of character for Lina to reveal much about herself to even her closest friends, let alone a stranger. But this was the time of the "Great Snap," and Lina's sanity tank was barely running on fumes.

"He has been cheating on me. He's never home, he gambles…" Lina's eyes began to fill, but she managed to hold it back.

"Infidelity and money issues can be a real challenge in a marriage," he said with a warm smile.

"Yes, I guess they can," said Lina with a nervous laugh that Tom took as a flirtatious one.

He suddenly felt more comfortable and confident as he sat taller and continued to speak with her. Lina assumed that Tom Kowalski was a priest, but he was in fact a deacon. Instead of becoming a priest, he had been ordained a permanent deacon in his youth, as he had always held out hope of meeting a woman and having a family. While the Catholic Church required deacons to already be married at the time of ordination, he knew the church sometimes made exceptions. He had already decided that if God had ever sent a woman his way, he would take that as a sign to leave the church. He hadn't been happy lately. And at age forty-seven, he wondered if he needed to follow a different path. Lina was beautiful and obviously unhappy in her marriage. He had always thought she was gorgeous, but even at age forty, she was still stunning.

"It can be very helpful to talk about it, though...and I am here for you. We could even talk about it outside of church if you wanted," he said as he placed his hand high on Lina's thigh, which was not covered by her skirt.

With that, Lina reflexively jumped from her seated position in the pew, bumping her knee. "Oh, well...that's so nice of you, but I just realized I need to be somewhere," she said, walking backwards from the pew.

Startled and embarrassed, Tom rose from his seat. "Oh, well, you know where to find me if you want to talk. Remember, it can be helpful."

"Thank you, Father. Well, I'll see you around," she called while walking quickly up the aisle.

"I'm not a priest," he uttered to himself in her direction.

Lina made it through the parking lot and was now in her vehicle. She fumbled for her vape pen which she kept in the center console. Her hands were shaking as she thought about Father Kowalski and how even working for God didn't give you immunity from a mid-life crisis...or horniness, obviously.

Praying definitely isn't going to help me, she thought as she pulled her cell phone from her Michael Kors bag. *God helps those who help themselves, and I am out of shits to give.* She remembered that Ricky had mentioned that he would be free that day if she wanted to grab lunch or something. She sent him a text, "Look fabulous and be ready in 10. We're going to play blackjack. I'll honk."

Ricky was already waiting outside of Motown Mood Café on Main Street wearing his lucky blue suede suit. He had assumed they were going to one of the casinos in Downtown Detroit and had excitedly packed all his frequent player cards into his wallet. Ricky didn't gamble often, but he was great at blackjack and poker. One time, he had even managed to have a crowd around him, cheering him on, when they met up in Vegas while she was living in California. While Lina loved to watch Ricky play, just as she had her late grandfather, she was awful at card games and never seemed to win at anything, even the slots. She needed his help to try to get the money for the kids' cheer and football registration. Lina pulled up to the curb and Ricky hopped inside.

"Hey Chica! I must say, I am very relieved that you have left your house. I am so ready to get out too!" said Ricky.

"Yeah, well I went to church today. Since I was already out, I felt like we should definitely do something fun."

"So, did you want to eat at the casino? Because I was thinking that maybe we could stop for a late lunch in Birmingham on the way home. Maybe take a stroll in their downtown area like we used to? And it's still early, so we have the entire day…and you are kid free!" said Ricky, smiling and clapping his hands together with excitement.

Lina was beginning to feel bad about her alternative gambling plans. Ricky noticed that instead of heading south on Rochester Road towards I-75 to Detroit, she was driving east.

"Um, where are you going?" asked Ricky with an unsure laugh.

Lina was bad at two things. Math and directions. He assumed this was accidental.

"Oh, well…we aren't going to Detroit," she said.

"What do you mean? Where are we going then?" asked Ricky cautiously.

"We're going to a place my grandpa used to take me. I mean, I haven't been there in ages. I'm not sure it's even still there, but I figure it would be safer than Detroit, yah, know?" Lina said, trying to make it sound reasonable.

Ricky's mouth fell open as he stared straight ahead and held up his palm towards the windshield. "Whoa! Wait! So, because you think the casinos in Detroit are dangerous, you're taking me to an illegal Sicilian gambling ring instead? Awesome," said Ricky, sarcastically. "Let me out of the car!"

"Come on! It will be fine. I really need to see if it's still there. I've been wondering about it for a long time. And if it's not, we'll head to Detroit instead. Please, Ricky."

"Wait, you said we're playing blackjack. But you don't play blackjack because you can't count up to twenty-one without using your fingers. Lina, I need some information here."

Lina was embarrassed as she explained her lack of funds for registering the kids. Ricky didn't have it to lend either, not until Friday, which would be too late. Lina instructed Ricky to go into her purse and remove the three hundred dollars in cash that she had been stashing in a fire-proof safe.

"Please, Ricky. Try to make it six hundred. If you can't, I won't be mad. I take full responsibility," she pleaded.

"But why not just go to a regular, legal casino?!" asked Ricky.

"Because, from what I understand, the legal casinos take a percentage of your winnings. The Perillo Gambling House doesn't. I need every penny you can win for me!"

Ricky conceded, as he thought that the illegal gambling house was probably long gone and that they would end up at one of the casinos in Detroit anyway. "Okay, babe. For you. But just so you know, the casinos in Detroit have very safe parking and are loaded with security." He looked at her blank expression as she continued to drive and added, "Okay, just sayin."

Lina was afraid that if they continued to talk about the gambling house, that Ricky might change his mind. Eminem's song "My Name Is" was playing on the radio, so she cranked the volume. Ricky watched the scenery from the window as every gangster film he had ever seen raced through his mind.

After what seemed like an eternity, Lina's Ford Flex reached the old, gravel driveway. It reminded her of the driveway at Fairview, but it still seemed shorter than how she remembered it. Slowly approaching the old, redbrick house, her tires picked up tiny little rocks that made clinking noises as they flew up and tapped her car. There were several other cars parked on the grass, which Lina took as a good sign that the house might still be in operation.

The gambling house had fruitfully stayed afloat for all of those years. Although the house was technically illegal as it was not operating in accordance with gambling laws, the owners were more afraid of armed robbery than getting busted by authorities. The house had lasted that long because it was a place for Italian men to go and escape from their wives. A place to socialize, have some drinks, smoke cigars, and gamble. Most patrons didn't know that the gambling house had been serving as a bank for several rings across the country, making it quite lucrative. This was a guarded secret that would not come to light for years to come.

"It looks like it's still in operation, Ricky!" said Lina with nervous excitement.

Ricky suddenly felt like he may vomit. If he had known they weren't going to Motor City Casino or MGM Grand, he would not have agreed to go. He had never accompanied Lina and her grandfather to the gambling house before, but he had seen enough mobster movies to know he didn't want to gamble with them. Joe Pesci shooting a kid for saying he was funny was a movie scene that was running through his head.

"So, there's no way you could do…like…a late registration for the kids? I can lend you money on Friday…"

Lina turned and looked Ricky in the eyes. He could see that the window panes to her soul were cracked. They were beautiful but fogged and tattered with pain. Something that only her closest friend could see. Lina needed the money, and he was going to try to get it for her. For his unofficial Godchildren, he would try. They both took a deep breath and exited the vehicle.

As they began to walk, Ricky stopped and suddenly wanted back in the car.

"Don't you think *they* might think it's strange for a curvaceous blonde and a gay, black Jew to just show up, out of nowhere, to gamble?"

Lina turned and spoke in a loud, frustrated whisper, "Would you just chill? I remember the password."

"You remember a password from what, thirty years ago?" asked Ricky, as he finally let out a big sigh and began following Lina again. "Fuck me hard," he whispered to the sky.

The two made their way through the old maze of bushes she remembered, and she easily found the hidden back door. Although everything seemed smaller, it was just as she remembered. Ricky and Lina looked at each other cautiously before Lina gave a nervous knock to the door with the back of her hand. After what seemed like an endless pause, the door opened slightly with a chain keeping it secure. Lina took a surprised, nervous breath and blurted out, "Pistachio pudding!"

The elderly Sicilian immigrant on the other side of the door hadn't heard that one in decades. The door closed shut, so the chain could be removed, then reopened. Sal Perillo stood before them. Lina recognized him and smiled.

The beautiful woman standing before Sal Perillo looked slightly familiar, but he couldn't place her.

Before Sal could think too much about Ricky and his blue suede suit, Lina spoke, "Mr. Perillo. I'm Nicolina, the granddaughter of Frank Mancini. I used to come here with him when I was a girl. I'm sure you wouldn't remember me…" She looked down at the ground.

Frank had been a third cousin of Sal's, which made Frank's granddaughter a relative too. He remembered the quiet, pretty little girl who would come with Frank all those years ago. He stared, slightly in awe, of this stunning Italian *woman* that now stood before him. Sal was instantly charmed and threw the door open for them. He gave Lina a kiss on both cheeks and shook Ricky's hand as Lina introduced them.

"Bella Nicolina! Yes, I miss my cousin, Frankie. So good for you to come!" gushed Sal as he motioned for them to follow him to the rock tunnel that led out to the separate, secure gambling house hidden in the woods. Ricky looked at Lina with wide eyes as Sal led them to the tunnel. She gave him a firm look before taking his arm and following Sal.

As the three entered the gambling house, Lina immediately noticed it had been updated. It was far more luxurious and fancy than it had been. Even the bar seemed to be covered in Italian marble, which glistened in the sunlight of early afternoon.

Sal extended his arms, motioning at the whole room, and exclaimed with his thick Italian accent, "Make yourselves at home." He smiled warmly and motioned Ricky towards the bar. He didn't know the strange man in the blue suede suit and thought it best if he had some alcohol before gambling. Lina and Ricky both nervously ordered white wines, which they nursed, barely sipping.

Lina took in the Mediterranean atmosphere and thought about her grandfather. She noticed all of the snake plants and horns evenly distributed about, to ward off the "evil eye" or *malocchio* in Italian. This was a Sicilian curse that could be cast upon an enemy by giving them a malevolent stare. Lina had already decided the curse didn't work. *I did that every time Carol turned her back to me for the last year, and that bitch hasn't dropped dead yet,* she thought as she noticed a seat opening at the blackjack table.

"Okay, there is an open seat," said Lina to Ricky in barely a whisper. "I will place a super small bet, so it doesn't look bad, since we know I'll lose."

Ricky nodded and took a sip of wine to try and clear the nervous knot from his throat. Lina took a seat and quickly lost.

That was fast. Shit. he thought to himself.

Lina wandered over to sit at one of three slot machines. She didn't want it to look weird with her hovering over Ricky, plus she was too afraid to watch. She just wanted the end result news. She prepared herself for the worst and switched to diet pop as she played quarter slots and watched Ricky take his seat at the blackjack table. She couldn't believe the place was that busy on a weekday at noon, but she was happy to soak in some of her culture, make small talk with some men speaking broken-English, and reminisce about her times there with her grandfather.

After what seemed like forever, Lina's thoughts were finally interrupted by the touch of Ricky's hand on her shoulder and a whisper in her ear.

"We got it, baby," said Ricky, trying to remain calm and hoping to get out of there immediately.

Lina was silently elated as she scoped the room and noticed Sal Perillo, the owner, standing by the door where she and Ricky were headed. As the pair reached him, she thanked Sal and gave him a kiss on the cheek.

"You are welcome anytime, Bella," said Sal before coming in close to whisper in her ear. "But next time, you leave your friend at home, k?"

Lina blushed and nodded as she gently nudged Ricky towards the door. It was clear to Lina that Sal did not want a blackjack champ coming in there and winning. That was bad for business, but Lina's plan had worked and for that she was grateful.

"You're my hero!" exclaimed Lina to Ricky as the two piled into the car and quickly drove off.

"Okay, I need lunch and a drink after that!" said Ricky as the excitement of winning for Lina suddenly kicked in. "I just won at a muther fuckin Sicilian gambling ring!" He counted the cash with a big smile. "Who is gangsta now, bitches?"

The two of them burst into laughter.

###

The friends were now seated on the outside patio at Main Street Pub for lunch in Downtown Rochester. After they both ordered iced tea with lemon and club sandwiches, they sat and enjoyed the outside atmosphere while they waited.

Lina thought about how much her hometown had changed since she last lived there. Many of the young adults in town had been small children when she left. The people her father's age, parents of friends, were either retired and living somewhere warm or getting ready to retire. So many new homes had went up since she had left, that even most people her own age didn't look familiar. Unless she was dealing with a business owned by one of the original Rochester families, her maiden name didn't mean much anymore either.

Times had changed, but Lina noticed that most townies who had known her before seemed to think she was still an eighteen-year-old girl, frozen in time. The people didn't see Lina evolve into a woman. They didn't see how Bill had cut her off months after moving to California for school and how she had managed to survive. They didn't know that she had landed a fantastic job in San Diego and had never asked her father for anything. They didn't see how Lina's lip had quivered as she looked through the racks at Walmart for jeans that would fit her after working hard and losing the baby weight. Other women she knew were giving themselves mini-vacations and designer bags to reward themselves for all their hard work dieting and exercising post baby. Luke's poor financial decisions had prevented Lina from even being able to buy a decent pair of pants to fit her. Nobody knew her struggles in life, and she was tired of feeling disrespected.

Her thoughts were interrupted when Ricky spoke, "Okay. So, you look fantastic. Body is looking good, tan is coming along nicely, but you *have* to do something with your hair. Eyebrows could use an update too."

"I know. I just haven't had any time to spend at a salon. I'm not even sure where to go."

"Well, my ex, Mario, owns that new salon in town. I can get you in. Plus, it would give me an excuse to call him and mention my new relationship," said Ricky, with a devilish grin.

"Yeah, that really *is* the perfect excuse for you to call your ex. Okay, make me an appointment."

"Okay, I'm on it!" said Ricky.

They both giggled and made eye contact as they sipped from their straws. Lina was suddenly overcome by her love for Ricky. Those beautiful, brown eyes of his had seen her through so much in life. *What would I do without this man?* she thought. *What would have become of me had I not had the love and support from Ricky and his mothers?* It was one thing to lose her father, but the thought of losing Ricky made her want to vomit.

"So, what do you want to do after lunch?" asked Ricky as he shoved a fry into his mouth, breaking Lina's thoughts.

"How do you stay in such perfect shape eating like that, Rick?" she asked, her eyes still glistening with love for her friend.

"Moderation, baby," he said with a wink, barely looking up from his plate.

Lina sat quietly with her hands in her lap. Deep in her own thoughts, her eyes rested on Ricky as he voraciously soaked up every last drop on his plate with his sandwich and stuffed it into his mouth. He let out a moan of pleasure as he chewed and smiled. Ricky had always been one of those people who could eat anything and never gain an ounce. All those years as a dancer, and now a dance instructor, had kept him looking as svelte and sexy as ever.

"And how does Carol own a restaurant on wheels, yet look so anorexic?" asked Lina, suddenly losing her appetite.

"Anorexic?" Ricky laughed. "Let's be fair. She's only ten pounds lighter than you, tops! Look, I don't like her. I think she inherited enough property that she doesn't need to stay living at your mom's house. I think she's a bitch and I suspect she used your dad, but she's attractive for a woman in her fifties."

"Well, I think she looks like a flat chested version of Natasha from *Rocky and Bullwinkle,* but that's just my opinion." stated Lina, before lifting her fork to her mouth.

"Maybe we need to find her a Boris, to keep her busy." joked Ricky.

"I think I deserve a new car," she stated, completely switching gears.

"Um, with what money? he asked, laughing as he pulled out his card to pay for lunch.

"I have money coming soon. I just don't know from where or when exactly," she said with a frown. "I've been so focused and consumed with Carol being in my mom's house...I need to call Jack's law firm and talk to that other lawyer he said to meet with. I just haven't wanted to deal with it."

Ricky handed the leather cardholder to the server as she walked past.

Lina continued. “I need a car that accurately represents who I am now. That I’m an upstanding adult in this community and should be taken seriously.”

“Mitch Marquette from high school works at Hillview Cadillac now,” stated Ricky with a smirk, waiting to see Lina’s reaction.

“Oh, my gawd. Remember those songs he used to write for me in high school?"

They both laughed at the memory of poor Mitch trying to win Lina over with his musical ambitions.

“A Cadillac *is* exactly what I have in mind though. Maybe just a test drive?”

###

Ricky continued to fill Lina in on Mitch Marquette as they drove south on Rochester Road towards the dealership.

“He works at Motown Mood as a stagehand right now to supplement his income at the dealership. I guess he isn’t very good at car sales. Anyway, my Mom, Greta, felt sympathy for him and gave him a regular morning gig playing on weekdays. It was pretty much just retired people and Mom’s groups at that hour. People started complaining that they couldn’t hear to have a conversation over his music, so she had to let him go. She told him that “Fuck Face” O’Malley had complained and that there was nothing she could do. Luckily, he bought it. I guess he’s living in the backroom at the dealership now too.”

The pair parked and walked into the dealership. Ricky had texted Mitch, who was excitedly waiting to greet them. He gave Ricky a fist bump before turning his attention to Lina.

“Looking good, Lina! Hey, it’s really cool of you guys to come in and support me like this," said Mitch as he tucked his long, dark hair behind his ears.

A middle-aged woman waved at him. “Excuse me! Could I get some help?”

Lina and Ricky noticed her, but Mitch didn’t seem to.

“People just aren’t buying cars right now," said Mitch.

The woman dropped her arms, exasperated. Ricky and Lina felt bad for her as Mitch led them back to his office/apartment. It was a small room with a rollaway bed and a microwave. The mattress had no sheets, and it smelled like a locker room. Lina and Ricky shot each other a quick, grossed-out glance as Mitch pointed to his prized possession.

“These speakers used to belong to the Nuge himself!" bragged Mitch, proudly.

“To Ted Nugent?" asked Lina. “Wow."

She thought to herself that they looked like her dad’s speakers from the early nineties. Mitch bent down and pulled a cd out from a drawer.

“I have an extra special treat for you guys," said Mitch as he held up the cd. “I collaborated with this really cool chick from Detroit. She goes by ‘Eight Mile Mary.’ Anyway, she sings in the style of Yoko Ono. So check this out...One day, ‘Eight Mile Mary’ met Yoko in New York City, just after taking a hit of acid. Anyway, Mary somehow channeled Yoko’s energy. She just channeled it in.” Mitch became more intense as he spoke. “And now it just flows freely through Mary’s instrument, man. Also, Yoko Ono is not given the credit she deserves, by the way. Obviously, if John Lennon thought Yoko was good, then she was.”

“Mitch, we’d like to test drive the red Escalade out front," interrupted Ricky.

Mitch grabbed the keys and led them out to the new Escalade. He handed Lina the key fob.

“Thanks so much, Mitch. How long can we test drive it for?" asked Lina, hoping she and Ricky could enjoy it for a while.

"Well...normally, they say for people that we know, to have it back in like, thirty minutes," said Mitch as he looked both ways over his shoulders, "But my cd is three hours long, and I know you guys are anxious to check it out on the car speakers. Plus, I need the cd back for my date tonight. Just have it back in three hours." He gave Ricky a pat on the shoulder as he stepped up into the passenger seat and popped the cd into the deck. The two waved as they pulled away. After about four notes of "Eight Mile Mary's" singing, Ricky popped out the cd and threw it in the console.

"Jesus Christ, dude. You could have prepared me better for dealing with Mitch. He hasn't changed at all!" said Lina, laughing.

"I almost feel like this car is too fancy for us," said Ricky as he examined all the bells and whistles. He let out a chuckle.

"Naw, everyone knows that Cadillacs are for Italians and Blacks, so we are *perfect* for this car, actually," said Lina, smiling.

"That *is* accurate, I'd say," agreed Ricky while checking out the moon roof.

The new luxury vehicle embarked upon the enormous hill on Rochester Road, that led back down to Main Street. Lina looked for a parking space along Main, so they could show the car to Denise and Greta. She located a spot and parallel-parked across the street from Motown Mood Café. They both spotted what looked like a red-carpet grand opening right near where they had parked.

"Oooh!" they said in unison, clapping their hands together.

"Let's go check this out!" said Ricky.

The summer day had turned into a beautiful early evening. The pair were happy to investigate what new business was opening and sample any free champagne they might be offering. As they reached the red carpet, Lina saw her old babysitter,

Connie Mavis, dressed in a long, gold gown. She was standing at the doorway and smiling as her picture was being taken. The pair shared a big smile when they recognized Connie.

“Hi, Connie," said Lina, greeting her childhood sitter.

Connie’s face lit up at the sight of Lina. Then she noticed Ricky. “Hey, you guys!" exclaimed Connie, giving them each a hug. “Welcome to my grand opening! The Mavis Art Gallery! Lina, you must have gotten the invitation I sent to your dad’s house. I’m so glad! I didn’t have your new address. Help yourselves to some champagne." She smiled and made her way to greet someone else.

“Don’t mind if we do," said Ricky, quietly to Lina, as they each took a free glass of champagne from the server’s tray.

Lina wondered what other mail for her had landed in Carol’s hands, that she hadn’t received, as the pair remained near the red carpet. They noticed several familiar faces who were older than them, but younger than their parents. All mostly people Connie’s age, who were in their late forties and early fifties. As they finished their first glass of free champagne and reached for another, Lina saw a skinny woman wearing a dress she recognized walking towards them.

This dress was no ordinary dress. It was a 1985 black Oscar De La Renta. A vintage, ageless dress that had been gifted to Lina’s late mother, Fara, to wear to the funeral of Bill’s mother. Aunt Isobel had bought it for Fara in fear that she might wear something inappropriate for a Carlson family funeral. When Fara had passed and her clothes were donated, this was one of the dresses that had been specifically kept and properly stored for Lina.

Connie and some other old acquaintances were now talking to Ricky. Kermit Karnes arrived and greeted him as he reached for a glass of champagne. Ricky was internally thrilled to see Kermit as Lina stared past at the woman in the dress.

Connie saw Lina look at Carol, who was approaching them, and smiled. She, along with the other female acquaintances, knew Carol was Lina's stepmother. They knew that her father had just passed, but didn't know that the two women didn't get along. Everyone standing around was suddenly anticipating a nice, surprise reunion for the stepmother and stepdaughter. Connie was about to explain to Lina that she had invited Carol to the grand opening, thinking Lina would appreciate that people were still including Bill's new wife, even though he was gone. Everyone was smiling sweetly when Carol reached the red carpet.

"Why are you wearing my mother's dress, bitch?"

The entire crowd gasped with surprise as they clutched their imaginary pearls. Ricky simply stood with his jaw ajar. Carol, not expecting to see Lina, shared Ricky's expression. Carol had chosen the dress to fit in with Bill's crowd. She was not about to let Bill's social status slip through her fingers just because he had died. She wanted to use the Carlson name to get her as far as she could. Lina had shown the dress to Carol back when things were still civil and had referred to it as a timeless classic.

"I *said*, why are you wearing my mother's dress?" demanded Lina, now standing toe to toe with Carol. "Take it off! TAKE IT OFF RIGHT NOW! I DON'T WANT YOUR PIT SWEAT IN *MY* DRESS!"

Ricky gently placed his hands on Lina's arms and spoke to her softly. "Honey, I understand you're upset, but she can't just take it off and be naked. Nobody wants to see that," he added loudly so Carol would hear. He wanted to make sure he still got an insult in on her since he had saved her from being naked.

Carol was visibly embarrassed and smiled in apology to the women standing around.

"You see, with my dear husband just passing away, I've had no time to shop. This dress was in my closet," she explained with her slight European accent. She pretended to hold back tears with a wave to her face.

The women looked at her sympathetically.

"Oh, boo *fucking* hoo, Carol," whispered Lina, as she stepped to the side of her. Lina bent in closer. "If you weren't wearing my mother's dress, I'd dump this champagne all over you, bitch."

Ricky grabbed Lina's champagne glass and set it on a table, thanking the crowd and whisking Lina off to the Escalade. The pair didn't notice as a man walked up from the back parking lot, and over to Carol.

Ricky guided Lina to the passenger side and buckled himself into the driver's seat.

As Kermit Karnes watched them leave, he silently wished he could get away with having a town gossip column in the paper he owned, *The Rochester News*. Between the funeral and this, Lina would be gold for him. Ricky pulled away, heading back to the dealership.

"I CAN'T FUCKING BELIEVE HER!" screamed Lina.

"Lina, I know that was upsetting. We will definitely discuss it, but first we need to think of words to say to Mitch about what we thought of his cd."

CHAPTER FOUR

1990/The Great Transformation
"Be My Lover"
by Alice Cooper

Fourteen-year-old Lina was at the Motown Mood Café hanging out with Ricky and his Moms. Greta had a stylist and make-up artist on location to get her ready for the Motown Music Awards ceremony at the Fox Theatre in Detroit.

Ricky sat at the counter, playfully teasing his best friend about her unruly, wavy brown hair. He began to brag about how his dark skin hides his pimples and Lina admitted he was lucky. Greta's make-up artist, Patty, overheard.

"Lina, if you want, I can try to do something with your hair. We could do a whole make-over, actually. Greta is my first client and I'm here super early." Patty offered.

"YES, please!" said Ricky, accepting the offer on her behalf.

Lina was terrified and didn't want anyone to fuss over her. "No, that's okay."

Before she knew it, Lina was upstairs with foils being pulled from her hair, after having her eyebrows waxed. Patty washed and performed a professional blow out, which left Lina's normally unruly hair, looking bouncy and beautiful. Lina was still dressed in her unflattering, baggy t-shirt and jeans. Luckily, Patty had several different bra and clothing sizes on her portable wardrobe cart, as Greta wasn't the only client she would be tending to that day.

Patty selected a cute, age-appropriate skirt and top for Lina before applying make-up to Lina's young face. Lina watched as

Patty gave her a tutorial on how to do her own cosmetics later. After Patty was satisfied with her work, she placed all the make-up used on Lina into a bag for her to keep. A size seven pair of heels were the final icing on Patty's masterpiece.

Ricky, Denise, and Greta made a playful, drumroll noise as Lina prepared to come out and reveal her make-over. Lina slowly walked out of the bathroom and into the bedroom that Denise and Greta shared. She felt uncomfortable being the center of attention but inhaled and stepped out anyway. When her audience caught their first glimpse, you could have heard a pin drop as everyone stared in silence. Then, to Lina's surprise, the room erupted with catcalls and applause. Still in awe and disbelief, Ricky walked to her and made her turn to view herself in the full-length mirror.

"Oh my God, Lina! You are HOT!" said Ricky with sheer excitement as the two of them continued to study Lina's image in the mirror.

"You look absolutely beautiful," said Denise as she came over and kissed Lina on the cheek, before stepping into the hall with the others. Greta stopped and wrapped her arms around Lina from behind. The two stared at Lina's reflection quietly for a moment before Greta spoke.

"The outfit is on me, darling. It's yours to take home."

"Really? Oh, Greta, thank you."

Greta walked away, turning one last time to flash Lina a loving grin before walking out.

Ricky bounced back into the room. "This is going to be so great for us in high school!" he exclaimed as he broke into a little dance of excitement. "You're wearing that outfit to school tomorrow, girl!"

Lina continued to look at the stranger in the mirror. She couldn't believe the image she was staring at was her. Lina said her goodbyes and made her way to the door.

The song *Heatwave* by Martha and the Vandellas began over the outdoor speakers. It was a sunny, spring day that brought everyone out of their homes and into town. The Detroit style "coney" hot dog cart was parked along the sidewalk, and people were moving along with the music as they enjoyed the weather and atmosphere. As fourteen-year-old Nicolina Carlson's first pair of high heels touched the sidewalk, it was as if she were stepping into womanhood. She had entered the café as a shy girl with bad hair and skin and was leaving as a bombshell. At first, she felt uncomfortable and silly as she tried to adjust her walking style for the heels and feared someone she knew might see and tease her.

Lina was feeling an unfamiliar streak of excitement, hopefulness, and vanity all at once. She would later recognize this feeling as sexiness. Lina was sexy for the first time in her life, which was amplified by the upbeat Motown sound as she began to walk in beat to the music.

The first few feet of walking were tricky, but suddenly all of Aunt Isobel's training with posture and etiquette, combined with her euphoria and love of music, all came together. She could feel her breasts bounce slightly with each step in her new, properly-fitting bra, and her hips began to take on a natural sway. Some older boys, wearing high school letterman jackets, did a double take.

One said, "Hello."

She shyly looked down before letting out a small "hi" as she walked past. Then she smiled to herself, feeling even more confident. As she glided through her hometown, it seemed as if everyone was looking at her with new eyes.

Seth Glickman, Lawson Jones, and Patrick "Fitz" Fitzpatrick were standing near the Coney dog cart as Lina came into view. Mr. Glickman, Seth's Dad, was buying their crew hot dogs.

"Hey, check her out," said Lawson to the other boys, thinking she was a stranger.

Lina's face came more into view as her young body bounced in tune to Martha and the Vandellas. She noticed the boys and became fearful that they would say something nasty to her. She made eye contact but said nothing. The three boys stood, frozen, as they tried to process what they were seeing.

Seth was able to utter, "Hi Li…Nic…ah, Lina" as she sailed past with perfect posture.

Mr. Glickman noticed her and leaned over the spellbound boys from behind as they stood speechless. "She's growing up nicely, eh, boys?" he said, smiling knowingly before turning to bite his coney dog, still moving his shoulders to the music of his time.

The three boys continued to drink in Lina's every move as her beautiful figure journeyed down Main Street.

Three businessmen were deep in conversation and didn't see Lina. Bert Walsh, an acquaintance of her father's, accidently bumped her as she passed. Mr. Walsh grabbed Lina's arm apologetically. "Young lady, I am so terribly sorry."

"That's okay, Mr. Walsh," said Lina as she looked him in the eye, smiled, and carried on her way.

Mr. Walsh's jaw dropped. "Was that Bill's daughter?" he asked the other two men incredulously.

It was that sunny, spring day in 1990 that fourteen-year-old Lina had experienced her "great transformation," as Martha and the Vandellas serenaded with their soulful "Yeah, yeahs."

It was then that she learned what properly-fitting clothes, undergarments, and make-up could do for a person. She never looked back. Bill's charge card for Mitzefeld's department store in town would now be used for both clothes and tailoring needs, as well as for regular appointments at their in-store salon. The fabric of who Lina would become was being rapidly woven together, and males of all ages seemed to be enjoying the results.

###

The following day, Charles "Chip" LeBeau was wandering the halls of East Middle School. He peered into classroom windows looking for friends he could tease while they sat in class. Chip was the athletic superstar of his eighth grade class and of the whole school. He had all-American good looks, an athletic, muscular build, and a keen knack for charming the socks off ladies of all ages. Even the teachers giggled and blushed when Chip paid them a compliment. During recent tryouts, Chip had even made the Junior Varsity baseball team for high school the next year. The coaches at Central High School had already decided that Chip should skip ALL freshman teams and go straight to Junior Varsity.

Chip looked into the classroom door window of Miss William's class. He didn't see any of his jock friends, but it was then that he first noticed Nicolina Carlson. She was sitting at her desk, her attention alternating between her notebook and Miss William's French instruction. She had luscious hair that seemed to glow, as the morning sunlight rested upon her from the classroom window. The bell rang before Chip had a chance to drink in anymore of this stranger. He scurried away as the classroom emptied.

Wearing her new outfit from the day before, Lina headed to her locker on the opposite side of the school. As she walked, a person was suddenly walking with her. It was Chip LeBeau.

"Hi, I see you're new here. I'd love to help you find your way around the school. I'm Chip."

"Yes, I know who you are," replied Lina, walking even faster now. She didn't know what the popular asshole wanted from her or what game he was playing, but she knew it couldn't be good. “I’m not new. I’m in your grade and have been here as long as you have.”

“Well, you’re new to me," said Chip as he got a better look at her. She had slender, curvy legs that were showcased by her white mini skirt. She wore a red, form-fitting knit top that hugged her perfect hourglass figure, and the little kitten heels on her feet were driving him wild.

“I’m going to call you tonight,” said Chip, smiling confidently.

“I didn’t give you my number," retorted Lina.

“I’ll get it," said Chip as he flashed his handsome smile and turned down a different hall.

Lina felt her skin become warm and her face blush. She was still unsure, yet bubbling over with excitement on the inside. Even the possibility that Chip was going to dial the number to her house and call her was enough to make her feel like she was floating, as she stepped into her advanced placement English class. She took her seat by the window and daydreamed about Chip, as her teacher shut the classroom door.

###

After the school day had ended, Lina exited the Rochester Public Library, floating on cloud nine. She had finally scored Judy Blume’s book, *Forever,* after several failed attempts. She had been desperately trying to get her hands on that book since the previous summer when she was “up north” at the family cottage at Crystalline Lake, Michigan.

The Glickman’s cottage was next door to theirs and Seth’s older sister, Macy, had been reading the book. Macy was only a year older than her but had proudly showcased Judy Blume’s more scandalous, mature novel. Lina was a huge fan of Judy Blume and thought that she had read all her books. Then she saw her favorite author’s name on the shiny, brown book cover held within Macy's fingers of chipped nail polish. Macy had explained to Lina that there was sex in the book, which definitely sounded like something Lina wanted to read. She herself had been experiencing sexual urges and needed Judy Blume to guide her, just as she had when Denise had lent her a copy of *Are You There God? It's Me, Margaret* when Lina had her first period.

Mitzy Hamilton's mother was the librarian and had previously refused fourteen-year-old Nicolina to check it out. Mrs. Hamilton believed it was filth and not for children, even though it was in the youth section. The excitement of finding the coveted book within the walls of her public library had been crushed as Mrs. Hamilton refused her.

Lina had staked out the library for months, waiting for Matt Munson, an older boy who had a crush on Lina, to be working the check-out counter. There had been many times since Mrs. Hamilton's refusal that Lina had spotted Matt working alone, only to find the book wasn't checked in. It always seemed to be checked out, but this day, the stars had finally aligned for Lina. The sexy novel was there, and Matt was working.

Matt felt a mix of excitement and nausea as his crush approached the counter. He was seventeen and chubby with large red pimples, glasses, and a love for dungeons and dragons. In his head, he referred to young Lina as his "Library Angel." She frequented the library the way some people frequent bars. And each time she walked through those heavy library doors, Matt felt it was a gift to him from God. As much as he rehearsed, he always tripped over his words every time he had a chance to speak to her. *She seemed really excited at the counter today,* he thought. *Maybe she likes me?*

Lina was at the corner, outside the library now, pressing the crosswalk button. As the robotic voice from the crosswalk counted down "five, four, three…," she spotted Kirk Kavanaugh walking on the opposite side of the street. He was now sixteen and the hottest, tannest lifeguard the community pool had ever seen. He saw her as she crossed University Drive over to Walnut Street where he was. Kirk smiled at her with his playful, almost snarky smile. He liked Lina. He liked her a lot, but he always teased her and acted like he didn't. She was younger and still in middle school. He didn't want his friends to know he liked an eighth grader.

"What's that?" asked Kirk, pointing to her book with an obnoxious laugh.

"None of your business," she said, holding the book to her chest so he couldn't read the cover.

"Judy Blume," Kirk said in a girly voice, gently teasing her.

"You on your way to work?" asked Lina

"No. I'm just in my swim shorts and lifeguard gear for no reason," he teased, while still grinning.

She gave him a half grin. As they reached the next corner, she headed the opposite way without saying anything.

Kirk called after her, still feeling playful. "This is the beginning of pool season! You should get some sun on that pasty skin of yours, all summer, before you start high school!"

Lina didn't even turn to look at him. She still had the biggest crush on that boy. No matter how much he teased and taunted her, she wanted nothing more than to feel his touch. She had inadvertently brushed shoulders with him at a party last Christmas and inhaled his sweet smell. Lina had decided that was the best smell in the world. She didn't know how to react to Kirk though. She was excited to start high school in the fall, but she knew Kirk would never be seen with a younger kid.

Lina reached her house and eyed the property as she walked up the driveway. She loved the color and architecture of their midwestern home. It was a two-story, brick house with a walkout basement. She admired the statues her mother had placed around the garden and looked lovingly at the trees Fara had planted before her death. Her home was all she had left of her mother, it seemed. Bill had wanted to remove all the Catholic statues, as he said they looked "ethnic." But he had seen how important they were to Lina, so he had let them be.

Fifteen minutes later, Lina was dressed in her new bikini that Denise had helped her find. It was her *first* bikini. And while she thought she looked good in it, she was still nervous about how the boys in town would react, especially Kirk. She grabbed a towel, jumped on her bike, and headed to the community pool.

Kirk was sitting on his lifeguard tower when she arrived. He watched with excitement as she secured her bike and headed through the pool gates. Kirk was still watching from above as she removed her cover up, revealing her skimpy suit. The bikini was yellow with tiny strings holding two little pieces of material over her young breasts. He sat frozen. His shorts had formed a bulge, and he was glad to be sitting where no one else could see. He tried to will his erection away. *Baseball, homework*, he thought. It still wasn't working. It was at that moment that Kirk knew he had to have her. He *needed* to touch her. His hormones caused him to feel like a starving man sitting in front of a juicy steak.

After two hours of reading her new book in the sun, Lina decided it was time to head home. The heat was exhausting, but she didn't dare go in the pool and mess up her hair and make-up. She wrapped a towel around her and headed to the restroom. As she reached the doors, Kirk came through the storage room entrance and silently but gently grabbed her by the shoulders and whisked her inside.

"What are you doing?" asked Lina, pretending to be annoyed.

Kirk said nothing as he gently pressed her against the wall, her towel dropping to the floor. He looked at her with a passion and intensity that she had never seen from him or any boy before.

He placed his right hand on her face, then bent down slowly, pressing his lips to hers. Lina felt her virgin body awaken as the kissing became more ardent. Kirk looked at her again briefly, before running his hand under her bikini top and resting it on her breast. She willingly followed his lead and ran her hands down his back, living out her nightly fantasy. He picked her up and gently placed her on top of an old desk. His expression was trance-like as he took her in. He quickly pulled down his swim trunks before pulling off her bikini bottom. Lina stared at him nervously as he hovered over her, moving the cups on her bikini top along the string, to the sides of her breasts. He paused breathlessly, in awe of her body, before touching her breasts and moving his hands to her lower region. He massaged her in places that had never been touched before, and she surprised herself when a moan released from her lips. Then, without warning, he entered her, causing her to suck in her breath. It was painful, but she didn't want him to stop. A few seconds later, he removed himself, leaving evidence of his lust on her stomach. They both paused, awkwardly. Kirk handed her his towel to clean herself, as he pulled up his shorts. Suddenly, Kirk seemed to snap out of his trance and back to his normal self.

"Okay, well…you have to go now before someone sees," ordered Kirk.

Lina's hands were still trembling as she fumbled to get her suit back on. She walked out and began to ride her bike, before quickly realizing that was a painful option. She decided to walk her ten-speed home.

Still reeling in euphoria, Lina arrived at her house and parked her bike in the garage. She heard drilling sounds as she entered her home. She was relieved that her father was busy and wouldn't pay that much attention to her. Lina was paranoid that Bill would be able to tell she wasn't a virgin anymore simply by looking at her. She knew that was ridiculous but couldn't shake the possibility. She followed the noise to the bathroom where Bill seemed to be hanging something. She decided she should say a quick hello, so he wouldn't come to check on her.

"What are you doing?" Lina inquired. She saw the bathroom mirror was down. The wall it had hung on had a large hole inside with shelves.

"Good, you're here," said Bill. "If anything happens to me, you need to know where the goods are hidden."

Bill produced a small velvet bag. It was the size of a deck of cards. He removed the bag to reveal it contained what appeared to be a large block of gold. After her eyes wandered up, she saw there was jewelry and other items of importance on the shelves.

"This is a bar of gold, Lina," Bill confirmed. "If anything happens to me, you need to remember that this is here. Do NOT *ever* sell this house without removing the mirror and taking these items first. Everything of value is in this fireproof safe." Bill put more items in the safe and placed it in the secret spot. "It's *imperative* that you remember this stuff is here." Bill smiled at Lina as he watched her impressed expression. She helped him hold the mirror in place, while he fastened it securely back on the wall.

She headed to her bedroom to change out of her bikini. As she pulled on an old tee-shirt and shorts, the phone rang. It was Chip LeBeau.

CHAPTER FIVE

2016
"Hello Detroit"
-Sammy Davis Jr.

Lina was sound asleep, dreaming. She and Kirk Kavanaugh were together in her childhood backyard. He was apologizing for his failure to ever return and professing his love for her. Her eyes watered with sheer joy at Kirk's admission of love as he pulled the brick of gold that her dad had hidden behind the mirror in her parent's house from his pocket to present to her. Then the twins made a noise which interrupted her slumber. *Crap. Reality*, she thought.

Lina was awake now but still lying in bed. The Carol saga had made leaving her covers increasingly difficult in the weeks since her father had passed. She was so stressed out and full of anger at Carol that she would wake in the night full of rage. She was livid with her father too. It was an odd thing to be so angry with a dead person, and she would never have the satisfaction or release of yelling and screaming at him or telling him off. All she could do was carry the burden of her anger and resentment.

In the past few weeks, even when things seemed calm, Lina would suddenly remember Carol's existence and instantly catapult into an angry state. It didn't matter what she was doing, anytime her stepmother entered her mind, she would whisper under her breath, "That fucking bitch" or "That fucking whore." And when it was time to shower, Lina would even turn her hatred for Carol into a full Broadway musical, as she'd belt out, "You

Fuh-king *b i t c h*, I wish that you'd fuh-king *d i e*. Bomp! Bomp!"

But this August morning, she had an appointment with Ricky's ex-boyfriend, Mario, at his new salon. She knew she needed to pull herself from bed, as this was a much-needed appointment. At age forty, Lina had roots that were not only dark, they were becoming full of grays as well. It had come to the point that she couldn't bear to walk past the mirror. She also knew she could no longer procrastinate a meeting at Jack's law firm with his partner. *I need some coffee to get me going today*, she thought as she left her bed to go make some.

After walking back to her room with two cups of coffee, she flipped on the TV to find her favorite local morning show on Fox 2 Detroit. She was excited to see Jessica Starr, Marielle Lue, and Dina Centofanti were hosting the show that morning, and Adam Graham from the Detroit News was about to give his movie recommendations for the weekend. She never went to the movies anymore but liked hearing Adam's reviews anyway. Lina watched while sipping her coffee and trying to come alive. She had a salon appointment at nine and a late lunch with Aunt Isobel before taking the twins to football and cheer registration.

Thanks to Ricky, she had the money to register the kids, and Greta had insisted on paying for her salon day since she had admitted she couldn't afford an appointment with Mario that soon. It was going to be a full day, and she hoped the law office would be able to squeeze her in so she could get several tasks completed all at once. An animal abuse commercial came on, so she quickly changed the channel. *I do not need anything else to upset me right now*, she thought.

She flipped the channel to find the old movie *Gone with the Wind* in progress. It was a movie she had seen parts of but had never watched in its entirety. It was at the part where Scarlet O'Hara is on her knees at her family's Tara Plantation.

"I'm going to live through this and when it's all over, I'll never be hungry again. No, nor any of my folk. If I have to lie, steal, cheat, or kill. As God is my witness, I'll never be hungry again!" said Scarlett.

The character's words struck a chord with Lina. For the first time, she understood Margaret Mitchell's book character. *Yes, Tara is the equivalent to my mother's house,* she thought. *And Kirk, wherever he is, is my Ashley.* She thought about it some more. *And Carol...Carol is the Civil War*, she decided as a look of conviction came over her face. She took a hit from her vape pen.

The movie then went to commercial, and she realized she needed to finish her coffee and jump in the shower. It was August, so she also needed to fix breakfast for the twins and get them brushed, dressed, and delivered to Motown Mood where Denise and Ricky would watch them for her.

She walked into the kitchen long enough to place her coffee mug in the sink and cringe at the mess the kids had already produced while fixing their own cereal.

"Better clean up, or you'll end up like Sarah Cynthia Silvia Stout!" called Lina to the twins, as she turned in the direction of her bathroom.

"Who?" the twins asked in unison.

"Nevermind!" said Lina as she made a mental note to order a copy of *Where the Sidewalk Ends* by Shel Silverstein.

She showered and shaved her legs but left her hair dirty, since she was on her way to get highlights and dye. It was a hot, humid day, so she made herself up and slipped on a form-fitting, sleeveless dress that would be both cool and appropriate for lunch with Aunt Isobel later.

"I'll be ready in ten minutes!" she yelled out her bedroom door to the kids. "Start getting your stuff together!"

Lina applied her red lipstick, stuck it in her purse for touch-ups, and slipped on her strappy heels. She exited her bedroom with purse in hand and made a quiet noise of disgust as she entered the mud room. Luke had dumped all the dirty camping equipment there upon yesterday's return for Lina to deal with. She decided to let it go for now and loaded the kids into the car.

Ricky was waiting outside of the Motown Mood Café to grab the twins as they pulled up, so Lina wouldn't have to search for a parking spot. As the kids jumped out, Ricky leaned in the passenger side window.

"Now, don't forget to say my new boyfriend is super-hot and rich," reminded Ricky.

"I'll be sure to say that, even though I haven't met him yet," she said, laughing. "I love you. See you later. Thanks again!" She pulled back out into traffic.

Denise was upstairs in their apartment happily making the kids pancakes in anticipation of their arrival. Greta came out in her robe and gave her wife a kiss on the cheek as Denise lowered some fresh hot cakes onto a plate with her spatula.

"Somebody seems extra chipper today!" said Greta, taking a seat at the table.

"It's just so good to have kids in the house again!" said Denise.

"Yeah, it is," agreed Greta. "I just wish Ricky would give us a grandbaby, too."

Although Denise had always been the primary caregiver when it came to Ricky, Greta adored being a mother and had secretly wished that Denise would go out and get pregnant again, back during her childbearing years. She had even half- jokingly suggested it as the two embraced each other in bed one evening not long after they had first moved to Rochester. Denise had thrown her head back, laughing at the idea, before the two had fallen into a romantic kiss.

“There is still time for Ricky to have kids." said Denise, optimistically, as Ricky arrived with Frankie and Marty. “Who’s ready for pancakes?!”

Lina dialed the number for the law office while at a red light. As the light turned green, she began to accelerate.

“Law offices of Jack Nelson," the receptionist answered.

“Yes. Hi, this is Nicolina Carlson," she said, purposely leaving out the Pratt extension of her married last name. “I need to make an appointment with Jack’s partner." It was two minutes until her appointment, so she was becoming distracted by the time.

“Oh, hi, Lina,” said Linda, Jack’s long-time receptionist who Lina had known since childhood. “Let's see, he could squeeze you in around twelve?”

“I’ll take it. Thanks, Linda,” she said hurriedly before parking and dashing into the salon for some much needed T.L.C.

At eleven forty-five, Lina emerged from the salon looking like a million bucks. Her hair was highlighted and styled, her fingers and toes were polished, and her eyebrows were perfectly arched. She also felt she had done an excellent ‘wing man’ job for Ricky with Mario. She was now a perfect package; thanks to the outfit she had selected that morning. She jumped in her car and headed back downtown for her appointment at Jack’s office. After finding parking and feeding the meter, her heels were back on the pavement.

Lina felt beautiful and confident as she strutted down Main Street to the beat of the song “Ain’t Too Proud to Beg” by The Temptations that was playing from the outdoor speakers at Motown Mood. She noticed men stealing glances and smiling at her with appreciation as she walked by. Her thoughts drifted to the day of her “Great Transformation,” when she had first caught the attention of the males in town. She smiled at the memory as she turned the corner to Walnut Street, entered the building, and climbed up the narrow stairs that led to The Nelson Law Firm.

She opened the door and saw Linda, whom she had seen recently at her father's funeral.

Linda smiled. "Hi, Honey. Kirk is expecting you. He'll be right out. Go ahead and take a seat."

Lina took a seat by the window and thought about what Linda had just said, *Kirk is expecting you*. It was a first name she didn't hear a lot. But when she did, it always made her think of *her* Kirk. She remembered her dream from that morning and made a mental note to look up what that dream could mean later.

CHAPTER SIX

1992-Ricky's Great Coming Out
"I'm Coming Out"
by Diana Ross

Lina and Ricky were fastening tape to the back of the poster they had stayed up all night working on. It was for the tenth-grade convention, and their chosen topic was gay rights. It had to be submitted for approval by seven-thirty that morning in order to be showcased along the hallway. All students in the school would be voting on the issues after the debates in the auditorium, so having your poster displayed beforehand could help aid your side in winning. Lina had been sure that if their team's point of view won, it could be the beginning of changing minds all over the world.

They were both pulling pieces of tape off the dispenser and balling the strips into little rolls. Their poster was large and heavy, as they did not think it through in the beginning. Lina had proclaimed that bigger was better and had insisted that they purchase the largest piece of poster board that Green's Art Supply had to offer. Now getting it to stay up was a challenge. They were both tired from staying up late to finish it, and they just wanted the damn thing to stay on the wall. They were on their third try now, adding additional tape to the back.

Chip LaBeau was sitting on the floor of the library watching Lina instead of helping his girlfriend Jeanette, a gorgeous girl with flowing auburn hair and dark eyes, finish their poster. Their chosen topic was "zero tolerance for adulterers in the workplace," an issue that Jeanette was passionate about since

Chip had cheated on her several times throughout their almost two-year relationship. Presidential Candidate H. Ross Perot had promised to fire all adulterers and gays if elected, and Jeanette thought that made good sense. She also hoped it would make Chip see how morally wrong it was to give into temptation.

Lina glanced over at Chip, who was dreamily smiling at her. He silently mouthed *hi* to her and winked, while his girlfriend was distracted with their poster. Lina melted before quickly mouthing a *hi* back to him and shyly looking back down at her poster.

"Oh, my gawd. I saw that," said Ricky, rolling his eyes.

"Just help me get this thing up," said Lina, slightly embarrassed, as she and Ricky lifted the massive poster again.

"He totally screwed you over. I don't know how you can even be civil to him," said Ricky.

"Oh, whatever. I see you making eyes with Kermit Karnes all the time, and it's no different," stated Lina, defensively.

"Whatever. At least Kermit isn't a total asshole like Chip," said Ricky as he sneaked a peek at Chip.

Ricky secretly thought Chip was hot too, but he would never admit it. He hated Chip for asking Lina to be his girlfriend over the summer before high school, only to dump her the second week of ninth grade.

Chip had really wanted Lina to be his girlfriend from the moment they first spoke in their final days of eighth grade. After spending the summer together, Chip had officially asked Lina to be his girlfriend. The first week of high school had been incredible. Lina felt special. Everyone wanted to know who Chip's girlfriend was, who the *chosen* one was. Everything was like a dream until Jeanette Horton moved to town.

Lina had found out that she and Chip were over when she saw him kissing Jeanette in the hallway. Jeanette was just as attractive as Lina, but Jeanette played sports. She was on the basketball, volleyball, and tennis teams, which had been the deciding factor for Chip. Now that he had been with Jeanette for two years, he was wishing he hadn't dumped Lina. She seemed to grow more attractive with each passing year. Sometimes when he walked past her at school, he felt as though he might explode with lust.

The poster seemed to be sticking to the wall this time, and Ricky and Lina did a high five before gathering up their books for class. Just as they were satisfied with their work and about to leave, Mitzy Hamilton pulled it from the wall and ripped it in half.

"HEY! WHAT THE HELL?!" screamed Ricky at Mitzy.

"It wasn't an approved poster. It needed to have a mark from Mr. Kurtz in the corner showing it was approved," stated Mitzy, holding a clipboard in her perfectly-manicured hand.

"It DOES have an approval mark from Mr. Kurtz!" said Ricky as he grabbed the torn poster to reveal the teacher's tiny initials in the corner.

"Oops, sorry," said Mitzy with a smile that said otherwise. She turned and continued to check and destroy more posters.

Ricky and Lina stood together in disbelief as they surveyed their torn project lying on the floor. They knew that even if they complained to the principal about Mitzy's actions, the poster was already destroyed. Mitzy would get away with the murder of their artwork.

Later that day, Ricky and Lina walked with their lunch trays in the cafeteria. They saw Mitzy Hamilton, the perfect blonde, at her usual table. She sat with Heather Helmsley, the statuesque redhead, and Jeni Wilcox, the skinny brunette with no curves. Ricky and Lina privately called them the "Sea Wees," since there was one with each hair color, just like the mermaid toys that Lina used to play with in the tub. Fitz was next to Jeni, doing something silly with his milk straw and making the girls laugh.

"Don't make eye contact," whispered Ricky to Lina as they approached the popular table.

"Hi, Lina," said Fitz with a shy, sincere smile.

"Hi," she said back before suddenly hearing Heather's loud, obnoxious voice.

"Look, it's the fag and the fag hag!" shrieked Heather as everyone laughed, "Mitzy ripped up their faggy poster today too!"

Lina stopped in her tracks and turned to look at the seated mean girls.

"Wow. Fag and hag rhyme. You're a genius, Heather," said Lina in her best Aunt Isobel impersonation, as she smiled coldly and headed toward her usual lunch table.

The faces of the "Sea Wees" dropped as they looked down at the table, feeling slightly stupid. The truth was, they didn't like that she took the attention of the boys at school. Lina was pretty, dressed just as nicely as them, and had a perfect figure. The girls had tried to recruit Lina to their crowd two years prior, after the great transformation. But Lina wasn't interested, and this insulted them.

Mitzy had invited Lina to her birthday party in ninth grade, but Lina had declined the invitation as it was the same day as Ricky's birthday. This infuriated Mitzy as she expected Lina to be *honored* to be invited to *her* party. She couldn't understand why Lina would want to spend the day with that queer, Ricky, instead. Plus, she had told all the boys that Lina would be attending, in hopes that it would spark more enthusiasm for the event. She had jealously watched as Lina got up in class to sharpen her pencil and noticed all of the boys staring at her in a dream-like state. Mitzy had decided then that Lina should definitely be her new best friend, so she could control her. When

Lina wasn't interested, it infuriated her. Mitzy never forgave the perceived snub of the party invitation and made sure nobody else in her crowd did either. Any chance Mitzy got, she would go out of her way to try to make Lina look bad, although it never seemed to work with the guys.

The two continued to their usual table of artists, musicians, and other various misfits. As they sat, Lina saw Chip and Jeanette join the others at the popular table. Chip winked at Lina when his girlfriend wasn't looking. Lina rolled her eyes at him and began eating, when suddenly she noticed the cowboy boot of Mitch Marquette planted next to her on the bench. She looked up to see he was strumming his acoustic guitar, before singing his lyrics.

"Your love is like a dove, that chirps a bed of fire, then flies up to my head, making me insane, 'cause your love is like acid RAIN. ACID RAIN BURNING MY BRAIN!" Mitch concluded by giving his guitar a strong tap for effect. A table of freshman girls broke into applause. He smiled graciously their way as he tucked his long, dark hair behind his ear and looked to see if Lina noticed the attention he was receiving. He walked over to greet his fans, saving her.

Lina noticed the new girl, Nora Layman, who had been introduced earlier that day in geography class. She was overweight with fuzzy hair and glasses, making her an easy target. Nora struggled to balance her lunch tray as she nervously made her way through the cafeteria.

"No fat chicks at *our* table!" called Heather, just loud enough so everyone could hear, without any proof that it was directed at Nora.

"Or people who wear clothes from the K-mart discount rack," added Jeni Wilcox quietly, as they all began to giggle.

Fitz looked embarrassed by the girls at his table, and Chip continued to try to flirt with Lina, seemingly oblivious to the situation. Ricky and Lina looked at each other.

"Did you just hear that?" asked Ricky, disgusted.

"Yes. And I think there is only one thing to do," she said as she stood, smiling. "I am going to invite her to sit with us!"

Ricky sat up proudly in his seat, and the other misfits smiled and uttered things like "that's cool" in support of Lina as she walked over to Nora Layman and invited her to join them. As Nora followed Lina to the table, Fitz looked on with admiration.

"That was actually really nice," said Fitz to his table, which was met with cold glares from the girls.

As the tenth graders finished lunch and began to filter out into the halls, Lina stopped at her locker. She was annoyed to see that the popular crowd had gathered near, and she tried to ignore them. She heard Seth Glickman's booming voice announce, "I'm ready to party tonight!" as he joined the crowd. She opened her locker and began rummaging around when Kirk began to approach her but was interrupted.

"Kirk!" called Jeni Wilcox from the social circle that had formed by Lina's locker.

Kirk was a popular senior, while Lina and the others were sophomores. She would often get jealous when girls in her own grade would flirt with Kirk or try to get his attention. She wished so badly she could just tell everyone that she lost her virginity to Kirk almost two years before. She had fantasized that Kirk would put his arm around her in the hallway and kiss her in public. Be her actual boyfriend. But that just wasn't Kirk's style. He was very private and especially wouldn't want to go public with a tenth-grade girlfriend. He was dating an older girl who was away at college, which Lina was grateful for. He rarely got to see her, and it kept him taken so none of the girls from school had a chance either. She especially liked it because it meant more late-night taps on Lina's window, when Kirk would crawl inside and into her bed.

Kirk diverted over to the circle at Jeni's request.

"Hi, Kirk," said Jeni with a giggle, as the others did the same. The tenth-grade guys thought Kirk was cool too, so they always kissed his ass.

"Sup?" asked Kirk with a grin.

"My parents are out of town, so I'm having a party tonight. Wanna come?" asked Jeni with puppy-dog eyes.

"Does he wanna cum? I bet he wants to cum!" said Lawson Jones, laughing immaturely and poking Fitz who began to laugh too. Glickman had gravitated to some freshman girls standing nearby to see if they'd be allowed to join the festivities that evening.

Kirk gave a condescending half-laugh in the direction of the younger boys, and they immediately stopped laughing and stood up straight, looking embarrassed.

Chip's girlfriend, Jeanette, interrupted. "Oh, I meant to tell you. I can't come tonight. I'm going out of town with my parents," Jeanette told Jeni as she leaned against some lockers with Chip's arm around her shoulders.

Kirk took Jeanette's interruption as an opportunity to switch his attention back to Lina, who was still searching her locker and had heard everything.

"What are you doing tonight? Do you want to go to her party?" Kirk asked Lina as he pointed his thumb back in Jeni's direction.

This question intrigued the tenth-grade boys who were suddenly silent as they waited for Lina's answer.

"Um, sure. Yeah, I could go."

"Okay, I can drive us. I'll pick you up around eight?" asked Kirk.

With one arm still around his girlfriend's shoulder, Chip chomped on his gum with a big smile as he thought of Lina being there that evening with Jeanette being out of town. He figured he had better moves than Kirk and looked at it as a challenge. The rest of the sophomore boys were now standing around Lina in a circle.

"What kind of beer do you like, Lina? My brother is buying for me tonight, so I can get whatever you want," offered Fitz.

"Yeah…and I mean, if Kirk can't drive you, I could pick you up," offered Lawson before noticing an annoyed glare from Kirk. "I mean, if there's an emergency or something."

Jeni, Heather, and Mitzy were not amused. Mitzy shot Jeni a look of urgency, commanding Jeni to put an end to this with her eyes.

Jeni blurted out, "You can't come to my party. She can't come." Jeni shook her head at everyone. "Sorry, my parents said I can only have…a *certain* number of people, so we're all filled up."

"All filled up," commented Lawson, laughing hysterically at his own joke. Fitz gave him a half smile.

Everyone knew that Jeni's parents were out of town and weren't even permitting the party, let alone a certain head count. Ricky had already walked up by this point, and had been there long enough to witness the humiliation of his best friend.

"That's okay," said Ricky. "Lina and I were invited to a college party with older people tonight anyway, so we're going to go to that."

Lina nodded along, even though there was no such party. Kirk smiled and walked off to class.

Chip and Jeanette walked by slowly, Chip's arm still around her shoulders. As the couple continued to stroll, he turned his head and looked at Lina before performing the perfect 'Chip LaBeau' move. This suave move was noted only in Lina's mind, but it consisted of a wink, a shot from a pretend gun that he formed with his thumb and forefinger, two quick chomps of his gum, and a quick grin, before placing his hand back on his girlfriend's shoulder and turning his head forward as they walked.

Even though Lina hated Chip for the way he dumped her, that move still made her weak in the knees. Ricky noticed the interaction and rolled his eyes.

###

The school day had ended, and Ricky and Lina were walking home. She pulled a pack of Virginia Slims from her backpack and lit one. She had stolen two cigarettes from a pack of Aunt Isobel's previously. She decided she liked them and that they should be her brand too. She thought they looked sophisticated, but Ricky found them disgusting. He had tried and liked marijuana but found cigarettes to be gross and pointless.

"I can't believe she did that to me!" exclaimed Lina, venting about Jeni's exclusion. "What a stupid fucking bitch! And they wonder why I don't want to be friends with them."

"Well, would you expect anything different?" asked Ricky, feeling bad for Lina. "And hey, I feel really awful that you get called names on my account. It's one thing when they call me a fag, but when they bring you into it…it makes me feel like…like I'm doing you a disservice by being your friend."

"Ricky! Don't ever say that! You are my *everything*, and I wouldn't have it any other way," assured Lina as she stumbled to pull some change from her backpack while still smoking her cigarette. "Come on, let's do our daily random acts of kindness."

"Ugh," moaned Ricky, rolling his eyes. "Do I have to go poor myself in order to spread kindness? Smiles are free, right?"

"We're only going to put change in a few parking meters today. I'm running low on change myself," she said with an angelic grin.

"So," started Ricky before taking a deep breath. "Since you are having dinner at my place tonight anyway, I thought I might take the *opportunity to* come out to my moms." He turned to Lina with a serious, pained expression.

Lina mimicked his serious expression for a moment as she looked into his eyes. Then she burst out laughing. "Are you serious?!" she asked, now bent over laughing as they walked. "Because I'm pretty sure they know. There was that whole *relationship* you had with Vin from the summer drama workshop last year, plus I really don't think they are going to have a problem with it!"

Ricky had joined the summer drama workshop offered at Oakland University in Rochester. It was there that he had met his first love, Vin Henrickson, a college student of Norwegian descent. Vin was tall, blond, muscular, and chiseled in every way. Ricky couldn't believe that Vin was showing an interest in him. His only relationship experience had been his ongoing flirtation with Kermit Karnes, which had still never blossomed into anything. Vin was twenty-one, experienced, and headed to Hollywood, which had been a dream for Ricky as well.

"Yeah, but my moms didn't know Vin was a guy! Vin can be a girl's name too."

"Um, every time I came with Denise to pick you up, you were always standing with a tall, blond guy in tight short shorts. Standing very close, I might add," said Lina. "You cried for a month when he moved to L.A.! The three of us took turns spoon-feeding you. I'm pretty sure they knew it was over the guy who totally looked like his name would be Vin, and not some girl they have never seen," she added, laughing. "Also, your bedroom is full of dance competition medals and you love Madonna."

"Well, some people don't know. I feel like I need to officially come out, so that people will know I'm gay and available. Then my moms can talk openly about me being gay and maybe help hook me up," he said shyly, looking over at Lina.

"You want your moms' help with finding guys?"

"Hey, they are a good advertising device! You get asked out all the time by guys, Lina. I want to be asked out by guys too. It's hard enough meeting other gay people. I need to be completely out."

As they continued to walk past Walnut and onto Main Street, Lina thought about how her grandpa might be the only person who didn't know Ricky was gay. She was pretty sure he still thought Denise and Greta were just roommates like "Laverne and Shirley."

The music from the Motown Mood Café speakers were now audible, and Madonna's "Vogue" was playing. The two sixteen-year-olds were now in front of Mr. O'Malley's store. Ricky immediately started vogueing like the expert he was and serving invisible competitors with his skills. Lina joined along to the best of her ability as Mr. O'Malley's grumpy figure entered his doorway. Lina spotted him and cut him off before he could complain.

"It's not turned up too loud!" she informed Mr. O'Malley.

"THAT'S NOT THE POINT! NOBODY WANTS TO SEE HIS PANSY ASS PRANCIN AROUND OUT HERE! THAT'S BORDERLINE OBSCENE! THERE ARE GOOD PEOPLE AROUND HERE THAT DON'T WANNA SEE THAT SHIT!" yelled Mr. O'Malley, motioning to a lady smoking a cigarette and people off in the distance who didn't seem to notice or care. He slammed his door.

As the two continued on their way to the Motown Mood Café for Ricky's coming out, Lina commented reassuringly, "He called you a pansy ass. See! Even "Fuck Face" knows you're gay."

The two entered the upstairs apartment at the café, kicked off their shoes, and threw their backpacks on the floor. Denise was watching Bill Clinton speak on TV as she munched from a bowl of Doritos. Lina bent down and put her arms around Denise's neck from behind, as she kissed the top of her head and paused to watch her favorite presidential candidate speak.

"I think he's gonna win," said Lina before grabbing a Dorito from Denise's bowl and heading towards Greta. "I just know it!"

Lina entered the kitchen and gave Greta a kiss on the cheek before shoving the Dorito into her mouth.

"Hey! Where did you get that?" Greta asked Lina. "Denise! I said no snacking! Dinner is almost ready. I'm just finishing up!" called Greta towards the living room.

"What?! It's an appetizer!" Denise called back.

Greta didn't cook often. Denise was the usual cook in the house, but Greta had a few specialties that she liked to make every so often. Denise had been feeling overwhelmed with household chores lately, and Greta was trying to do more around the house. Running the business and booking musical talents had been Greta's main role, but she could tell when Denise was beginning to feel underappreciated. She had even made Denise's favorite cake for dessert.

Greta brought the food to the table, and the other three filed into the dining area to sit down. Ricky looked at Lina and gave her a nod before taking his seat at the table. Lina remained standing and cleared her throat.

"Tonight...is no ordinary dinner," announced Lina. "Tonight will go down in history." She paused for dramatic effect, "When we recall this evening one day, it shall bring a tear to our eyes."

The two mothers looked at each other with impressed expressions.

“Well, this sounds very exciting," said Denise as she and Greta smiled at each other.

Ricky rose and took a deep breath, before closing his eyes. He always did this when getting into character for his drama class. “I’m gay!" he blurted out.

Lina was surprised. She thought Ricky would give some sort of speech before diving right in. His two mothers looked at each other. Ricky stumbled, not sure what to do with the silence.

“So, um…”

“Ricky, I have some pamphlets on how to tell your parents that you’re gay in the back room," offered Greta before giggling and standing to put her arms around Ricky.

“You thought we didn’t know?" asked Denise, confused. “I mean, we survived the whole Vin thing.”

“Vin can be a girl’s name too!" insisted Ricky before falling into a hug with Denise.

“So now you guys can do your Jewish matchmaking stuff with Ricky!" offered Lina before shoving some bread into her mouth.

There was a knock on the door. Lina got up to answer, as they were expecting her grandfather to pick her up after a church activity he had been attending that evening.

“Grandpa!" she said, opening the door.

“Hi, honey.”

“Come on in. Ricky just had his big coming out.”

“Comin outta what?" asked Grandpa with his Italian accent, as everyone stifled a giggle.

“Nevermind. Come on in and have some food," she said, kissing him on the cheek and taking his arm.

###

Grandpa drove Lina home that evening. She entered the house and saw that Bill was home watching the news.

"Hi, Dad! I'm home!" called Lina as she grabbed a can of soda from the fridge and headed into her bedroom.

She shut her door and made herself comfortable on her bed. She was obsessed with the V.C. Andrew's *Heaven* series and couldn't wait to get back to her book. No matter what happened in her life, it was never as messed up as the lives of those characters. As she began to drift into a fictitious place and time, there was a knock at her window. She smiled and placed her bookmark back inside. She knew it must be Kirk. She had wondered if he was still going to go to Jeni's party.

She quickly checked her reflection, before pulling up her window shade to find Kirk's handsome figure in the moonlight. She slid her window open.

"Hey. What are you doing?" asked Kirk.

"Just reading. Just got home from Ricky's."

"Come out."

"My Dad is still up watching TV. It's only ten o'clock," she said, wanting to go outside and be with Kirk more than anything. "It's our last week before you go. Before everything changes." She began to feel overcome with emotion.

"I know. That's why I want you to come out. Screw your Dad, he won't notice. Just quietly walk out the front door."

Lina agreed and made a quick trip to the bathroom to brush her teeth before sneaking a peek at Bill. He was snoring in his chair with the TV still on. She made her way outside and to the very back of her property, behind a shed, where she and Kirk had often met. He led her through the dark to a picnic blanket spread under a large oak tree. The two teenagers got comfortable on the blanket, each lying on their sides and looking into each other's eyes. Lina enjoyed the scent of Kirk's Drakkar Noir cologne and smiled, knowing she would be wearing the same scent by daybreak.

“I saw you and your grandpa at church last Sunday. What did you think of the new deacon?”

“Yeah, I saw you too. He was okay. We stopped and talked to him on the way out. Seems nice. He’s young.”

“Yeah," said Kirk before an awkward silence. “So my parents are selling the house.”

“What?”

“Yeah, my parents don’t need the big house anymore. I’ll be studying abroad for two years, and they want to retire somewhere warm.”

“What if I never see you again?" asked Lina, feeling sick.

“Of course you’ll see me again, silly. I’ll be back in Michigan, hopefully going to Wayne State Law, eventually. I’ll come back for you. I’ll be back when you graduate from high school.”

With that, he closed in on Lina’s lips and began to explore her beautiful body. He made love to her that night under the stars like he would never make love again. He was excited for his future and naively thought she would be right there, waiting for him, in two years.

###

The next morning, Bill was up drinking coffee. He had an early tee time with Jack, Brad, and George at the club. Lina was entering the kitchen in her robe and socks, still blissful from the night before.

“Good Morning. I’m running late to play golf with the guys. I’d like you to pick up the rent check from Walt Weimer. The cop in the red house," he said as he pointed up to the house through the window.

She remembered which tenant Walt was because he creeped her out. She wanted to like him because he was a police officer, but the way he sometimes looked at her just seemed icky. He looked at and flirted with her the same way that boys in school did. Many grown men had begun to look at Lina differently, but in a respectful, gentleman-like way. Walt simply made the hairs on her neck stand at attention, and not in a good way.

"Okay," she sighed.

Lina had nothing planned for the day except reading her book, but she showered and got made up anyway, just in case Kirk decided to stop by unannounced. She threw on a comfortable pull-on skirt and t-shirt. *Nothing fancy but still cute.* She slid on her leather flats and headed up to Walt Weimer's, passing her father's REELECT BUSH FOR PRESIDENT lawn sign.

Walt answered the door still wearing his police uniform, unbuttoned to reveal a white "wife beater" sleeveless t-shirt.

"Hey there, beautiful lady. What beckons you?"

"Hi, my Dad said to pick up the rent check," she said with a polite smile.

"Well, why don't you come inside and see what I've done with the place?"

She stuck her neck inside the doorway. After looking around, she stepped back and said, "Yep, nice."

"Well, the check is in the kitchen. Come in," he said, smiling to reveal crooked teeth.

She begrudgingly entered her father's rental house. She just wanted to get this over with. Walt shut the door.

"You know, I felt an instant connection between us, Nicolina. Or should I call you Lina?" he asked, smiling with endearment. "You see, I've earned my certificate in paranormal consciousness, and I attend many workshops. I have a sixth sense when it comes to feeling cosmic connections. I can even make the flame of a candle move using only my mind."

"Oh, cool," she remarked as she looked away and rolled her eyes.

"Some people are just more sensitive than others, and through study, I've really been able to *hone in* on my abilities. It's all about astrology."

"Well, I'm glad you've been able to *hone* and everything. You got that check?"

"You're sixteen, right? That's the legal age of consent in Michigan. I saw a thing on TV where a sixteen-year-old ran off with a thirty-year-old. I'm twenty-nine," he said, smiling like they were meant to be.

"Oh, so I really gotta get goin-"

"Don't fight God, Lina. You don't think there was a reason that God made me rent from your dad?"

"Because it was available you answered the newspaper ad?"

Walt took both of her hands and looked into her eyes for a moment, before quickly grabbing her and lifting her into his arms. It was then that she realized she was in danger. She tried to grab the edge of the wall to free herself, but he kept walking to the bedroom. He placed her gently on the bed.

"Sixteen is the legal age for marriage in Michigan. I mean, your dad would have to say okay. But I'm a cop and everything, so I'm sure he'd approve."

His expression and demeanor then turned serious and cold as if a lustful demon had taken over his body. He pinned Lina to the bed, holding her down with one hand and unzipping his pants with the other. As he penetrated her, she lay frozen, her mind racing. He was being gentle. She was the legal age for consent in Michigan, and he wasn't a stranger. He was a cop, so was this really rape? Was it really okay for her to kick a cop in the balls? She remained still, unsure of what to do, and waited for it to be over. When he finished and rose to button his pants, she jumped up, found her panties on the floor, and immediately headed to the front door.

“Aren’t you forgetting something?" he asked, holding the check.

As she went to grab the check from his hand, he whipped it away.

“Now we can have fun like this every month when you come to collect the rent. It will be our special time," he whispered, kissing her forehead. “And who knows? After today, we might be having a baby too.” He looked hopeful, then his personality seemed to shift again. “You’re the age of consent and you came over here begging for it. I am merely a son of God who was tempted by the evil Eve.”

She snatched the check from his hand, pushed past him, and raced home. It didn’t seem real, and she was still out of breath from the rape, but she just kept running to the safety of her bedroom. There was a sunny spot in the corner where the sunlight rested. She sat there in a fetal position, feeling an odd comfort from the warmth. She wished her mom was there. She sat there until the sun set, then took a long shower. She thanked the Lord with tears of relief, two days later, when her period arrived.

Lina never told anyone. She found ways to get Ricky or her grandfather to collect the rent check on her behalf. A few months later, Walt purchased the house from Bill, leaving no more rent checks to be collected. She avoided Walt like the plague for the next two years, before moving to San Diego for college.

CHAPTER SEVEN

2016
"The Walk"
by Mayer Hawthorne

Lina continued to ponder her dream about Kirk. She checked the time on her phone.

"Nicolina Carlson," said a man's voice.

She looked up and into the eyes of Kirk Kavanaugh. She froze and struggled to catch her breath as her heart began to race. His light-brown hair was now mostly gone, his once toned body was larger, but those eyes still pierced into her as they always had. Yes, this was *her* Kirk standing before her. Kirk Kavanaugh, to whom she had lost her virginity and waited for. Her lost love, who now wore a band of gold on his ring finger. He stood grinning at her with a slightly-flushed face and nervous yet flirty eyes. She was so taken by surprise that she could hardly respond. In all the madness, it hadn't even occurred to her to ask or even Google who Jack's partner at the law firm was. She finally had the sense to stand.

"Kirk?! My God, is that really you?" she asked, smiling and awestruck. "Did you know it was me that Jack was sending to you?"

When she extended her hand for him to shake, he held onto it with both of his for a pause. They looked into each other's eyes before breaking their contact. He wanted to grab her and kiss her, but he knew that would be inappropriate under the circumstances. Plus, he wasn't sure how she would feel about him at this point. He had excitedly flown to Michigan in August

1994 with hopes of reuniting with Lina, but he had been crushed to find out that she had just left for California the day before. It was then that he had made the decision to reunite with his ex-girlfriend, whom he had met in college, and get married. After he graduated from law school, opportunities presented themselves in his hometown. That's where he and his wife settled to raise their children. He had thought about Lina often but figured that she had probably long since forgotten about him.

"Yes, and I'm so sorry about your father. Come on in and have a seat."

Kirk led Lina into a conference room which had all the necessary paperwork already organized and stacked neatly in piles. Kirk extended his arm and motioned for Lina to take a seat.

"Fine wine ages, and you do not," said Kirk, pausing to grin at Lina before pulling something up on his P.C.

Lina could feel her face blushing. This was the first time Kirk had ever outright complimented her. His attention in the past had always been through teasing.

"So, I guess you're all caught up on me," she said, motioning toward the large stack of paperwork. "Why don't you tell me where you've been all these years? I was hoping to see you before I left for college, but you never seemed to return."

Kirk inhaled. "I did return, but you had already left." He paused. "You know my parents moved to Florida."

"Yes, I know. So, is that your wife and kids?" she asked, pointing to the family portrait on his desk and changing the uncomfortable subject.

"Yes," he said, picking up the photo. "This is my wife, Kitty, and these are my kids. Joe is fifteen now and my daughter, Rachel, is twelve."

Lina tried not to laugh that his wife's name was Kitty. Her mouth formed a smirk instead.

"What?" asked Kirk with a chuckle.

"Nothing. You have a beautiful family, Kirk."

"Okay, so your stepmother," he said, stopping to look at her name on the paper. "*Carol* hasn't signed the paperwork yet to have the investment funds split up and allocated. She will need to sign those in order for things to get moving."

"Jesus, that woman is such a procrastinator. This will never get done," said Lina, breaking from being formal now that they were down to business.

"Well, that's why you have a great team of lawyers, Miss Carlson," Kirk said with a smile. "I will call her this afternoon."

Lina secretly loved how he addressed her as a single woman, even though he knew full well she was married.

"Next business," continued Kirk. "It seems that you have a set of tenants who haven't paid their rent in three months. Jack brought this up to me before he left. Apparently, your Dad had nothing but problems with these people. He suggested we serve them with an eviction."

"Okay," agreed Lina, thankful that they seemed to have that situation under control for her.

"Sounds good, we'll have them served by tomorrow morning."

Kirk pushed a document across the desk for Lina to sign. As she scribbled her name, he stole a long look at her cleavage which was popping through her tight, V-neck dress. He remembered how he used to long for her breasts as a teen boy and how great she had looked in a bikini that day he stole her innocence. His thoughts were interrupted when she pushed the signed document back his way. Kirk looked down at the next set of paperwork, read for a moment, and then spoke again. "Okay, and you're aware that your aunt is running low on money? I have a copy for you of the budget arrangement your dad made for her."

Lina sighed. Aunt Isobel was ten years older than her father and had been married five times. Her son, Miles, worked on Wall Street and rarely came to visit. Isobel had become Bill's unofficial responsibility once Lina's grandparents died. Isobel had moved into Fairview with her parents not long before they had passed away, and that is where Isobel remained when she wasn't staying in England with family or traveling.

"Now, about your dad's house," said Kirk, moving the business meeting along.

"My *mom's* house," Lina corrected. She didn't want it referred to as his house.

"I'm assuming Jack went over this with you?" Kirk inquired.

"Yeah, about that. The conditions. Jack said that per the prenuptial agreement, I own the house, but she gets to live there as long as she wants. She is allowed to stay as long as she continues to pay the mortgage, the taxes, and the upkeep of the house. He said she can't sell it because it's not hers, it's mine. How am I supposed to know if she's meeting all those conditions? Carol won't let me into the house or speak to me, so I don't even know the mortgage account number," Lina explained as the anger started to rise in her again. "And how is there even a mortgage? I was under the impression that it was paid off decades ago!"

"Well, it looks like it *was* paid off, but your dad took out a home equity loan to purchase a vehicle."

"What?"

"It's quite brilliant actually," Kirk said smiling. "That way he could write off a mortgage on his taxes, essentially using his car payment as a tax break. This could actually be a good thing, Lina." He tapped his pen on the paper before him with excitement. "At least there is a mortgage for her to possibly not pay." There was a long pause as Kirk continued to look at the paper and think. "Okay, here is what I suggest. Don't ask her for the account number. You don't want her to know you're keeping tabs. I know this is hard. Jack told me how difficult the funeral was for you. Don't worry. That's what I'm here for."

Hearing those words from Kirk's lips made her melt inside. That was the first time anyone had said anything even remotely comforting to her. Her husband, Luke, had barely said a word to her or given her a hug for that matter. Here was her long-lost, forever crush sitting before her and offering to protect her. To be there for her. Her eyes began to water, and she suddenly felt like going across the desk and kissing him. She wanted him to take her right there on his desk, like the first time he had taken her on the desk at the swim club. Her emotions were everywhere, and she wasn't sure she could trust any of them. She looked into Kirk's dilated pupils and sensed he wanted the same. They shared a long look before Kirk glanced at the clock and spoke again.

"I have another client coming. I apologize. Normally, I would allocate more time, but we wanted to fit you in. I was waiting for your call, Lina."

Kirk walked around to her side of the desk, and Lina stood for a hug. The chemistry between them was undeniable. Like two magnets struggling to come apart, the lust was magnified with the friendly embrace. Without thinking, Kirk tightened his grasp around Lina's waist and gently pressed her against the wall. He looked her in the eyes with the same intensity he had the day he deflowered her. Kirk was unhappily married, and he loved his kids, but Lina looked so good. He wasn't expecting her body to have the same effect on him that it once had, or for the chemistry between them to be so electric. He too had thought of Lina over the years. He had wondered who was looking into her exotic eyes, what she did for a living, if she was married, and who was making love to her. He knew now that she was married, but he also noticed she wasn't wearing a ring.

Kirk gave in to temptation and pressed his lips firmly against hers, before gently pressing his tongue into her mouth. Lina slightly resisted at first, then slowly reciprocated. Kissing Kirk was the closest thing to happiness she had experienced in ages, even if it was wrong. Lina was so thirsty for affection, for comfort, for the touch of a man. And this was Kirk. The boy, the *man,* she had thought of all those years. Here he was, his warm flesh encompassing hers.

The kissing became more intense. Kirk placed his right hand over her breast and his left hand up her skirt, as he continued to lean her against the office wall. She felt his fingers penetrate her as she pulled her face from Kirk's, breathing heavily, eyes closed. He continued to pleasure her with his fingers, causing her to let out a quiet moan. She instinctively reached for his crotch and began running her hand up and down his trousers in one spot. He was fully aroused and becoming more passionate in his kiss and touch. Then there was a knock on the office door before it began to open. They both jumped back into reality.

"Mr. Kavanaugh, sorry to interrupt," said Linda, oblivious, as she entered with some papers.

"Well, I should be going," said Lina, straightening her dress behind Linda's back.

"Yes, I'll let you know what Carol says after I call her. And we'll serve the eviction notice to those tenants. We'll be in touch," Kirk said, acting as if nothing had happened and hoping Linda wasn't noticing the bulge in his dress pants.

Lina saw herself out and stepped back onto Main Street, feeling a mix of cloud nine and nausea. On one hand, she knew nothing could ever come of this. On the other hand, she just had the sexiest experience with her childhood crush. She smiled as she strutted to "Brick House" by The Commodores, playing from the Motown Mood speakers that ran all along the street. She felt floaty with butterflies as she jumped into her white Ford Flex and headed to the Grand Park Hotel on University Drive to meet Aunt Isobel for lunch. She pulled up to the valet, took her parking stub, and walked inside.

As she entered the swanky hotel, her eyes scanned the beautiful marble floors and the signed photographs of presidents and world leaders that had stayed there in the past. The Grand Park was well known as being one of Metro Detroit's finest places to dine and stay. She knew that although Aunt Isobel was treating, that it was going to be charged to the Carlson account, which meant Lina was actually paying. She felt a bit sick, since she wasn't sure how to pay that bill right now. She hoped Kirk would get Carol to sign the papers in order to at least get some money to start taking care of the things she had to. She started to become angry at how Carol's laziness or just lack of care had been what was holding up Lina's part of the monetary inheritance. It was bad enough that this stranger was taking a large chunk away from Lina and her kids, but she at least wanted what was supposed to go to her. She decided to push that from her mind before she went into a rage. She needed to keep her composure in order to have a pleasant lunch with her aunt.

There was no sign of Aunt Isobel or her driver yet, but she recognized a cackling laugh followed by the familiar voice that went with it. *Fuck, it's Heather Helmsley*, she thought as she hurriedly moved to the back of the lobby behind a giant marble column. All of Lina's horrible memories of Heather came flooding back. She remembered how Heather's obnoxious mouth used to call her a "fag hag," and how she used to refer to Ricky as "she" just to be a bitch in high school. She sneaked a peek from around the column to see that it was in fact Heather, and she also noticed that Heather had gained a significant amount of weight since high school. Her spying was suddenly interrupted by a flamboyant young man in his twenties with perfectly manicured eyebrows.

"Is there anything I may assist you with, Ma'am?" asked the maître d.

Startled, but immediately noticing that the hotel employee played for Ricky's team, she responded, "Oh, hi. Yes, could you tell me how long the wait is for a table? I'm meeting my aunt, *Isobel Carlson*, for lunch. As you may know, she's elderly. I wouldn't want her to wait for too long."

"I overheard my colleague at the restaurant check-in telling some other guests that the wait time is *thirty*. Have you checked in and put your name on the list yet?"

Lina thought fast. She only had about fifty extra dollars from Ricky's winnings, the rest had been deposited into her bank account, to register the twins for football and cheer later that afternoon. She reached into her bag to retrieve a fifty.

"I haven't yet. But I'm wondering if you might be able to assist me. You see that loud woman over there?" She motioned to Heather, who was loudly talking with a friend, "In high school, that lady used to call me a "fag hag" and bullied my gay best friend, Ricky, mercilessly." She showed the young man her fifty-dollar bill. "Is there any way my aunt and I could be seated before them? Like in a really obnoxious fashion?" She looked at him with hopeful, big eyes.

The man looked over at Heather and friends, then turned back to Lina with an evil smile. "Is it Ricky Goldman you're referring to?"

Surprised, Lina said, "Yes, you know him?"

"Let me put it to you this way, the boys and I love when your friend and his tight dancer's body comes in. He is one *hot* older man. Total snack. His mom Greta is a legend too," he finished, smiling. "Put that fifty away, girl. You said you're with Ms. Carlson, correct?"

"Yes. I'm Lina Carlson," she said smiling back, not sure of what was happening.

The young man held up his finger to signal that it would be just a moment. Then he went to the host station and whispered into his co-worker's ear. She saw that same evil smile come over the host's face, and Lina realized that he must be gay too. She then noticed her aunt being escorted in by her driver. Lina didn't want Heather to notice her, so she quietly made her way over to greet Isobel, as Heather was heavy in conversation with her friends. Lina thanked Fred, the driver, and gave him a kiss on the cheek before he headed back outside to wait.

"Sorry that I'm a tad late, dear. The traffic in this town is absolutely atrocious. There are just too many cars on the road at the same time! I'll be sure to address the mayor about this. You *do* understand, darling."

"Yes, of course, Aunt Isobel," she said, giving her air kisses.

Feeling confident, thanks to her morning salon visit, she took Aunt Isobel's arm and walked confidently towards where Heather was chatting. She gently nudged in front of Heather to check in with the host.

"Yes, hi. Carlson is the name. Table for two, please."

"Lina?!" exclaimed Heather.

Lina turned to follow the voice and acted like she didn't immediately recognize her. "Yes. Oh, *Heather*? I didn't recognize you," said Lina, giving her a once over followed by a fake smile. "How *are* you?"

"Well, we'd be better if there wasn't such a long wait," she complained, giving the host an annoyed glare as if it was his fault.

The host interrupted, "Yes, the two lovely Carlson women. Right this way, please."

Lina turned to Heather. "Well, I guess *our* table is ready. Nice to see you, Heather."

She saw Heather's face turn red, as her jaw began to drop. Aunt Isobel, who always expected that kind of treatment at the

Grand Park, didn't seem to notice their preferred status. She simply nodded in the direction of Heather and her friends as the first Maître d that Lina had spoken to, hurriedly came over to escort her. After their chairs were pulled out for them, the two ladies took their seats.

As he pushed her in, Lina whispered in the young man's ear, "Thank you so much."

"My pleasure. Tell Ricky that Jordan at the Grand Park says hi."

"Will do," she said, smiling up at him.

Lina then turned her focus on her seventy-five-year-old lunch companion. Her aunt was perfectly put together in a navy Ralph Lauren dress. Lina thought about how Ricky had always said that her aunt looked like novelist Jackie Collins. Aunt Isobel wasted no time, and went straight to something she had been considering.

"So, I was thinking," began Isobel, "I should move into your father's house while Fairview is being renovated. It would help Carol out with housing expenses, and I could avoid staying in some dreadful hotel. Which would also help *me* financially, of course."

Lina stared at her father's older sister, dumbfounded. She had previously mentioned the conditions of her father's prenup to her aunt. If Isobel moved in and helped Carol with housing costs, there was no hope of Lina getting her house back anytime soon. Her only hope was for Carol to fail in meeting the prenup conditions concerning residency of the home. Lina *needed* Carol to not be able to afford the mortgage, taxes, and upkeep. Lina *needed* Carol to give up, so she would leave. That was the only way Lina could legally take custody of the house that she legally owned. Closing her open mouth and struggling to keep her composure, Lina spoke.

"*Isobel*, I thought you were going to England for six months? *That* is when you said you'd have Fairview remodeled!"

"Well, yes, darling, but you know how long contractors can take. If I move out now and let them get started, it will be finished by the time I return from England. That would give them a full nine months. You know how much I hate to be inconvenienced with all the dust and noise."

"*Isobel*, you know you are on a tight budget these days, yes? Dad said he went over all of this with you before. Arnold's pension has run out and your inheritance from Grandpa and Gran is dwindling. It's *imperative* that you stay within your budget that my dad set up for you! Why will it take nine full months? Did you *add* to the budget?"

Lina saw the uncomfortable look on Isobel's face and softened. Isobel was grieving too. Her world was changing as she struggled to cling to the only lifestyle she had ever known.

"Isobel, I'm asking you to stay out of my mom's house. I *need* you to stay out. I really don't appreciate being stabbed in the back," Lina said firmly, staring her elderly aunt dead in the eyes.

"Well, I'm *hardly* stabbing you in the back, darling. It was just a thought," said Isobel, seemingly surprised that Lina would have such a problem with that arrangement.

"We will discuss the renovations and schedule another time, but I must insist you stay *out* of my mom's house, Aunt Isobel. *Please*."

They were interrupted by the server coming to take their order. *Thank God*, thought Lina. *Saved by the bell*. She was becoming so angry and upset that she needed that interruption in order to prevent her from saying something she might regret.

Lina barely managed to make it through the rest of lunch with Isobel. She was highly irritated with her aunt's suggestion and felt betrayed. After what seemed like an eternity, Lina signed their tab. The two women said their goodbyes as Fred escorted Aunt Isobel into the backseat of her old Mercedes. Lina stood alone now, waiting for the valet to bring her car. She texted Ricky that she was on her way to collect the kids. She thought about her conversation with Kirk, and how life insurance money would be coming soon.

Lina texted Mitch Marquette, "I'd like to buy that Escalade."

After her car arrived at the curb, she tipped the valet and headed out to collect the twins for football and cheer registration.

Lina pulled up in front of the café and honked her horn. Traffic in Rochester was especially bad at that time of the day and Main street was jammed with cars. Annoyed drivers honked their horns, trying to get around her in their lane.

Ricky came running out with Frankie and Marty. He had been working with Frankie to refresh her cheer moves for the beginning of the new season. As a professional dancer, Ricky was great with choreography and stage presence. He enjoyed working with Frankie and was so glad Lina was back home. This not only enabled him to have Lina back in his life full-time, it allowed him to form a bond with her kids.

"Bye, Uncle Ricky," they sang in unison as they piled into the car and fastened themselves. Ricky poked his head in through the open door on the passenger side.

"She is doing great! We will be ready for another winning season of competitive cheer!" he called out to Lina.

"Thank you!" she called back. "Text you later!"

She drove to the high school where registration and practices were held. This was Frankie and Marty's second year with Metro Detroit Competitive Cheer and Football (MDCCF). The previous fall, Marty's football team had won the league Superbowl and Frankie's cheer team had won first place at the Midwestern Cheer Competition in Chicago. The entire town was ready for the new season, and Lina was looking forward to seeing the kids advance even further this year. Being brand new in town, it had been an important achievement for the twins.

The trio arrived at the high school and headed out to the football field where registration was being held. The August afternoon felt like a sauna, and Lina wished she was in her pool instead. She remembered how chaotic the registration had been the year before and just wanted to get it over with.

The football field was lively with footballs flying past and girls practicing their cartwheels. Lina found the correct cheer booth and began filling out paperwork and writing checks. As she looked over the forms, she saw the name of the new cheer coach, Jeni Wilcox-Slade. Her stomach turned as she heard a familiar voice right behind her.

"Nicolina Carlson? Is that you?"

Lina turned to see Jeni Wilcox from high school. The cheerleader who, all those years ago, had humiliated her in front of everyone by telling Lina she wasn't invited to her party. The bitch who had snickered when Mitzy ripped Lina and Ricky's convention poster from the wall and had delighted in Greta and Denise being called dykes. Jeni's big, fake smile made Lina want to use it as a punching bag. She was emotionally fragile and could not believe this was happening.

"It's me, Jeni Wilcox…well, *was* Jeni Wilcox. My married name is Slade. I thought you might be the Nicolina Carlson listed on the Mom roster, but then I thought you would be married by now…," said Jeni with a smiling mouth and bullets for eyes.

"Yes, that's me! I *am* married, but I guess I accidentally put my maiden name when I signed up! How exciting that you'll be coaching my Frankie!" She lied.

"Well, you know I was the head cheerleader in high school. And the previous coach moved to Nebraska, so I was the obvious choice!" bragged Jeni.

"Oh? Do you have kids on the team?"

"No, my son is a senior in high school now."

"Oh, wow. You started early, then."

"Yes, I was able to *find* a husband with no problem. Looks like you started a little late," said Jeni with a smirk.

"Yes, well, I was busy with the whole successful career thing."

"Oh? What did you do?"

"I sold medical supplies to hospitals," said Lina, aware her former job didn't sound that cool.

"Oh, how exciting," stated Jeni, flatly.

It was now obvious to Lina that Jeni had not changed and was purposely being a snot. *It's on*, thought Lina. She looked Jeni up and down as she spoke. Then she focused on Jeni's nose, and then her breasts. Both had obviously been altered. Lina smiled.

"Well, I'm so glad you said something to me, Jeni! I'm not sure I would have recognized you! You look so *different*. It's a *big* improvement," she said as her gaze went back to Jeni's chest. Then, making it as obvious as possible that she was focused on Jeni's new, much-smaller nose, Lina grinned. "Did you do something different with your hair color too? Something else is different, but I just can't put my finger on it." She casually brushed her finger against her own nose.

Jeni's eyes grew large with embarrassment. "We'll catch up more later," she said as she turned to the crowd of girls and mothers who were finishing paperwork and gathering now.

"Okay," said Jeni, clapping her hands together to get everyone's attention. "Welcome to the 2016 MDCCF cheer and football season! Please find the sign-up in your email for snacks! I have very strict dietary guidelines for our athletes! With a new coach comes different rules! I want healthy snacks. Healthy does not include cheese sticks or anything that contains animal fat!

Such items will constipate our girls and hinder their overall performance! I became a vegan six months ago, and it has changed my life. You will see the exact options for snacks listed in the sign-up!"

Lina could hear the subtle groaning within the crowd of moms as Jeni spoke. It made her feel some relief knowing that others seemed to find the new coach annoying by their own accord.

As soon as Jeni began to wrap up the meeting, Lina made a beeline for the football registration booth. She saw her old classmate, Fitz, throwing around the ball. She was already reacquainted with Fitz, as he was Marty's coach the previous year and would be again this year. He was the general manager of their organization and was also a popular realtor in the Greater Detroit area. "Fitz gitz it sold!" was the slogan on his park-bench advertisements. Fitz noticed Lina approaching and gave her a friendly wave as she started writing more checks and filling out paperwork. She heard a man behind her address the teenager handling the booth.

"Yeah, I need to register Logan LaBeau."

Lina knew that voice and last name. She could feel her spine stiffen and her face turn red. She slowly turned and saw Chip LaBeau standing behind her. The teenager was handing him the forms.

"Chip?" asked Lina in disbelief.

Chip stared at her for a second, and then his face and eyes instantly brightened.

"Lina? NO WAY! Did you move back?" asked Chip, astonished.

"Yes, my kids are on the team. I mean, my son is on football and my daughter does cheer," said Lina as she nervously tripped over her words.

The teen briefly interrupted to tell Chip about one of the forms. He asked the teen if he could hang on a second, as he turned to Lina.

"Hey, so do you want to exchange numbers so we can catch up sometime?" asked Chip.

Lina agreed. The two quickly exchanged numbers as she turned in her completed football paperwork and Chip continued with registration. She stopped to address Fitz as she passed him.

"Hey, Fitz! How are you? Did you notice Chip LaBeau is here?" she asked, smiling.

"Hey, Lina. I'm doing good. Yeah, Chip lives in my old sub, next door to my ex. I told him about the organization, so his son is starting this year. If his son is as athletic as his dad, this will be a great season!" said Fitz, smiling with enthusiasm.

Chip and Fitz had played varsity football, basketball, and baseball together in middle and high school, and Fitz couldn't have been more excited to coach young Logan. Both of Lina's children came running up.

"Okay, well, I guess we're all set. See you tomorrow at practice," said Lina as she and the children began to walk off the field and back to the car. Lina looked back and saw Chip looking at her. They exchanged a wave, and she turned to keep walking.

The trio pulled into their driveway, just north of the Rochester city limits. The twins ran inside, anxious to get back to their tablets and video games, and Lina decided to get the mail from her box at the end of her driveway. She smiled as she took in her surroundings. It was a beautiful summer day. She felt grateful that they were able to afford a nice home, thanks to the sale of their much more expensive but significantly smaller home in San Diego. The trees were lush and green and almost seemed to make subtle, clapping sounds as the wind blew through them. The slight humidity made the breeze feel warm in the early evening, and she savored the smell of the natural vegetation. It was something she had missed while living in California.

As she opened her mailbox and began to flip through the junk and bills, she silently reflected on her day and smiled. This was the first moment she had been alone to even try to digest that she had not only seen Kirk, but Chip also. She thought about her inappropriate rendezvous in Kirk's office and began to tingle all over. Then, just as quickly, she reminded herself that while the chemistry was definitely still there, they were both married. Even if she did consider her marriage to basically be over, his wasn't. She couldn't give in to her feelings. Then she remembered Chip. *Mmm, man did he look good,* she thought, beginning to feel giddy again. *I wonder if Chip is married. He has kids.*

From the corner of her eye, she saw a white Mercedes pull up and stop near the end of her property. She figured they were there to visit the Weiss's next door and continued to look through the mail pile as she headed to her front porch.

"Lina!" called the man who was exiting the Mercedes. "What's up?!"

It was old schoolmate and next-door neighbor at the Carlson cottage up north, Seth Glickman. She had seen him at her father's funeral and had spoken to him briefly, mentioning that she was currently living in Rochester Township.

"Hey, Seth! How are you?" she asked, feeling confused as to why he was suddenly at her home unannounced. "Whatcha doin?"

"Well, I didn't have a chance to tell you at your dad's funeral, but I'm actually the mayor of Rochester Township," he touted, proudly.

"Oh, really?" asked Lina, confused, as she wasn't aware the township even had a mayor.

"Yes, well, I'm the township council president, so it's basically the mayor," he informed, smiling and standing tall.

"Cool! I did not know that," she stated, still wondering why he was there.

"Yes, I like to drive around my district often to make sure everything is in order," he said, now leaning against his car. "Then I remembered you were now living within my jurisdiction, so I figured I'd stop by! I think it's important to check in on my constituents."

"Oh, well thanks for checking in! We're fine!" she said with an awkward laugh.

Seth Glickman's face then turned serious. "Lina, if there is *anything* I can do for you. I mean, *anything*, please let me know. I'm here to serve," he added almost seductively as he looked down at her cleavage in the dress she still had on since that morning.

"Well, I will keep that in mind," she said, smiling. "Thanks. Oh…and tell your dad I said hi!"

"Will do!" said Glickman. He gave her a card with his contact information and then tripped over the curb as he tried to get back to his car.

She watched him leave and waved as he turned around in the cul-de-sac.

She exhaled and thought, *This was an excellent day to go to the salon! I ran into everybody today.*

Inside now, she saw that the kids were in the basement playing video games. She poured herself a diet Faygo, a popular Michigan brand of soda-pop that she had often craved while living out west, and flipped on the TV. Donald Trump, who had just announced he was running for president, was speaking live from a rally. Oddly, the words coming from his mouth were making sense to her. Lina had never voted for a Republican before, and the idea of her doing so would be absurd to anyone who knew her. But this was 2016, the year that Lina had snapped. The year that would later be recalled by Ricky as the "Year of the Great Snap" when speaking about it to Lina's adult children one day.

"That's right! You can't just come into OUR country and start taking things that aren't yours!" yelled Lina at the television, as she thought about Carol.

Lina puffed on her e-cig, as she listened intently, sipping her pop. Trump was talking about illegals coming in and taking our jobs, committing crimes, and abusing our system. Lina thought about Carol's unidentified foreign accent and how she had just moved into Lina's mom's house and started taking over. As soon as Bill and Carol had wed, she started making changes to the house. Remodeling, new paint colors, new cabinets. The list went on and on. This had been enough to get under Lina's skin, but now this woman was acting like she owned the house. She had seen a stranger's public post with pictures on Facebook thanking Carol for giving her kids all those new toys. Those "new toys" belonged to Lina's children. Her father had kept toys there for when the family visited from California, and then just for visits after the family made the move to Michigan. She picked up Seth's business card and flipped it around in her fingers. She thought about it for a moment, then sent Seth a text.

"Hi, Seth. It's Lina. Do you think you could use your mayoral powers to find out if the property taxes are up to date on my parent's house?"

Her focus turned back to the TV and talk of illegal immigrants. *The nerve of that bitch to give away my children's toys*, she seared. It was wrong enough for Carol to give away Lina's things - she had seen other posts with pictures of dishes and silverware that had belonged to Lina's mother - but stealing and giving away the twins' toys was a whole other level of evil. For the first time, Nicolina Carlson was considering a vote for the Republicans.

CHAPTER EIGHT

1994-The Great Transition
"Human Nature"
by Madonna

"Oh, great. I think I'm allergic," complained Ricky with a sneeze. "Where are we taking these live animals to now, genius?"

Lina and Ricky were frantically pulling out of the Larke Dennis Pharmaceutical Company's parking lot in Lina's red convertible. There had been a large animal rights protest on that May afternoon and Lina had convinced Ricky that it would be more productive to actually break in and rescue some rabbits. The pair had done just that, while everyone was distracted with the large crowd of protesters.

"To the high school biology room," said Lina. "Mrs. Hellman will take them in."

"Oh, good idea!" said Ricky, relieved.

The high school seniors stopped at a red light.

"Gee, this isn't obvious at all," said Ricky, holding the giant cage with live animals on his lap. There were four additional cages full of rabbits in the back seat, poking out of Lina's convertible. He gave a subtle wave to a vehicle full of young women who were staring. "Hi," he mouthed to them with an awkward smile. "Oh my gawd, Lina." Adrenaline pumped through Ricky's body. "I can't believe you smashed that window inside! We rescued the animals, but that's vandalism. We're vandals...and thieves! What if we get arrested?"

"Oh. So, you getting arrested is worse than what those poor animals were enduring? Wow, Ricky," said Lina as she lowered her car visor and pointed to the Gandhi quote she had pinned to the fabric.

It read, "The greatness of a nation and its moral progress can be judged by the way its animals are treated."

"Okay!" surrendered Ricky. "You're right. *Gandhi* is right."

"Besides, it's not like your moms would get mad if you got arrested for that." She laughed.

"Yes, but my mothers also have no control over me having a criminal record, which I do *not* need as a black man. We are eighteen now and about to graduate from high school. I don't need to create any other obstacles in my life."

"It's me who should be worried! My dad would kill me if I got arrested for this. He actually believes that animals need to be tested on in order to find cures. You have absolutely no idea what it's like to have no mother and a close-minded father," stated Lina as the light turned green.

"I'm a Jewish, black man who was raised by two lesbians and never had a father, so back that truck up!"

Lina looked down in embarrassment. "You're right. I'm sorry."

Luckily, the high school was only three miles from the pharmaceutical company, and they arrived quickly and without incident. Their biology teacher had been an old hippie who took in many animals to live at the school. Each of her students were assigned a different animal to care for each week, and many volunteered to bring them home during breaks and over the summer. Both knew that this was the perfect place to bring the rabbits and that Mrs. Hellman wouldn't have a problem with what they had done. Luckily, the school was open for a baseball game, and the pair were able to leave the rabbit cages outside the biology door where they would be safe.

As Lina's convertible pulled back onto the road, Ricky felt something in his pocket poke him. He reached inside and pulled out a bag of weed and a new glass pipe that he had purchased one month before at Hash Bash, an annual marijuana rally that took place the first weekend of April at the University of Michigan. Lina had spotted the beautiful colors of the hand-crafted glass pipe and had suggested it to Ricky.

"Wait, you had pot with you this whole time and you were worried about getting arrested for protesting?" laughed Lina, relieved that they hadn't had any interaction with police.

"Oh, yeah," said Ricky as he laughed at his own stupidity. "I didn't want to leave it at home, so I brought it with me."

This was something the two had begun enjoying only recently but really liked. *No hangovers or regrettable hookups!* the high school seniors had proclaimed. Something Lina wished she had discovered before drinking too much and hooking up with their guitar-playing lunch table mate, Mitch Marquette. That had been the same drunken night that Lina had walked in on Ricky and Nora Layman, just moments after Ricky had lost his hetero virginity. She cringed at the memory as she continued to a shortcut through a downtown neighborhood, to avoid an area that was undergoing road repair.

When they pulled onto the posh residential street, Lina and Ricky both recognized Seth Glickman's blue Trans Am, which was smashed, along with three other vehicles that were parked on the street, surrounded by police cars. They saw Mrs. Glickman, arms flailing, standing with two uniformed officers. Seth stood with them, holding his head in shame.

"What is going on *here*?!" asked Ricky. His interest was sparked when he saw that Kermit Karnes was standing in a crowd further down with other teen boys from school. "Park the car, so we can inquire."

Lina obliged and parked her car at a safe distance from the commotion. The two exited the car and headed to the crowd of teen gawkers standing near. Lawson Jones's portly body came jogging over to greet them as they approached.

"Did you guys see what Glickman did?!" asked Lawson, laughing so hard he was red-faced. "Fuck, man!" he added before walking with them back into the crowd.

It was then that Lina noticed Chip LaBeau was there, as well as his girlfriend, Jeanette. Kermit Karnes was silently pleased that Ricky was randomly present, and Fitz was in the crowd sharing everyone's pleasure at Glickman's stupid mistake.

"What happened?" asked Lina.

"Glickman was smoking a joint on his way to hang with us at Chip's place," said Fitz, motioning to Chip and Lawson. "The hot on the end of his joint fell off and got trapped between his balls and the seat. He stood up to try to grab it and slammed into all these parked cars." Returning to hysterics, he gave Lawson a high five.

"What a fuckin idiot!" laughed Lawson before holding his fist to his heart and proclaiming with a leftover tear of laughter in his eye. "I love that guy."

Jeanette was quietly giving Chip a lecture about his friends and how she didn't want him hanging out with them anymore. She was always looking for a way to isolate Chip from the friends she didn't approve of, which was all of them. Chip had already decided that this was the last two weeks of his relationship with Jeanette. He planned to be a free man upon high school graduation and had already been rehearsing his break-up speech. His attention turned to Lina and how beautiful she looked dressed down and natural. *If I get rid of Jeanette, maybe I'll have a chance to hook up with Lina again before I head to Michigan State*, he thought as he ignored the ongoing lecture and smiled sweetly at Lina.

Now that Lina knew what had happened, she was ready to leave. These people were not their crowd. And although those guys had matured and had been friendly the last few years, she still couldn't bear the sight of Jeanette with Chip. Although Lina was sickened with the way Chip had love-bombed her only to retreat to another girl, she still found Chip overwhelmingly electric. He was just so charming and good-looking, it seemed to erase her memory when he looked her way. There had been many nights when the memories of Chip had pleasured her while alone in her bed.

Before Lina could recover from Chip's smile, Mitch Marquette appeared with his guitar. He lived on the street and had heard the crash. After spotting Lina from his window, he decided he should take the opportunity to perform the new song he had written for her. Mitch had written several songs in Lina's honor, but after their one-night-stand six months prior, he was sure it was pure love. The reality was that Lina had been at a party drinking and secretly longing for Kirk to return to Detroit. She had been hormonal and feeling extra hopeless that Kirk would ever come back, as she hadn't heard from him, so she had given in to Mitch's affections. Before she could think, Mitch was strumming his guitar.

"You're so hot, your sweat tastes pretty. Let's travel 'round the world, let's skin this kitty."

"Wait!" she said, holding her palm to him. "As an animal rights activist, I don't like that lyric."

"Oh," said Mitch, slightly irritated. "Well, it works with the song, so..."

"Right. Well, it's a good song, Mitch. Thank you. I gotta go. Ricky and I are late," she lied.

"The pleasure is all mine, Lina," said Mitch, romantically. "Call me anytime. We're in the phone book."

Lina walked over and interrupted Ricky and Kermit's conversation.

"You ready to go, Ricky?" she asked.

Kermit was visibly annoyed. And as Ricky went to shake hands goodbye with Fitz, Kermit whispered in Lina's ear as he passed. "Cock block."

Lina had no clue what that meant, so she ignored it and motioned for Ricky to join her.

"You may as well just stay parked here. The Spring Flower Fest is going on downtown," he reminded her. "You won't be able to park any closer, anyway."

Lina agreed and went to her car to retrieve a cigarette before lighting it and locking her car doors. She looked over at Seth Glickman who was still being questioned and laid into by his mother. Everyone else had dispersed as well, and Ricky and Lina began their walk to his apartment.

Ricky was quiet for a moment as he prepared to ask Lina something. "So, I'm wondering if you would be willing to attend a gay dance with me tonight."

"A gay dance? Where? At that Club Havana in Detroit?"

"No, it's at an old church in Royal Oak. It's just for teens. Kermit invited us. Please!"

"Kermit did *not* invite *me* and you know that." She laughed. "Am I even allowed to attend a gay dance? Don't you have to be gay?"

"No gay requirements. I *did* ask Kermit that. Please?! It will be fun! He said there's dancing, and it's for lesbians too. Gays and lesbians."

"And straights?" She smiled. "Okay, it *does* sound very intriguing. What time?"

The conversation continued as they approached Main Street. They immediately saw that it was not only Spring Flower Fest, but that the Leader Dogs for the Blind were practicing with the dogs in training. This was not unusual, as the Leader Dogs for the Blind was headquartered in Rochester, and events were the perfect time to really test if a dog was ready to graduate. She knew it was a great organization, but she couldn't help but feel sorry for the dogs. They had no choice.

Ricky and Lina were now giggling, as Lina teased him about his Kermit obsession.

"I know he's a douchebag, but he is so fucking fine. I don't know what's wrong with me when it comes to him! I just need to experience him, maybe?"

Lina wasn't sure, but she completely related. Chip was a douchebag, but if she were to find herself alone with him, she knew she would crumble in a second.

"I totally get it, Ricky."

"Whoa. Check out all the flowers! They really went all out this year." Said Ricky.

The old Main Street in suburban Detroit was adorned with colorful flowers for as long as the eye could see. Crowds drifted from store to store to purchase a variety of arrangements for charity, and children enjoyed their ice cream and desserts from local shops. She noticed Mr. O'Malley stuffing a sandwich into his face and cringed before seeing a police officer. Her stomach dropped in fear that it was her father's old tenant, Walt Weimer. She was relieved to see it was Officer Brady, a dark-haired, dark-skinned police sergeant who was well liked in town. He had served on the local police force for over thirty years and knew everyone. He had even let Ricky and Lina play with his flashing lights and sirens once when they were younger.

As the teens drew closer, they overheard Officer Brady's heated conversation with a stick-skinny woman in her early thirties with long, black hair. The woman appeared to be selling food from a gray truck.

"Ma'am, we went over this. You don't have a permit to sell food! Plus, you're obstructing the view! Nobody can see!" shouted Officer Brady, suddenly realizing the streets were filled with blind people and guides who were testing leader dogs. "I mean, the dogs can't see where they are leading people! It's a hazard!"

"This is pretty good. You have any sauce for it? Ranch?" interrupted Mr. O'Malley, who had just purchased a sandwich from the woman.

"Zen, why is it okay for zat hot dog stand to be here?" demanded the woman with a foreign accent.

"Because they have a physical restaurant down the way, lady," he said, pointing in the direction of the restaurant. "It's a different situation altogether!"

"You really are obstructing my view. How the hell am I supposed to see the damn flowers?" interrupted Mr. O'Malley again. The woman shot him a look of death.

"You just said you liked my food!" she yelled.

"I already bought my lunch, now I don't need you here," growled Mr. O'Malley.

"They don't have zeese issues with food trucks out west! I don't know what the problem is!" shouted the woman to Officer Brady.

"Detroit ain't west, lady! You see that clock up there?" said the officer, pointing to the clock on the old bank. "This is the eastern time zone! That means *east*. You can pack it up and drive it to the fruits and nuts out west all you want. I don't care, but you can't be here!"

The crowded sidewalk had slowed Ricky and Lina's passing of the food truck, which had enabled them to hear the entire conversation. Officer Brady gave the kids a wink of acknowledgement as he pulled out his pen and pad of paper. "Now, what is your name?" he asked the woman.

"What? You're going to write down my name!? Ugh. It's Carol, I'll spell the last name, it's L-I-P…"

As they finally passed, they looked at each other and released their giggles.

"That lady reminds me of Natasha from that Rocky and Bullwinkle cartoon," giggled Lina.

"Oh my God! She totally does!" said Ricky, falling into giggles as the two did a low high-five in acknowledgement of her accurate revelation. "Exactly like her!"

The best friends continued their silliness as they reached the Motown Mood Café and entered. Denise was behind the counter, polishing up some glasses in preparation for the evening rush, while watching the local news. Greta was facing the stage in deep thought over how she wanted that evening's entertainment to play out, which was very normal, as she was a perfectionist.

"Where have you two been?" asked Denise.

"We were at a protest," answered Ricky.

"Which one?!" asked Denise as she motioned to the TV behind the bar. "There is a 'Free Dr. Kevorkian' rally at the courthouse."

"Nope, we missed that one. We were at the Larke Dennis protest for animals," said Lina.

"Oh, yeah? How'd it go?"

"It went *smashing*," answered Ricky as the two teenagers laughed in unison, thinking of the window Lina broke, to rescue the rabbits.

Local news reporter, Mort Crim, was now giving commentary on the Tonya Harding and Nancy Kerrigan scandal. Just four months earlier, Ricky, Lina, and Denise had watched in horror as Nancy Kerrigan screamed "why?" on live television. The Olympic trials had been held in Detroit at Cobo Hall that year, and the trio had been watching the live news coverage when everything had taken a very sudden and unexpected turn. Mort

Crim was now reporting that Tonya Harding was having her National Championships title revoked.

"All kinds of excitement going on today," said Denise absentmindedly as she continued to tidy up behind the bar.

"Okay, so what time tonight?" Lina asked Ricky, getting ready to make the walk back to her car. "We're going to a gay dance," she informed Denise.

"A gay dance? Why wasn't I invited?" asked Denise, laughing.

"It's for teens only, Mom. In Royal Oak. Pick me up at eight-ish?"

"Okay," said Lina, turning to leave.

"Well, that was a short visit!" said Denise with a laugh.

"I didn't know I was going to need to get ready for a dance when we first started walking here," giggled Lina with a wave as she exited the main door.

###

Lina's Mustang convertible pulled up to the former church in Royal Oak, Michigan, which was a trendier, more forward-thinking suburb, not far from Rochester. As the pair tried to find parking, they passed a large group of protesters holding signs that read things like "God hates Fags," "Go Home Dykes," and even "Kill Yourselves."

"Jesus Christ," said Ricky as they drove past with their convertible top down.

Lina could see the fear, sorrow, and even shame that was coming over Ricky due to the hate that was being cast their way. She could feel her cheeks flush with anger. *These assholes don't know jack fucking shit about my dear, sweet, loyal friend till the end. How dare they make him feel bad about who he is!* Tears of frustration formed in her eyes. She struggled to see the road as they continued to circle in search of parking. She didn't want

Ricky to notice her emotional state. She felt she needed to be strong for him. She cranked her stereo system in an effort to block out the hatred that was polluting both the air and the ears of young, impressionable Detroit teenagers. The new song, "Human Nature" by Rochester-native Madonna was now filling the ears of the haters.

"Shut the fuck up, Satan's spawn!" shouted a greasy-looking man in his forties to a young girl.

"How Christian of them," commented Ricky as he watched crowds of gay and lesbian teens being escorted in for safety by some good Samaritans.

They finally found a parking space after waiting patiently for someone else to pull out. Ricky spotted Kermit with two guys he had never seen before. Kermit noticed them and waved as he stood waiting.

"Oh, my God. He is waiting for us," exclaimed Ricky, taking a deep breath and putting his thumbs and middle fingers together in meditative form. "Phew, Phew," he said with nervous exhales.

Lina put the top up on her car, and the two walked up to Kermit, whose friends had begun talking to other dance attendees they knew.

"Hi. Thanks for waiting for us," said Ricky, flirtatiously, yet nonchalant.

"Well, I figured we could walk in together since we know each other. For *safety*," said Kermit.

Lina lit a smoke as she stood uncomfortably while Ricky and Kermit shared a romantic gaze. She didn't want to interrupt their moment, but she also felt like a third wheel. She realized what Kermit had meant by 'cock block' earlier in the day. She figured she would need a cigarette anyway, since they had quite a crowd of hate to face before reaching the safety of the dance. The smaller clusters of people became larger ones as they made their way closer to the church across the street. Lina had chosen a dark-blue, v-neck t-shirt and jeans for the occasion. She noticed that many of the girls her age were wearing identical sandals to hers. Black with a two-inch block heel and one thick strap across the toes. Ricky was looking extra handsome in his tight, short-sleeved sweater and jeans with tennis shoes.

As they reached the corner of protesters, they saw that the three local news channels were there. The man who had called the young girl "Satan's spawn" was speaking into the Channel Four microphone.

"These children are an abomination of God! And all who host this evil shall perish in the depths of HELL!"

A sudden burst of confidence and anger came over Lina as she neared the anti-gay activist. She stepped in front of the man's microphone which was being held by a field reporter.

Denise and Greta were behind the bar at the Motown Mood Café watching the news with some customers, when Lina appeared on the screen. A regular customer recognized her.

"Hey! Isn't that Lina?! Oh, and Ricky!" he exclaimed, pointing to the TV.

Denise excitedly turned up the volume and Greta waved at the customers to be quiet so they could hear.

Lina spoke, "Actually, this man is the one going to hell. He isn't following the teachings of Christ. But from the looks of him," she said, standing aside to look him up and down, "he is probably illiterate. So, if there are any volunteers who could read the Bible to him and save his soul…"

Back at the café, Denise raised her arms in the air and cheered. "YES! I'm so proud!" Greta smiled at the television, looking on with pride.

The man's eyes became wild with hatred. Lina stepped away, and he began to point at each teenager individually. "You're not a Christian, you're not a Christian, YOU'RE not a Christian," he said, pointing to Ricky.

"You're right! I'm a Jew!" called Ricky as they continued down the street.

They had become separated from Kermit, and Ricky scoured the crowd frantically for him as Lina pulled his arm away from the drama. "Come on. I have an idea."

She began running and waved for Ricky to follow. There was a grocery store around the corner. Lina remembered how she and Grandpa Mancini used to go behind grocery stores to find produce. Grandpa had assured her that there was nothing wrong with most of the food that was thrown out, and the two had used discarded tomatoes in many recipes. They found the dumpster out back. Luckily, there was a cardboard box of tomatoes sitting next to it.

"Grab as many as you can!" she instructed as the two used the bottoms of their shirts to carry them.

"I can't believe Kermit ditched me. Where did he go?!" asked Ricky, almost in tears.

"Come on. Let's go back to the car. We're going to practice our gym skills," said Lina.

"What gym skills? I'm a *dancer*," he said in the snooty way he always said that. "My muscles have to be kept in dance form. You know I don't do the ball sports."

"Oh, don't you?" joked Lina.

They shared a laugh as they reached her car. After lowering the top, they pulled out onto the road.

"There is Kermit!" exclaimed Ricky with excitement as Kermit stood on the sidewalk across from the protesters. He watched them pass with his palms up.

"Get ready to throw!" called Lina.

As the convertible passed the angry crowd, who were now shaming other teens, Ricky did his best and used those dance muscles to pummel the haters with tomatoes. The greasy man didn't know what hit his sign and began to run after the car speeding away to safety. Ricky looked over quickly to see that Kermit was watching and had seen his courageous act. That was all Ricky needed to feel energized and triumphant. Although they didn't make it to the dance, he didn't have to worry about what to say to Kermit, or what moves he might make. He knew his retaliation on the protesters would impress his crush beyond anything else he could do. He imagined Kermit was thinking of him as a protector, a strong man of integrity.

Lina was flipping radio stations and the song "It's a Shame" by The Spinners was in progress.

"Yes! This!" yelled Ricky as he cranked the volume even more. He turned around in his seat and pressed his belly against the backrest, singing loudly to the last big chorus of the song with his arms extended into the dark, spring air. He was feeling so electric and for some reason, that old song was resonating with him. It was a shame the way the strangers wanted to hurt him. It was a shame the way Kermit played with his emotions. With the melting of the snow, a renewal had emerged within them both. Graduation day was approaching, and the season of their lives were about to follow suit. As he sang along with the tune, it was as if his soul was being emptied of childhood challenges and making room for new experiences. Lina danced in her seat as she drove, occasionally singing along.

###

Lina pulled up to her house after dropping Ricky off. She recognized the car of her father's close friend, Brad, parked along the street with four others. She pulled into her usual spot in the driveway and walked around to the back door, which was always unlocked. As she stumbled in the dark through her backyard, she remembered that Brad had just had his third divorce. This always meant he would be around more. As she opened the back door, she could hear Marvin Gaye singing "Let's

Get it On" and the sound of women giggling flirtatiously. One was heard saying, "Oh, Brad! You're too much!" Lina rolled her eyes and stepped inside cautiously, hoping to sneak past and into her bedroom.

She followed the first set of laughter and voices to the hot tub in the sunroom, located to her right. She saw Brad, her father, and two unknown ladies in bikinis enjoying the warm bubbles, all with cocktails in hand. The women looked to be in their late twenties, and it was clear that Brad was running the show with his usual charm. She was startled when she heard voices and laughter coming from the left, in the den. *Crap*, thought Lina, as that was her only other route to her room without directly passing the sunroom. Trying not to be seen, she moved closer along the wall until she could see inside the French doors, which were slightly cracked open.

The jazzy opening notes of the song "I Like It" by Debarge could now be heard. She saw it was Mr. Glickman, Seth's Dad, entertaining another set of ladies in private. She watched as Mr. Glickman raised the volume before picking up a cocktail glass, snapping his fingers with the other hand twice, and doing a spin before stopping to make a drink. He stumbled a bit on his turn, making it obvious that wasn't his first drink of the evening, but Lina found it impressive nonetheless. *I bet he was like Chip LaBeau when he was a teenager*, she thought. Lina had developed a crush on Mr. Glickman in recent years as she thought he looked exactly like an older Rob Lowe. It was hard for her to believe that Seth could be his son, as he looked and acted nothing like him. *I wonder if he knows his son crashed up his new car today*? she thought. *How could his kid be such a fuck up?* She began to feel jealous of the older girls Mr. Glickman was with. She saw Mr. Glickman was still making the ladies drinks. This time when he spun charismatically for the girls, he dropped some ice and flashed a drunken grin before kicking it under Bill's couch. *That's going to stain the floor*, she thought. *Oh, well. That's Bill's problem.*

She decided to walk past the sunroom where her dad was entertaining and hoped he would be too distracted to notice her. Just as she passed, "Lina!" called her father's voice.

Shit.

"Lina, do you have any smokes I can borrow?" asked Bill as he hurriedly approached her, shirtless and holding a towel around his waist.

She rolled her eyes before turning around to face Bill. "Yes, hang on," she said as she fumbled in her backpack. She removed her copy of Sylvia Plath's *The Bell Jar* which had now been traveling with her for three months as she just couldn't get into it. She finally produced her pack of Virginia Slims and shook a couple of cigarettes loose for her dad.

"You only have these?" asked Bill, disappointed. He hated girly cigarettes and said they were like smoking air. "Well, I guess I can cut off the filter." He looked over his shoulder anxiously, worried that Brad might steal the more attractive women. Lina began to turn away.

"Hey, there's something else we need to talk about!" he said in an angry whisper. "My secretary called me tonight. She was all excited that she saw you on the news attending a function for gays." His face turned red with anger that had been brewing since the call. "Do you have *any* idea how embarrassing that is for me? Do you think that's good for business?"

"*You're* embarrassed?" she asked, looking around for emphasis. "I'm not the one who has a bunch of hoes in the hot tub."

"Stop being crass!" Bill commanded. "These *women* consist of Mr. Glickman's secretary and some of her friends. Tonight is his fortieth birthday, and we are celebrating. He just got separated, so there is nothing wrong going on here." he added firmly.

They both winced when they heard Mr. Glickman attempt to sing along with the high notes at the end of the DeBarge song.

"Anything else?" she asked.

"No, and thanks for the smokes," he said as he dashed back into the action.

A bunch of men in their early forties acting like teenagers. "Mid-life crisis, much?" she muttered quietly as she lit a smoke and shut her bedroom door.

CHAPTER NINE

2016-Back to The Snap
"The Love You Save"
by The Jackson 5

It was a rainy August morning, which Lina had decided was a license to be lazy. The twins were happy to follow their mother's leisurely example and were enjoying YouTube in the other room, while they ate Fruity Pebbles in their summer pajamas. Lina wore a tight, cream tank-top and an old pair of yoga pants that she had cropped into shorts. Her blonde hair was still loosely tossed into a bun she had absentmindedly created before brushing her teeth.

The anger continued to keep Lina awake at night, often flying into a rage and punching her pillow. Her summer tan from being in the pool all season was the only thing keeping Lina beautiful. Without the sun's saving rays, the lack of sleep would most certainly have shown on her face.

She was watching yet another Trump rally as she sipped her coffee in bed. As Lina continued to fall under Trump's spell, she noticed a familiar smell coming through her bedroom window, which was cracked to hide her vaping from the kids. It smelled like a skunk, and Lina hoped it was something else that smelled exactly the same. She sat up in her bed to get a better look and saw her college-aged neighbor outside with a friend. They were unsuccessfully trying to conceal themselves behind a bush while they smoked a bowl of weed. Lina got excited. *Maybe they can hook me up. I could really use some,* she thought.

As she slipped on her flip flops in preparation to go outside and talk to them, she saw a woman in her fifties approaching the two young men. *Shit*, Lina said to herself as she thought fast and grabbed some cash from her purse.

Lina walked quickly to the bush where the young men stood. Looks of fright took over their faces when they spotted who Lina assumed was somebody's mother.

"Hi! Hi there!" Lina exclaimed nervously. She approached the young men and older woman, slightly out of breath. "I'm your neighbor, Nicolina. The guys were just waiting for me while I ran in to get some cash!" With a polite laugh, Lina extended her hand to the tall, heavy-set woman in her fifties who seemed to be the mother of the familiar-looking young neighbor.

"Ethel Weiss," said the woman, visibly confused, as she shook Lina's hand. She was on the verge of anger.

"Oh, you must be so proud of these boys! I'm assuming you're the mother of…" Lina looked to the boys for help.

"Roy," filled in Roy. He hoped his instincts were correct and that this hot mom from next door was on their side.

"Roy!" Lina exclaimed, pretending she already knew him and was his pal. She continued while putting an arm around Roy's shoulder as he and his startled friend looked down at Lina's braless body.

"I'm Tom," the friend volunteered, staring at Lina, his jaw slightly ajar.

"Well, Mrs. Weiss, you have raised a wonderful person. I suffer from a *disease* for which I have a medical marijuana prescription. I was having a flare-up and didn't have time to get a proper patient care card here in Michigan. My prescription was from California. Well, anyway, I asked around…and these boys," Lina said, conjuring up a fake tear and swallowing hard, "these boys, out of the kindness of their hearts, found me a caregiver who could get me the medicine I need to survive. They said that while they completely disapprove of marijuana use, they just couldn't stand by and let someone suffer. They had to help." She gave a teary smile of adoration for the young men and Mrs. Weiss.

"Oh, I see," said Mrs. Weiss, suddenly softening and following Lina's lead of having adoration for the good kids. After all, she had seen her attractive neighbor and her children playing outside. Lina had moved in a year before, but they had never met. Ethel had only watched her from the window, but Lina seemed to have it all together. She didn't look like a junkie or troublemaker.

"I had taken a couple of puffs before I realized I needed to reimburse them," she said with a false, embarrassed laugh as if she were talking about accidentally leaving on the curling iron or stove. "I ran in…and here you are! I sincerely apologize for any confusion I might have caused. Again, you truly raised a great man. Going against his moral beliefs to aid another human, a *mother*, in need."

"Oh, well. Yes, I'm glad he could help you," said Ethel, convinced. She gave her pretty neighbor a smile.

Lina handed Roy a fifty dollar bill and took the sandwich bag of marijuana.

"Now, are there instructions?" Lina asked, pretending that the caregiver may have given them instructions for her. Both young men slowly shook their heads in unison, mouths still agape.

"Nice to meet you. I'll head inside now, so Roy can tell you privately about your medication. I always said Roy should be a *doctor*, but he's into his computers," said Ethel as she walked away, hoping this would prove to Roy that he had a natural calling for medicine.

Lina smiled at the two young men as they stared back at her, dumbfounded. Tom was wearing glasses that were fogged from the weather and maybe from the heat he felt when looking at this older woman.

"Wow, thanks," said Roy, still in disbelief.

"No problem. I was young once," Lina said with a slight smile. "Was fifty dollars enough?"

"Um, yeah, I mean…you don't have to pay," stated Roy nervously.

"It's all good. Just hook me up when I need it. I may need a favor one day too," she said, smiling and heading toward her yard.

"I like your toenail polish," uttered Tom in her direction, still amazed.

"Hey, what disease do you have?" called Roy as the milf continued to walk.

"Boredom," said Lina with a wink and a smile as she continued to her house.

Roy and Tom, twenty-one-year-old techie virgins, decided that they were in love with Lina.

###

The cloudy morning had turned into a dry, warm afternoon. Lina drove the twins through Rochester, past the bustling crowds on Main Street and the beautiful park. They stopped to let a deer cross as they pulled into the high school parking lot for football and cheer practice. The dry sun on Lina's face lifted her mood and dried the bleachers on the field as they made their way to practice.

Lina and the twins were now in a familiar routine for practices. The trio's first stop was where the cheerleaders were gathering to drop off Frankie. Lina saw Jeni doing stretches, which made her breast implants more obvious. They reminded her of Tori Spelling's choppy boob job from the nineties. Lina approached Jeni and handed her the snack from Whole Foods, carried in a designer "shopper" bag that Greta had received as a gift and had no need for. Lina was always happy to take Greta's free celebrity gift bags off her hands.

"Oh, per-*fect*," said Jeni in her chipper, condescending way. "These vegan smoothies are SO much better for their *digestion*."

"Yes, well, like you said, we don't want the girls constipated. And it seems like you know *a lot* about that," said Lina, mirroring Jeni's attitude.

Lina turned without waiting for Jeni's reaction and followed behind Marty as he ran off to join his teammates. She spotted Fitz holding a football and looking at her. She walked up to greet him.

"Hi there, Lina," said Fitz, standing tall with his chest out and smiling.

"Hey, Fitz. It's another warm one, huh? Sun is drying everything up in time for practice!" she said with false cheer. She was still highly irritated from her brief encounter with Jeni.

"Yeah, drying everything up," he said, smiling at her in a way she hadn't seen him smile at her before. The way men smiled when they were interested in a woman. Lina remembered that Fitz was the chapter president of the MDCCF and had the final say in all hiring for the organization.

"So, how long have you been divorced now, Fitz?"

"We filed a year ago, but it's been final for about six months now. It's rough being a single dad," he threw in for sympathy. Lina knew through the "grapevine" (Kermit Karnes) that the kids were living with their mom and only saw him at football practices, games, and every other weekend. She decided to feed into it though.

"Well, if you ever want to go out sometime. I mean, my husband is always out of town, so I may as well be single," she said with a flirty laugh. Giving Fitz the message that things are not well in her marriage.

"I would *love* that!" exclaimed Fitz. "We *definitely* should. This week! Definitely. I will text you. I have your number on file. I mean, if that's okay."

"Absolutely! Please, let me know," said Lina with what appeared to be an interested smile. She winked at Fitz before turning and walking toward the bleachers. She was hoping to see Chip but hadn't seen his son Lance yet.

Lina sat in the bleachers, enjoying the warm sun on her face. She watched Fitz throw the football with another coach as he stole glances up at the bleachers to see if any of the moms were watching him. Fitz was in textbook, mid-life crisis mode. Like many others their age in the community, Fitz was recently divorced, living on his own in an apartment, and trying to prove he still had "it." Something Lina could relate to and didn't judge him for. It was just an observation. Something she saw in Fitz that she also saw in herself.

Fitz had been a popular boy in middle and high school due to his athletic abilities and all-American good looks. The girls used to swoon over his crystal-blue eyes and thick, blond hair. The only athlete better than Fitz in their high school had been Chip. Lina imagined that Fitz was probably reliving his glory days through coaching the team. As Fitz caught the ball, he stopped and looked up at Lina for a long moment and smiled.

"Hi, Lina," said Chip's sexy voice from behind her.

"Hi there!" said Lina, surprised. She had quietly zoned into Fitz and hadn't noticed Chip.

"I wasn't sure if you or your wife would be bringing Logan today," she said, trying to decipher if he was married or not.

"Nope, it's just me these days, actually. I'll be the one taking Logan to most practices," informed Chip, smiling shyly. Lina knew there was nothing shy about Chip but melted for his performance anyway. She took his answer to mean he was divorced.

"Hey, since we have two hours before pick up, why don't we grab some coffee and catch up? There is a new coffee place right next to my gym," invited Chip without asking or caring what Lina's relationship status was.

"Sure, why not?" said Lina with a slight laugh. It was clear that Chip hadn't changed. He still had to mention he worked out whenever he could slip it in. She could tell by looking at him that he was in great shape. His tanned arms were muscular and his body was toned, right down to his perfect calf muscles.

"Great! Let's do it! I'll meet you there! It's right across from the old high school, next to the new gym," said Chip, looking fine as ever.

The two vehicles reached the gym parking lot. Chip pulled his Ford Explorer next to Lina's new, red Escalade and put his window down to talk.

"Hey, I realized how late in the day it is for coffee. I'll never get to sleep if I drink it now. Do you want to park over on the side by the gym and talk?" suggested Chip as he pointed toward a more secluded parking area on the side of the building.

Lina agreed. She put her car window up and silently freaked out as she followed Chip's car. *Oh my God,* she thought. *I'm so glad I took a shower and brushed my teeth right before leaving for practice. You've got this. Deep breaths.*

Chip exited his vehicle and went to the passenger side of Lina's car. She turned off the ignition and unlocked the door for his entry. When he got in, she could smell the peppermint from his fresh piece of chewing gum. He looked into her eyes for a moment before breaking out his foxy grin and leaning in for a hug.

"It's so great to see you, Lina. Wow!" he said, staring at her with what seemed to be genuine awe and adoration, while lightly chewing his gum. The same cute way he had chewed his gum in high school.

"Yeah, it's incredible that our kids are in sports together. It's good to see you too, Chip," said Lina. She quickly looked down and smiled like she was fourteen again.

"So, are you still married?" asked Chip.

"It's complicated," said Lina with a sigh.

Chip took a breath, knowing what that could mean. He spoke softly. "I remember the day I heard you were engaged. A bunch of us guys were hanging out and Glickman told us. I remember feeling really, really sad," said Chip, looking very serious and somber at Lina. "You were always my favorite girl. I always hoped you would return from California. And here you are."

Lina nervously broke from Chip's intense gaze, not knowing what to say.

"So, what are you doing for a living these days, Chip? How long have you been divorced?"

Chip did his famous, sexy half-laugh. He would grin with a closed mouth and almost make a hmm sound. Then he made seductive eyes and chewed his gum like only Chip could. There was almost an art to his sexy charm, which he had long perfected back in middle school. There was just something about everything that Chip did. The way he would do little half chomps on his gum, the way he would wink at her in the halls at school, the way he could so easily conquer any woman.

"I'm actually a private investigator now," said Chip, completely ignoring the second half of Lina's question. "If you need help investigating your husband…I mean, if you suspect him..."

Lina began to think about how she could use his help, but not with her husband. She already knew that Luke had been cheating since before they had moved to Michigan a year ago. Lina had been busy taking care of her father, and battling Carol the whole time. She had been busy with the twins and their new routines. Luke had begun staying in Detroit at a company apartment during the winter months to avoid the long commute in snowy weather. Lina had been left alone to deal with her misery. She had so many other things going on at that point, she simply could not take on the arguments and legality of a divorce. *Not now*, she had thought. *Not until I get my mother's house back and everything else from my father's estate in order. One stressful legal battle at a time.*

Lina was about to ask Chip about investigating Carol when she caught him staring at her longingly with his sexy grin. The two seemed to fall under a spell as they stared into each other's eyes. It was as if they were not sitting in a parked car in the lot of a popular gym in daylight. Lina had been so thirsty for love and affection. She was crazy about Kirk, but he was married. Lina was in dire need of a distraction from Kirk, and Chip was here looking hot and offering it to her.

"So, this is a pretty cool ride you got here. Look at you," said Chip as he gently touched her chin and smiled. "Do you mind if I take a look at the third row? This car is huge." Chip climbed into the back, gently grabbing her arm to signal her to follow his lead.

Lina gladly complied, happy to show off her new car to Chip. The old classmates sat in the very back. Lina nervously looked at Chip, and he went in for the kiss. She was hesitant at first, then reciprocated with full force.

Chip's lips felt the same as they had all those years ago. The taste of his peppermint gum and smell of his skin sent all reason out the window. His hand slowly moved to her breast as he passionately kissed her. Both had electric bolts of lust going through their bodies, hitting all the right places. Lina could feel the blood rush to her private area, making her panties wet. She stopped for a moment and gazed at him passionately.

"Chip, we shouldn't," she said.

He ignored her, embracing her face with both hands and kissing her again. Chip knew she wanted it, and she did.

Lina began to massage Chip through his cargo shorts. He was rock hard, which made Lina even more excited. The legendary ladies' man of Rochester then stopped, grabbed Lina by the waist, and pulled her down so she was lying on the seat. He looked down at Lina with one knee on the car seat and the other foot on the floor. He slowly grabbed each of Lina's ankles and removed each sandal, kissing her ankles and resting her feet on his shoulders. He was sweating from the summer heat in the car as he slipped off her shorts. He unbuttoned his khaki cargo shorts before flashing a look of pure lust and tasting her treasures. Chip continued to savor Lina's delectable delights as his heart pounded with every lick. He then sat in the middle of the back seat and pulled Lina on top of him, so her legs straddled his perfectly-fit hips. He grabbed himself and looked her in the eyes as he located her opening and pulled her down upon him with full force.

Lina and Chip were both dripping with sweat as they moaned with pleasure. Chip then repositioned her, so she was facing the windshield. He continued to enter her from behind as she grasped the two seats in the row before her. Chip reached around and massaged her pleasure center, as he continued to have his way with her. He then pulled her shirt off and lifted her bra up so it rested above her breasts, exposing them. He cupped them before he let out a loud moan as he finished deep inside of her.

This brought Lina back to reality. They were in a public parking lot in broad daylight at the gym *everyone* in town went to, having sex like they were in a hotel room. She nervously looked around as she got dressed, her hands shaking. Chip pulled up his shorts and zipped them. Lina started the ignition and blasted the A/C. Chip exited the vehicle and walked around to Lina's car door. He opened the door and pulled her out, smiling.

"That was incredible," he said with a slight, sexy laugh. "I think we should do this more often." He gave her a hug, and then put Lina's back against her car. He put his hand on the car next to her head and leaned in as he spoke to her. The same way he had spoken to her in ninth grade, pressed up against the lockers.

It was so public and wrong. She *was* a married woman, and anyone could be watching from the comfort of their cars or passing by to the gym. But the attention from Chip felt so good.

"Okay, well, we should go," Lina said, breaking into a nervous laugh and looking around.

Chip leaned in again and kissed her with one hand still pegging her to the car. "Text me," he said as he smiled slyly and got back into his car.

Lina got into her car, fastened her seatbelt, and waited for Chip to pull away first. "Upside Down" by Diana Ross was playing on her car radio. She began whispering to herself, *Oh my God, holy shit!* She pulled out onto University Drive and headed toward the new high school to collect the twins from practice. She sucked on her vape pen, alternating between naughty laughter and mild shame.

CHAPTER TEN

2015-Meeting Carol
"America"
by Simon & Garfunkel

Lina and her almost six-year-old twins were on a flight from San Diego to Detroit to visit her ailing father, Bill. The twins hadn't seen their grandfather since they were toddlers, when Bill last flew out to California. Although she had been assured by Bill that he was fine and that they were just running tests, she felt that it would be a good time to visit. She had been longing for a trip home to see Ricky and the moms anyway, as it had been six months since they had visited her in California. She was also hoping that some of the leaves had turned colors, so her children could experience the brilliant vision of changing seasons.

There was another huge reason that Lina felt compelled to make a trip home. Bill had suddenly eloped, just three months earlier. Lina had never met the woman and was completely shocked by the news of nuptials from her father. Although there were many times growing up that Lina had walked in on her Dad and his friends entertaining ladies, Bill had resigned to the bachelor life and had never been in a serious relationship after her mother's passing. Lina felt optimistic about this union and hoped that Carol would cause Bill to lighten up and not be so grumpy all the time. His moodiness had seemed to increase as he aged. And although she had never had a close relationship with her dad, she thought that love in his life may just be what he'd been lacking all of those years.

Lina directed the twins to look at the clouds from their airplane window. Finances and tensions had been running rampant through her unhappy household, so travel hadn't been an option. In an effort to smooth things over with Lina, her husband, Luke, had taken out a new credit card and purchased flights for the three of them to go home. Little did Lina know at the time, there was another reason he wanted the house to himself for a couple of weeks.

"As we prepare to descend into Detroit, please make sure your seat backs and folding trays are in their full upright position. Please fasten your safety belts," said the flight attendant on the overhead speaker.

Lina and the kids were exhausted after the long flight, which had forced them to wake at five in the morning. Happy to land, they made their way off the plane and to the luggage terminal. After collecting their bags and rejoicing that none had been lost, Lina spotted a driver wearing a chauffeur jacket and hat holding a sign that read "PRATT" in black marker. Bill had always ordered a metro car to collect anyone flying into town, and she was relieved that she had no issue spotting the driver. The older gentleman greeted them and loaded their belongings into the luxury sedan before making the thirty-minute drive to Rochester, Michigan.

When they arrived, Lina tipped the driver. Their belongings were unloaded onto Lina's childhood driveway. She took a moment to inhale the clean, fresh, suburban air and smile at her surroundings. She looked down the way towards Kirk's old house and wondered about the people who lived there now. She realized that her kids were investigating the neighbor's koi pond a little too closely and called for them to join her as she approached the front door.

The old, brass knockers on the double front doors each read "Carlson." She had forgotten about the nameplates and happily pointed them out to her kids. She took a moment to center herself. *What if she doesn't like me?* she thought. She consciously suppressed the negative thoughts. *Stay positive. She will love you.* She pressed her thumb on the handle and opened the door.

The children ran past her and into their surprised grandfather's arms. She was then startled to see that her father's new bride was standing there, looking cold and unamused.

"You always just enter people's homes without knocking?"

Before Lina could even begin to comprehend what was happening, Bill was there, giving her a hug.

"Honey! It's so good to have you guys here," he said as he added an additional squeeze with one arm. Bill was sixty-four years old now and still had his solid, six-foot-two build. Lina was an adult, but at five-foot-four she still seemed small and child-like to Bill. She was feeling a bit uncomfortable by her first exchange with Carol and emotions were already strained with her marriage, but she felt a sense of security while in the grasp of her only living parent.

"Carol, this is my beautiful daughter that everyone in town has been telling you about!" said Bill proudly.

"Yes," said Carol, as her dark eyes studied Lina with a coldness that gave Lina a slight shiver.

Bill quickly diverted Lina's attention to all the toys he had purchased the kids to keep at his house for when they came to visit.

"Santa dropped off some toys for my grandkids!" he announced as the twins excitedly darted in his direction and began to take stock.

After only three months of marriage, Bill had begun to realize that trying to keep Carol happy was nearly impossible. She had been the first woman to truly excite him sexually since his late wife had passed thirty years prior. With Fara, it had been about young love and true passion. But after losing his first wife, he had only committed to casual relationships with women. There just hadn't been anybody as naturally beautiful inside and out as his young, Italian bride had been. Then he met Carol who had done things to him in bed that he had only heard about and seen in adult films. His lonely, broken heart of thirty years had confused his sexual gratification from Carol with love. Bill was anxious with worry that his new bride might show her true colors while his daughter and grandchildren visited. He was feeling stressed, trying to keep up his happy facade. It also didn't help that he hadn't been feeling well and had been in and out of the hospital for testing. He still figured everything would be fine and that the results of his recent biopsy would reveal a clean bill of health.

Lina suggested that the children go outside and explore her old backyard and release some energy from being squished on a plane all day. After sending them out back, the three adults took a seat in the living room. Carol offered Lina a beverage.

"Oh, I'm fine. If I get thirsty, I'll just get it myself," she offered with a sincere smile.

The last thing Lina wanted was for Carol to be put out by her. She wanted to give a good impression and avoid coming off as a nuisance. Carol's interpretation of this was that Lina was a spoiled brat who didn't know boundaries. *How dare that little bitch come inside my house without knocking? And now she thinks she can just help herself to food and drinks?*

As she made herself comfortable on the couch, Lina noticed how skinny Carol was. With her long, black hair and dark, piercing eyes, Lina naturally wondered what her ethnicity was. She had also detected an accent, which Bill hadn't said anything about. Lina's father had told her that Carol was fifty-four years old and had never been married, but not much else.

"So, where are you originally from, Carol?" inquired Lina.

"Out west," stated Carol coldly.

"Carol was living in Portland up until recently. She owns a food truck. Business has always been easier for food entrepreneurs out that way."

Food entrepreneurs. Okay. thought Lina.

"I lived in zis area briefly in the nineties before moving my business out west. They are much more reasonable there," stated Carol, revealing that accent again.

"Oh? Well, how interesting," said Lina, who was now using her Aunt Isobel personality as a defense mechanism. "Where did you live *before* the nineties?"

"New York," she stated, still not giving any explanation as to why she sounded European.

Bill quickly changed the subject, acting like he and Lina had a close relationship and he was a fun-loving father. "Tell me, kiddo, what are your plans while in town? I'd love to take you for a drive and show you everything that has changed. You have to see how they converted the old…"

Bill was in mid-sentence, speaking directly to his thirty-nine-year-old daughter, when Carol decided to begin talking into Lina's ear. "The children will enjoy my grilled cheese. It has four cheeses. It's an adult favorite."

Carol clearly had no idea how picky most kids were.

"Oh, well...um," said Lina, turning her head to look at each, unsure of how to hold a separate conversation and answer both questions at once. "No, Dad I didn't know something was converted. Which building?"

"The old twist drill building has been made into…"

"Your father likes to go for drives."

"Yes, I kno-"

Bill was becoming irritated with Carol's constant interruption and offered Lina a change of scenery.

“Why don’t we go into the kitchen? I have a map from the city that highlights all the new changes in town," offered Bill.

Lina gladly accepted, jumping up from the couch to follow him. Her eyes darted to the filthy mess in the kitchen and she froze for a moment before taking a seat at the kitchen table. Bill had always been a stickler for cleanliness. She had even suspected that both of her parents may have suffered from OCD, as most visitors would comment that their house looked more like a museum than somewhere people lived. After Fara’s death, this chore had become Lina’s, and she had done an excellent job since age ten. Looking at dirty dishes piled in the sink and food splattered all over the stove was making her anxious and sick to her stomach. *Why is this woman treating my mother’s house like garbage?*

“Carlson’s building teamed up with the city of Rochester, and had this map of past and present printed for the town centennial coming up. Isn’t that cool?" asked Bill.

Still bothered by the filthy kitchen, she managed to conjure some fake enthusiasm. “Yes, very cool.”

Carol came in and sat at the kitchen table as Bill continued to point out things on the map to Lina.

“Did you forget to bring anything? Perhaps za both of us should go to the store," interrupted Carol once again, with a subtle leak to her foreign accent.

“Um, no. If I need anything, I can just take Dad's car later.”

“Oh, well, I’m not sure if the insurance allows outsiders to take our cars. Also, I wouldn’t want you to have to go alone.”

“Well, lucky for you, I’m very self-sufficient and not *needy* at all. I’m sure it’s fine to take my Dad’s car, as it has never been a problem ever before. You *are* allowed to let friends and family borrow your car," informed Lina firmly. “I had better go check on the kids.”

Lina found the kids deep in her old backyard. They were playing out behind the old shed where she used to play. She was glad to see her kids were enjoying the outdoor space, something their modest home lacked in southern California. But she also felt sick, deep in the pit of her stomach. Something was definitely off with her father's new wife.

The following morning, Lina and the kids rose late as they were jet-lagged from the three-hour time difference. Although it was ten in the morning eastern time, it was only seven California time. She threw a robe over her t-shirt and panties and exited her old bedroom. The house was silent, and she wondered where her dad and Carol were. She peeked into the spare room where the kids were staying and saw they were quietly playing together. She decided to leave them be and peeked out the front windows as she headed to the kitchen for coffee.

Lina glanced outside and noticed Peedy, the adorable poodle from next door. Peedy was well-loved by the whole neighborhood and would make his daily rounds to each house for treats. Bill had sent her numerous links to videos of Peedy that she and the children always enjoyed watching. As she wondered if her Dad had any treats that she and the kids could give to Peedy, her thoughts were interrupted by the sight of water drenching the dog as he ran away. Lina's jaw dropped when she realized that Carol was outside watering the flowers and had just sprayed beloved Peedy from the yard. Lina needed no other information at this point. She had been adamantly taught by both Greta and Aunt Isobel that anyone who was mean to or didn't like dogs was not a good person.

Lina fueled up on coffee, showered, and got the twins cleaned up and dressed before emerging into the main part of her childhood home again. She wondered if Bill was around now, since she hadn't seen him earlier. It was then that she heard the loud stereo system booming from the finished basement below.

Bill was showing off his toys to his grandchildren, just as he always had when his buddies came to visit. She followed the sound of Stevie Wonder's song "Reggae Woman" down to the basement. She was pleased to see that the kids were jumping around wildly to the music as her father watched them, beaming. Bill noticed Lina and lowered the volume on the sound system.

"Well, good morning! Or afternoon, I should say," said Bill, happily.

"Momma, can we go play outside now?"

"Yes! You should definitely be playing outside. Need to enjoy the open space while you can," said Lina. "I'll meet you out there in a few and show you the old, hidden creek."

"Yay," exclaimed the kids as they ran to the sliding basement door and out into the yard.

Lina needed to have a conversation with her father, which she had been dreading. Once Bill had cut her off at age nineteen, she had never asked him for anything. She prided herself on how well she was able to survive after being raised in an upper middle-class household. She had even managed to purchase her own condo in San Diego without help from anyone. Everything had been fine when Lina only had herself to worry about. It wasn't until she married Luke that survival had become nearly impossible. The high cost of living in San Diego with two children and a gambling husband had stretched Lina past her limit in both sanity and credit card debt. Luke had a high enough credit limit to get Lina and the kids plane tickets to Detroit, but that was all. Now they had to make the monthly payment on that card, and both of the kids needed new shoes. Lina had decided that if her dad could just lend them fifty dollars, it would be enough for two pairs of shoes from a discount store and some food at the airport when they traveled home.

Although they had just arrived, this was already a very real worry for Lina. She had become so poor through her marriage to

Luke and staying home with her kids that she had to take into account every little aspect of every little thing. *Was there going to be a charge for parking? Better not meet that friend who offered to take you out to lunch. Was there going to be a tip required? Better wash your own car. Would going to see a movie require a sitter? You're never leaving your house again.*

This had become Lina's sad reality and cause for descent into postpartum depression. She had been taking an antidepressant, which had helped, until they could no longer afford her prescription. She never rested, knowing that the slightest accident could cause them to be homeless. If Bill could just lend her fifty, at least the kids could have some shoes that fit. Their toes were beginning to hang off their flip flops.

"How are you feeling, Nickel?" asked Bill. Nickel had been a nickname that Bill had often called her before her mother had passed, when Bill was still happy. It caught her by surprise, as she hadn't heard him call her that in years.

"I'm okay," she answered, easing into her big request. "Dad, you know I hate to ask you for anything."

"Lina, what's wrong?" asked Bill, looking concerned.

"Well, I'm a little short on money. Again, I hate to ask you, but we have fallen on some hard times lately…"

"How much do you need?"

"If I could just borrow fifty, I could buy each of the kids new shoes…"

"Darling," interrupted Carol from behind the shadows. She had been listening the entire time. "Is zis conversation something your *wife* should be involved with? It is *our* money, and I should be involved in zis type of decision."

Oh no, she didn't, thought Lina. *What the fuck? Is this woman for real?*

"I'm only asking for fifty dollars, Carol," said Lina, swallowing her pride for the sake of her children. "I never ask my Dad..."

"I think that you are an adult, and that adults have to take care of zem-selves. I've never had to beg anyone for money, and you should not either. You should have some pride."

Lina could feel her face flush with anger. *How dare this bitch! She doesn't know anything about me. Of course, she's never had to beg for money, she's never had a loser husband or kids! Have some pride? You bet your ass I have some pride. I've accomplished incredible things in my life! My only mistake was getting married and trusting him to support us while he urged me to stay home with the kids!* Lina stood speechless, unsure if she should ask her father again or tell Carol to fuck off. And Bill wasn't sticking up for her either, like an animal who had been whipped into submission. She finally excused herself and went to find the kids.

###

She spent the rest of the day with Ricky and the twins, after texting him an SOS to pick them up. Denise and Greta met up with them for dinner at Mr. B's restaurant on Main Street that evening. Greta excused herself for the powder room.

"Order me the Matzo ball soup and a side salad," she instructed as she headed for the ladies' room.

The young waitress, with false eyelashes, came to take their order. Denise wanted to bond with the kids and had been secretly dying for a cheeseburger, something that was not kosher and not approved of by Greta. She decided to take the opportunity of Greta's bathroom absence and ordered. "The three of us would like cheeseburgers and fries!" said Denise, motioning to herself and the kids.

Lina smiled; she knew what Denise was doing. While Denise had a Jewish father and had been a practicing Jew ever since she had met Greta, she had been raised Catholic by her Irish mother. She missed cheeseburgers, ham, and shellfish. Ricky also smiled and gave Denise a pretend look of disapproval as Greta returned to her seat. The table of six began to chat and reminisce over the bottle of wine that Ricky had ordered, and Lina laughed as she hadn't in years. Something about being home with the people who cared about her and her children gave her a sense of peace, even though it was clear she and her new stepmother weren't going to be friends.

Lina had so looked forward to her visit home and didn't know when she would be able to return due to lack of funds. She was annoyed that Carol's negativity had put a damper on her vacation. Nonetheless, it warmed her heart and lifted her spirits to see Ricky and the moms interact so sweetly with the twins. If it weren't for Carol, she might even consider asking Luke to find a job in the Detroit area. The server brought the food to their table after setting the large tray of dinner for six on a fold out stand.

"Three cheeseburgers!" announced the waitress as she set them in front of the twins and Denise.

"Are you allowed to eat cheeseburgers, Denise?" asked Lina's daughter, Frankie. "My Mom told me you can't eat that if you're Jewish because it isn't kosher."

Denise looked in Greta's direction with guilt, as Greta's disapproving face raised an eyebrow.

"Whoops! I did not realize that was ordered! Oh, well. We don't want to waste food," said Denise as she stuffed a fry in her mouth, giving Greta a coy smile.

That naughty girl is going to get it later, thought Greta, beginning to feel excited and thinking that Denise should put on that new lingerie later. Lina saw the randy exchange between the moms, and while she was happy that their flame still burned after all those years, she also felt a ping of jealousy. She longed for someone to feel that way about her again. To pass sexy glances across tables to her, to touch her, to want her. Plenty of men in San Diego would look at Lina, but once they spotted the twins in tow, they would quickly look away. Now that they were growing older and more independent, Lina had begun to crave human touch again. It was something she rarely felt from her husband, and she was beginning to suspect he was giving it to someone else.

###

Later that evening, after dessert and more laughter at the apartment above Motown Mood Café, Ricky's car was pulling into Lina's old driveway to drop them off.

"Don't let that chick get you down," whispered Ricky as the kids exited the car. "Let's enjoy the time we have."

"You're right. It's just so hard. It's like I can't do anything right with that woman."

"It's so weird to be dropping you off at your old house," said Ricky with a sentimental smile. "God, I miss you so much, Lina. I wish you could move back."

Lina gave Ricky a peck on the cheek before getting out and shutting the door. Ricky waited for them to reach the front porch before backing out of the driveway, just as he always had. Lina unlocked the front door and was relieved that Carol and Bill were already asleep. She shut the door quietly and led the kids to their rooms in the dark.

Lina and the twins were beginning to acclimate to the three-hour time difference, and they rose at nine in the morning eastern time. She made herself some coffee with her father's Keurig and put some bread in the toaster for the kids. She was desperately trying to get as much caffeine in her body as possible before dealing with Bill and Carol, whom she hadn't seen or heard yet.

Then her luck suddenly changed, and Carol came in from the garage.

"Oh, hi, Carol," said Lina, trying to sound chipper. "I'm surprised to see you. I thought you'd be busy cooking and driving your food truck around."

"I have many employees now and five trucks. I take time off to get acquainted with my husband's family," informed Carol coldly.

It was clear to Lina at this point that Carol had no intention of really getting to know them, and she wasn't going to allow Bill that bonding opportunity either. Lina had been around the block in life enough to know that master manipulators always isolate their victims. This woman hadn't allowed Lina to engage in conversation with her father, even under her own watchful eye.

Carol hid in shadows to control what Bill gave his daughter, to monitor how and what she might use against Lina, to keep her in check. She didn't need to know Lina or her brats, she just needed to keep her away. *That spoiled bitch could ruin everything for me*, she had thought. *I am becoming a pillar in this society, thanks to my marriage. I will not allow this girl to interfere. I must not even give her a chance to interfere. I need to make sure she knows she is not welcome in this house anymore.*

"Well, how thoughtful of you," said Lina, with a narrow, firm glance before taking a sip of her coffee.

Just then, the garage door opened and in walked Bill with his best friend, Jack Nelson. They had been out skeet shooting all morning at their gun club, north of the city.

"Well, hello crew!" called Bill in good spirits.

"Lina!" exclaimed Jack as he went over to give her a big hug. "Long time, no see. Welcome back to town!"

Jack Nelson, Bill's lifelong friend and lawyer, looked the same, just older and grayer like Bill. She smiled pleasantly as it was nice to see him. He had always been kind to her as a child, and he was the friend of Bill's she had always known the best. As Jack greeted the kids, her cell phone rang. It was Luke.

"I have to take this, excuse me," she said to everyone as she answered the call and headed to her old bedroom for privacy.

"Hello," answered Lina.

"Hi. How is everything going there?"

"Okay, I guess. We haven't heard back from my dad's doctor yet. Maybe no news is good news."

"Oh. Well, I'm sorry you don't know anything about his biopsy yet, but there's another reason I'm calling."

"Oh?" she asked, hoping he had gotten a raise or won the lottery.

"You know my co-worker, Julie?"

"No. You speak of her often, but I've never…"

"Well, she just got transferred to our new Detroit location. So, she said I should look into it too, since they are staffing there internally first. Anyway, if you want to move back to Michigan and be close to your friends and your dad…I can do it!" he announced ecstatically.

"Oh, Luke. You know, I'm not sure about that. There are things we need to discuss about Carol. And my dad is probably fine anyway. He has been out shooting with his friend all morning. I'm sure there would be no need to uproot our lives."

"Well, I think it would be a good opportunity for me…and you're always saying how much you miss home," said Luke, sounding annoyed.

"Okay, well, can we talk about this more after I get back? It's not a *no*, I just don't know that it would be necessary. I mean…if my dad had some terminal disease, and I needed to take care of him…then yes. But like I said, he seems fine."

"Well, I'll need to let them know, Lina. I'll call you tonight to discuss it more?"

"Yes. Okay, we will talk later. I love you," she said.

Luke hung up without responding, and Lina felt sick to her stomach. She knew for certain that something had shifted between them, and now he was pushing a move to Michigan, which was extra bizarre. When she used to tell him snowy tales of her youth, he had always said he could never live in a cold climate like Detroit. She decided to push the subject aside for later and return to the kitchen, so as not to be rude to Jack.

She joined Jack, the kids, and Carol in the kitchen and made small talk with her dad's old friend. Bill emerged from the den, where his gun safe was, this time proudly holding his newest possession. He brought in his new Beretta rifle to show off to Jack.

"Check out my newest toy!" said Bill proudly. He knew Jack was going to be impressed and had been looking forward to unveiling it.

"Wow!" exclaimed Jack. "Is that a Beretta 687 Silver Pigeon?! How much did that set you back?"

"I got it from the gun show last weekend when you were out of town. Got it for two thousand!" bragged Bill.

"Yes, my husband works hard and deserves to enjoy the fruits of his labor," said Carol with a cold stare in Lina's direction.

"Okay," said Lina, heading over to her twins. "I don't think we need to do this right now with the kids in here." She was becoming more annoyed and angry by the second. "Kids, go brush your teeth and get dressed."

Lina was not only angry that a gun was being shown off in front of her seven-year-old kids, it was the fact that she had asked for fifty dollars to help Bill's *grandchildren* and was shot down. But a two-thousand dollar gun that he would rarely ever use was fine? And it had to be brought in and displayed before her face? It felt like a slap, and she struggled to contain her emotions.

The landline rang as Bill sat down at the counter. He looked at the caller I.D. “It’s my doctor," he announced before picking up the receiver and hitting the green button to answer. “Yes, this is Bill.”

The room fell silent as Bill spoke with his doctor. Lina watched and listened closely, trying to make sense of the one-sided conversation. When Carol began to speak, both Lina and Jack instinctively held up one hand to her, signaling for her to be quiet so they could hear. Neither of them were going to allow Carol to try to keep them uninformed. Lina was surprised and relieved when she sensed that Jack had seemed to reach the same conclusions that she had about Carol.

Lina watched as Bill’s demeanor changed. As the conversation continued, his shoulders fell forward with intense disappointment as both of his elbows pressed against the kitchen counter. She remembered this same body language after he had been on the phone with her mother’s doctor all those years ago. Lina had forgotten that until now, as all of those horrible, forgotten memories and feelings suddenly resurfaced. She didn’t know what her father’s doctor was saying, but she knew it wasn’t good. Carol slowly walked over to Bill and gently tried to take the receiver from his hand. He shook her off and motioned for his calendar, so he could make an appointment. His voice was full of sadness and uncertainty as he thanked his doctor and hung up the phone. You could have heard a pin drop as everyone waited for Bill to reveal his news.

“I have pancreatic cancer. It has already metastasized. It’s in my liver and lymph nodes. I go in on Wednesday to meet with the oncologist," he stated with strength that comes only with experience and age.

Jack, Carol, and Lina stood frozen as each tried to wrap their minds around this grim news. Carol ran over to Bill and embraced him. Jack placed his arm around Lina's shoulder for comfort, as he used his other hand to brace the counter for support. Lina could feel Jack's body shaking with concealed emotion as the reality of what they had just been told sank in.

CHAPTER ELEVEN

2016-Still Snappin
"Lust for Life"
by Iggy Pop

The remainder of August had become a steady routine of Chip, pool, sex, repeat. Lina enrolled the twins in a weeklong, free summer camp for city and township residents held at the park. On some days, Denise had insisted on taking the kids for overnights before school began. These were the days that Lina was allowed to be most free. No driving meant the alcohol could flow freely and Lina felt alive again. She was reliving her teenage years with Chip, and escaping from all of her problems. She often wished it were Kirk she was having these experiences with, but Chip was available and beyond sexy.

On one such occasion, the two were on Lina's sofa in shorts, with their shoes off like teenagers, hitting Chip's bong and drinking beer. The stereo was blasting Iggy Pop's song "Lust for Life," and Lina got up to jump on her fancy sofa while swigging a beer. She was happily wasted, and Chip, standing on the floor, pressed his body against hers as she danced. She wrapped her legs around his waist, and he twirled her away from the couch as she went to sip her beer. After discovering it was empty, she giggled and tossed it. Then Chip lowered her down to the carpet and laid on top of her. As he entered her to make love, she thought about how she really did seem to have a lust for life again with Chip.

###

Lina and the twins arrived downtown to have dinner with the Goldman's, in their posh apartment above the Motown Mood Café. There was no parking available on Main Street during the busy rush hour, so they pulled the car around to Walnut Street. The twins delighted in feeding the parking meter.

The Motown Mood Café was busy with college students and business people enjoying happy hour. Patrons of all ages and all walks of life enjoyed and were welcome at the café. Local musicians, some famous and some unknown, were delighted to play intimate shows there as well. Greta not only had the voice of a goddess, she was also a very smart business woman. Other establishments in Downtown Rochester had come and gone, but the Motown Mood Café continued to thrive. Greta had a knack for ensuring the café evolved with the times and was a stickler for customer service.

Lina and the twins entered the café through the rear door and made their way to the front.

"I want to request a song! Me too!" yelled the twins with excitement.

"The DJ doesn't start until eight o'clock, you guys. You can pick songs from the jukebox though," Lina suggested.

Lina divvied up some quarters from her change purse, and the twins excitedly ran over to select some tunes. As Lina went to zip her bag back up and follow, she noticed the new employee, Sheila, working at the counter. She stopped to introduce herself.

"Sheila, right? I'm Lina," she said, extending her hand. "Denise and Greta told me about you. You just moved to Rochester from Downtown Detroit, right?"

"Yes, that's me."

Sheila was twenty-one years old and had the face and body of a supermodel, but with a partly-shaved head and pink dreadlocks flowing from the rest. She smiled sweetly, as she had heard all about Lina and her twins. She loved Ricky so far, and knew that Lina was his best friend. Sheila was excited about starting her new life in Rochester. She had hopes that Greta would eventually allow her to sing there, even though her girlfriend wasn't entirely onboard.

"Well, welcome. It's nice to meet you."

The phone behind the counter rang, and Sheila went to go answer it.

"Motown Mood! How may I help you?"

A woman with short brown hair and Birkenstocks had been watching Lina and Sheila's interaction from the main entrance of the café. She was Maxi, Sheila's older girlfriend, who had a jealous streak. When Sheila had announced that she was moving to Rochester to work at the café, Maxi had not been thrilled. Then, to make matters worse, she had heard on a LGBTQ podcast about the female version of the "down low" that was happening with married women in the suburbs. The sight of attractive Lina shaking hands and talking to her girlfriend nearly made her explode with envy, and she was going to nip this in the bud. As Lina was about to join the twins at the jukebox, Maxi blocked her.

"I'm Maxi, and Sheila is my girl. Can I help you with something?"

"Oh, hi. I was just introducing myself to her-"

"Look. I don't know what your game is…"

"What? Um, I don't have a ga-"

Maxi put her finger to her lips. "Shhh." Then in a low, serious whisper, she said, "I'm not going to let anyone ruin my relationship."

"Well, I'm married. So don't worry about me, sweetie."

"My name is Maxi, *not* sweetie."

"Yes, *Maxi*. Like the pad. I remember," she said with a cold glance as she walked past Maxi and towards the kids.

The children had already inserted their change and selected their songs as Lina reached the jukebox. After a moment, the song "Oh, Sheila" by Ready for the World began to play loudly.

Shit. No! Of all songs, they pick this one? She is going to think that I picked it!

Lina froze and caught her breath before turning to view Maxi, now sitting at the counter. Maxi pointed two fingers at her own eyes, before shifting those same fingers back at Lina, with a glare of death.

Frankie and Marty danced to the song and jumped around joyfully while Lina was distracted. Just then, she felt the tall presence of someone standing behind her.

"Hi, Lina," said the man's deep, familiar voice.

Shivers went down Lina's spine. Her stomach dropped as she turned to see Walt Weimer standing behind her in his police uniform.

"Your kids are cute. Your daughter looks just like you," said Walt in his low, creepy voice.

Lina stood with her mouth slightly open. She was not expecting this. She didn't need this. She was shocked. Thankfully, she was saved by Denise's soothing, chipper voice as she enthusiastically hugged and greeted the twins.

"I...I have to go," muttered Lina as she walked away to join the others.

She looked back over her shoulder to see that Walt was approaching Sheila at the counter and noticed Sheila's eyes roll in disgust. Ricky was standing by the stairs to go up to the apartment, when Lina reached them. He could read Lina like no one else and knew something was wrong. Lina had never told Ricky, or anyone, about what Walt Weimer had done to her when she was a teenager, but he knew that Lina's whole demeanor would change anytime they had encountered him in the past. Ricky gave her a greeting kiss on the cheek.

"What's wrong?" Ricky inquired.

"Nothing," lied Lina. Ricky put his arm around her, and the two walked up the stairs. Ricky silently turned his head to look at Walt but said nothing.

Lina was now safely seated at the Goldman dining room table, behind the apartment walls and above the café, where Walt Weimer, Lina's rapist, couldn't harm her. Although she felt safe, it didn't stop the anger at the situation from merging with her already boiling kettles of emotion. This was making her even more self-righteous when politics were discussed at the table. "Well, I'm just saying, we can't let people just come into this country without properly vetting them first. I have kids!" Lina said before shoveling a mix of roast beef and mashed potatoes into her mouth.

"You got the word "vetted" straight from Fox News! And your grandparents were immigrants from Italy, not to mention your other grandma who was from England. Seriously?!" said Ricky with irritation as he also shoveled food into his mouth.

Political conversations in the Goldman apartment were almost always one-sided. Denise and Greta had always been huge democratic supporters, and Ricky had the same views. Lina had always been in agreement with them in the past, but this was the "Year of the Great Snap." Something had shifted in Lina when her father died and left her with all the stress. She had so much clouding her mind. Her marriage appeared to be over, but her husband wouldn't communicate with her. Carol was in her mother's house, she had the final building project downtown to complete for Carlson's, and she was evicting tenants from her father's apartment building. Now Kirk and Chip had resurfaced, causing all kinds of emotions. And that creep had spoken to her downstairs and commented on her daughter's looks. Lina tried not to think about Walt during dinner, but the anger was intensifying within her regardless. She angrily excused herself to use the bathroom.

Denise began to butter a roll for Marty, as Ricky watched for Lina to be out of ear shot. The twins began to act silly and converse amongst themselves. Ricky spoke to his mothers in almost a whisper.

"See! I told you she was supporting Trump! Can you believe her? I mean, I know she is going through a lot of trauma…"

"Ricky, all people handle trauma and stress differently. Some people shoot up heroin, others vote Republican. Regardless, we *have* to be *supportive,"* said Denise with her Long Island accent.

Greta sat smiling pleasantly at Ricky, her cheek resting on her palm. Both of Ricky's mothers were taking the news of Lina being a Republican as seriously as they had when Lindsay Lohan came out as a lesbian, which was not at all.

"Cheer up, Bubbala," said Greta as she gently touched Ricky's face with the back of her hand. "Remember your Aunt Ruth?" She smiled at Ricky reassuringly as she stood to clear some dishes.

"Sort of. Wasn't she the hippie who lived on a commune in the sixties?"

"Yes, that was her. Anyway, Ruth's husband died the same year that Ronald Reagan ran for president. She had been a Democrat her whole life, then blamo! Out of nowhere, she votes for Reagan. It was as if she had just snapped or something. Long story short, she was healed and back to herself by the next election. It will all be fine."

Lina emerged from the bathroom down the hall and went to take her seat. Everyone stopped and smiled at her as if she were a mental patient.

"You two are going to go out alone for a while to unwind," commanded Denise after a pause, motioning to Lina and Ricky.

"Greta and I are going to watch a movie with the kids. Go on, get out!"

Though they disagreed about politics, the pair could never stay angry with each other. Ricky and Lina both laughed at Denise's insistence. Lina made a motion as if to say *twist my arm* and thanked each of Ricky's mothers with a kiss on the cheek as they exited. She promised to be back by the time the movie ended.

###

Lina and Ricky sat parked in a secluded spot on a high hill overlooking Downtown Rochester. The city looked beautiful in the late August moonlight. At dusk, they could see the green trees in full bloom, some of the leaves just beginning to make their transition into fall. It had been their favorite spot to hang out as teens for sneaking beer and pot. This time they were forty-year-old adults sitting in Lina's new, red Cadillac. Lina and Ricky laughed hysterically as she put the windows down to air the pot smoke from her vehicle. The two had decided to make use of what she had confiscated from her neighbor.

"You're going out with a Korean Rock star!? No effin' way! Why didn't you tell me that?" Lina asked excitedly, still giggling.

Ricky pulled up his new boyfriend's picture on his phone to show Lina as they both grew more serious.

"I met him at the dance tryouts for his local shows at COBO Hall in June," admitted Ricky, beaming. "He wants me to go on tour with him for the next year, dancing in all his shows full time. All over the world!"

Lina's heart was full and happy for Ricky. She had watched him go from boyfriend to boyfriend over the years. None of them had lasted, but she could tell this time was different. She could see it in her best friend's demeanor, in his eyes. Then she quickly remembered Ricky's obligation to run the Motown Mood Café during winter months for his mothers. A new arrangement that Ricky had agreed to for all winters moving forward. Greta and Denise were growing older and wanted to transition Ricky into full management and ownership, in preparation for their retirement. They had purchased a lovely home in Miami and wanted to start using it during the harsh, Michigan winters.

"Wait, what about the café? Have you mentioned this to your moms?" inquired Lina, as Ricky's excitement turned to guilt.

"I haven't yet. We leave in January, after the holidays. I don't want to let them down, but this is everything I ever wanted. I have a full-time dancing gig, *and* I'm truly in love. You know I love the café, but this is my dream. I'm forty and have the chance to perform. That doesn't happen often. I love teaching dance part-time…but I still have it, Lina. I still have *it.*"

There was a long pause, and then Lina spoke. "Talk to them. They are the most understanding women I know. I'm sure they will understand, but you have to talk to them. Lies are what they have no tolerance for."

"You're right," agreed Ricky. "I need to sit down with them very soon."

"What will happen when the tour ends? Are you moving to Korea?"

"No, Jihoon is older. This will be his last tour. He is looking to settle down and loves the idea of settling here and running the café together."

"Well, that works out!" said Lina, relieved.

Ricky turned the conversation back to what had led them to this reveal.

"So, you really fucked Chip in the gym parking lot?" he said, laughing again, then turning serious. "If you get caught cheating…"

"Well," said Lina, cutting him off. "Luke has been cheating for years. I never see him. He hasn't been supportive through any of this. This marriage has been over a long time."

"I know. But you are going to have to face things," said Ricky, calmly. "We *both* have to face things and be honest. Plus, Chip? Really, Lina? He has always been such a jerk! Plus, I just saw Kermit Karnes at the café recently. Chip came up in conversation, and he didn't say anything about Chip being divorced. Kermit knows of all relationship statuses in town, and he hasn't mentioned anything about Chip."

"Why would he lie?" asked Lina, looking seriously into Ricky's eyes before they both broke out into laughter. "No, I'm sure he's single. And he's so friggin' hot! Hey, did you know Glickman is the mayor of Rochester Township? Not the city of Rochester, but the township part?"

"Yes," said Ricky before bursting into laughter again. "Mayor Glickman."

"But is he really the mayor? Like a city council president or something, right?" she asked as tears of laughter filled her eyes.

"I guess!" he exclaimed, laughing. "Remember what a fuck up Glickman was back in the day? Ha, crazy!" Then, Ricky turned serious. "But then again, anything is possible in politics."

Lina rolled her eyes in anticipation of where she knew Ricky was heading with that last comment. "Shut up," she said as she gave him a light punch on his arm.

Ricky began to open his mouth but then remembered Denise and Greta's advice.

"Why don't we finish this roach, then take a walk downtown. Maybe find some dessert," Ricky suggested as he tried to light up the last couple of hits without burning his fingers.

"Okay, just a second," she said as she picked up her phone to text Chip. "Hey Chip. I'm wondering if I could ask you a huge favor. I could really use some help getting info on my Dad's wife."

CHAPTER TWELVE

2016-Dominos
"That Girl"
by Stevie Wonder

The following morning, Lina was getting ready for her appointment at the insurance agency with Mitzy. She had been avoiding the meeting, but she needed to get the insurance for all the inherited properties figured out. It should have been done weeks ago. But every time she pictured Mitzy's nosey face at her father's funeral, or the mean way she had ripped down Lina and Ricky's poster in school, she would become infuriated. Everything infuriated Lina during the time of the "Great Snap," but Mitzy and her other BFFs just added fuel to Lina's anger at the world.

Ricky was already at Lina's with his new boyfriend, Jihoon Kim. They were drinking coffee and setting up music to work with Frankie on her cheer and dance moves. They had arranged to have Ricky watch the kids while she went to the insurance agency, but Jihoon was an exciting surprise for Lina and the kids. Jihoon was taller than she had expected, and Ricky had never looked more blissful as the two shared a kiss.

Lina saw the way Ricky and Jihoon lovingly interacted with each other as she exited her bedroom, fastening an earring. She paused for a moment with pure appreciation and happiness for the pair. She had hoped for so long that Ricky would find true love and companionship. Jihoon seemed to fit the bill on all levels, but she still worried about how Denise and Greta would react to the news that Ricky wanted to work in Jihoon's show, and go on tour when they needed Ricky to take over the reins at the café.

"How do I look?" inquired Lina while turning slowly for the group to admire.

"Like a movie actress, as always," said Ricky, walking over to kiss her on the cheek, before looking to Jihoon for approval.

"Fantastic!" exclaimed Jihoon with his thick, Korean accent.

"Better than Mitzy?" asked Lina, already knowing the answer.

"You could wear a potato sack with no make-up and still look way better than Mitzy," Ricky confirmed, smiling at Lina with confidence. "Now, go strut your stuff and show Mitzy and everyone in town who is boss!"

###

Lina found a spot to park on Main Street, but it was a few blocks down from the insurance agency. After feeding the parking meter, she smiled to herself as she walked down the street, bopping slightly to the music streaming loudly from the Motown Mood Café. Her pale-pink dress brought out her sun-kissed, summer skin, and her open toe stilettos gave an extra spring to her step.

Downtown Rochester was alive with excitement. The community had several events throughout the year. This week all the businesses along Main Street were participating in "Downtown Dominos," an event in which each business created their own unique domino display in their front window. They could paint the dominos any color and get as creative as they wished with design. She smiled pleasantly as she admired the mermaid-themed display at Green's Art Supply. Their dominoes were painted all different shades, resulting in a perfect mermaid portrait. Lina thought that Green's Art Supply would most likely win the contest. She closed her eyes and allowed the breeze of late August to cool her nerves. As she continued walking to her dreaded appointment, her brief encounter with contentment was suddenly interrupted.

“That goddamned music isn’t supposed to be so loud!" called Fuck Face O’Malley from just inside his shop, which now appeared to be mostly items to be sold on eBay. “Those are city rules! When are you going to get it through your head that not everyone wants to hear this crap?"

“Why yah yellin’ at me??? I don’t own the café! By the way, I was gone for over twenty years!" she called as she turned and continued walking backwards, facing O’Malley. “In case you hadn’t noticed! Get a fucking clue." She turned to walk forward again.

“Well, you look the same to me! A half-Guinea wop dressed up as a Carlson! You kiss your mother with that mouth?”

“My mother is dead, jerk! Thanks for bringing it up!" she yelled back, still headed to the insurance agency.

O’Malley stopped and thought for a moment, as he realized her mother had in fact been dead for decades. Then he closed his mouth, shook his head, and angrily shut his front door.

Lina crossed the street and arrived at the Hamilton Insurance Agency. She saw Mitzy in the window, working on their domino display with a younger female employee. The Hamilton Insurance Agency had chosen to do an elaborate but traditional domino display with all dominos painted pink for breast cancer awareness.

Lina entered, trying her best at faking a sincere smile.

“Lina!" exclaimed Mitzy as she carefully removed herself from their display area.

“Hi Mitzy! It looks like you ladies are hard at work on your Downtown Dominos project.”

"Well, it's all in place now. All that is left is to go through and glue each domino into place!" Mitzy exclaimed proudly as she motioned for Lina to join her in her office.

The two former schoolmates took their seats at Mitzy's desk.

"Now, whenever there is a death, it is *imperative* that the properties are insured under the correct owner or owners. So, the first order of business is taking inventory of who owns what," finished Mitzy, secretly excited to hear inside information. It was rumored that Lina got nothing.

"Well, the only properties that Carol owns, she already had insured with my dad. They purchased the two recreational properties right after they got married." *With my money*, she thought.

"And Fairview?" inquired Mitzy, as she took notes.

"Fairview is owned by my Aunt Isobel, my dad's sister. When she passes, her son and I take ownership together," said Lina.

Mitzy nodded. "And Carol owns your father's house now, I presume, since she is clearly still living there," said Mitzy, looking down at her paper with a subtle, evil smile.

"No, actually. I am the legal owner of the house. She is just *living* there," stated Lina firmly. The question and Mitzy's unsympathetic attitude were already making her blood simmer. She had a deep-rooted hatred for Mitzy to begin with. That was one group of people she did not miss while she was living in sunny San Diego, yet each one of them was magically back in her life. Like a sick joke from the universe.

"Oh, well in that case, we will need to have the property appraised and insured in your name," said Mitzy, slightly deflated. "Your stepmother will need to obtain renters insurance while she is living on your property."

This news lifted Lina's spirits. *She will need renters insurance while she is on MY property*, she thought, smiling.

"Renters insurance, yes. In fact, if you could *call* Carol and let her know she will be needing *renters* insurance to live in *my* house, that would be so helpful," Lina said, trying to hold in her enthusiasm at the thought of Carol receiving that call.

"Of course," said Mitzy, taking down a note, without detecting Lina's subtle delight. "Now, for the rental property downtown..." Mitzy stopped, put her pen down dramatically, and looked at Lina with fake sympathy. "It must be so hard to run those businesses when you had nothing to do with them before. You know, because *you* only own them because of *someone else's* hard work."

"Yes, the same way it must be hard for you to run this place just because your grandfather started it long before you were even born," said Lina, modeling Mitzy's tone as she smirked and stood before heading towards the office door. "If there is anything else you need from me, please send a text or email. I can print and sign documents, and then drop them back off. I really must be going now."

Lina exited Mitzy's office and entered the lobby. Standing tall with her small handbag hanging from her shoulder, she walked to the front desk with the imaginary book on her head.

"Ladies, it was so lovely to see you all today," said Lina to the girls at the front desk as she reached the door. She then spotted Mr. Hamilton, Mitzy's father. "Mr. Hamilton, good day! And please give my regards to Mrs. Hamilton."

After charming everyone in the office, almost on evil autopilot, Lina's designer handbag 'accidentally' tapped the end of Mitzy's domino display. The whole room gasped as each perfectly-placed domino fell one by one.

"Oops, sorry," said Lina as she turned her head to face Mitzy with an innocent smile. The entire lobby watched in silence as Lina finally achieved retribution for Mitzy tearing down the poster all those years ago. As she turned her head forward to reach for the door, her pseudo-polite expression turned to a satisfied grin as she strutted back out on to Main Street. She barely had time to think about what had just happened when she nearly bumped into Fitz, who was leaving the classic Dairy Bar restaurant.

"Lina! Well, hello, young lady! You are looking very nice," said Fitz as he eyed Lina from head to toe, stopping at her breasts which were highlighted nicely in the stretchy, knit material of her dress bodice.

"Fitz! Yes, hello, handsome! Sorry I haven't texted you back yet. I was wondering if we could talk."

"I just finished lunch and have no showings this afternoon. I was headed to my office. Would you like to join me? I could show you around," Fitz offered.

This wasn't planned, but the kids *were* already with Ricky. And she *did* look fabulous, she decided. She took Fitz's arm before the two took a leisurely stroll down the street to Fitzpatrick Realty.

His slogan - "Fitz gitz it sold!" - was painted on the glass door along with a headshot of himself confidently smiling in a trendy suit jacket. The two entered and Lina immediately noticed a large heap of dominos dumped near the store window. Fitz looked embarrassed.

"The ex-wife used to do the store window stuff," he confessed. Then he quickly shifted Lina's attention to his personal office, motioning with his arm. "Right this way."

As they entered his large work area, Lina looked around, acting extra-impressed.

"Wow, Fitz. I love what you've done with the updates. Was this your dad's office?"

"Yep, he is retired now, living in Florida! And hey, I know I've said this before, but I'm sorry about your dad."

"Yeah, it's fine," said Lina, caught off guard and waving off the statement.

Fitz stood near his desk as Lina continued to meander around the room, looking at trophies with exaggerated interest.

"Ooh, what is this award for?" she asked, pointing to an engraved, decorative sword on the wall.

"That was for Kendo, a form of Japanese fencing," said Fitz, standing taller with pride. "That was for a state-wide competition. I'm almost a black belt."

"Wow! Impressive. No wonder you stay in such great shape," she said with a flirty smile. "So, Fitz. That is really great that you take the time to volunteer as a coach for the kids. Everyone really appreciates it. *I* appreciate it."

Her sexy grin made Fitz's heart pound.

She casually walked over to another award and touched it gently as she thought about her next move.

"Yes, and I'm the general manager too, of course," touted Fitz.

"Of course! Yes, that's a pretty big deal too. I didn't mean to leave that part out," said Lina, smiling and giggling towards Fitz in the seductive way she had mastered years before. "I mean, you make all the hiring decisions for coaches and everything, right?"

"Yes, that's right," Fitz confirmed with pride, still standing near his desk, watching Lina admire his awards. "I have the final say on all decisions. Veto power too! I refused to make the kids have that extra practice in the rain. You see, my vision for the team has many levels. Physical health, mental health…it all comes together." He brought his palms together for a visual and smiled confidently. He was sure Lina must be impressed.

As Fitz spoke, she stopped at an award that was hanging on the wall and touched it gently. "So, tell me Fitz. Who do I have to *fuck*... to get Jeni fired?" asked Lina.

Fitz, caught completely off guard, briefly looked shocked. He then sucked in his gut and gave Lina a big smile.

Twenty minutes later, Lina emerged from Fitzpatrick Realty. She smiled to herself thinking, *Sometimes you have to take one for the team. Mission accomplished, and Fitz was actually really good!* She was trying to adjust her outfit and hair when she nearly bumped into Kirk.

"What are you up to, missy?" asked Kirk with a suspicious smile. "I saw you go into Fitzpatrick Realty with Fitz from my office window. Just came down to grab some lunch and here you are."

Lina was looking around as Kirk spoke, as if looking for a place she needed to be right away. She came up short.

"Are you planning to sell your house or something?" Kirk asked.

"Oh, no. I was just stopping in to talk to Fitz."

"Yes, I saw that. But about what?" asked Kirk on the verge of laughter. He looked pleased with himself because he knew he had her flustered.

Then the obvious excuse came to her. "If you must know, Fitz is the general manager of the MDCCF organization. We were discussing the team."

Even though they were outside on the street, you could still cut the sexual tension in the air with a knife. Kirk loved his family, but he just couldn't shake Lina. He thought about her day and night, especially when he had monthly sex with his wife. He pictured Lina's face as he hovered above Kitty, Lina's ass when he flipped his wife over, and Lina's mouth when his wife sucked him on his birthday. He thought about how he was the first one to conquer Lina, and in some ways, felt he deserved to be with her over anyone else, due to this fact. He had marked his territory with Lina long ago on that summer day at the pool. It was an image that was burned into his mind and recollected many times throughout his life. She was back in Michigan now. Here was his chance, but he was paralyzed with obligation to a cold, loveless marriage.

Lina was hopelessly in love with Kirk. So much so, that she would never do anything to risk his happiness. She knew if she proceeded to have an affair with Kirk, that the only available outcome would be heartache and misery. It would eventually end, and it would end badly. It would never have the chance to flourish and grow into a healthy relationship when it was rooted in lies and deceit. As much as she longed to be selfish and dive into bed with Kirk, she was wise enough by age forty to know hard, cold reality.

Lina's explanation made sense to Kirk, and he disguised his relief. The thought of her with Fitz, or anyone else, secretly made him sick.

"Oh, okay. Well, I was just teasing you anyhow, Lina. So anyway, while I have you, did you happen to get the mortgage account number for your parent's house yet? I've asked Carol repeatedly to send copies of the mortgage payment receipts, but they never arrive. She always seems to have an excuse. Honestly, Lina, she really does seem fucking crazy! I'll admit, I thought it was just you and the situation at first…"

"I *tried* calling to get the account number, but they won't give it to me! Said I need the account number to find out if mortgage payments were being made, but they won't *give* me the account number! *I'm* the owner of the house, but the bank won't give me *my* account number. They said they'll mail it to me at the house address…that I have no access to...ERRRR," said Lina, frustration and anger surging back as she recalled the bank situation. She took a deep breath to calm herself. "Also, I had the human resources secretary with Carlson's sign off on my dad's 401K. I mailed everything in, but haven't heard back yet. Fingers crossed that his original beneficiary forms still stand, regardless of the new marriage. I will flip out if that bitch takes that from me too."

"Okay, we'll figure this out. Beyond frustrating!" sympathized Kirk.

"I'll talk to you very soon!" she called back while heading away and back to the safety of her car.

###

Ricky and Jihoon said their goodbyes after watching the twins for Lina. She turned on the television and got comfortable on the coach. Amy Andrews from Fox 2 News was doing a story on school supplies for the underprivileged. Lina was thinking about how to get the mortgage account number for her parent's house. *Maybe going in person and pleading my case would help?* she thought. She remembered her grandpa telling her to always first "tell them who you are" when arriving at a place of business. "Use that Carlson name!" he would tell her. Grandpa knew the Mancini name had never gotten him anywhere in town, and had been pleased for his daughter and granddaughter to have a recognizable and influential name. He had always reminded her to use this power.

Lina went on her tablet and began looking up local branches of the bank that the mortgage was through. She looked at the website for the bank just north of town, and didn't recognize any employees. She remembered the branch right on Main Street in Rochester. *Duh*, she thought to herself. She opened the branch website and began to scroll through the employees. The first few weren't familiar, so she clicked on the branch manager. To Lina's shock and elation, it was none other than Matt Munson, the former librarian at the Rochester Public Library who had a crush on her back in school. The boy three years her senior who had allowed Lina to borrow *Forever* by Judy Blume from the library at age fourteen. *I wonder if he would remember me?* she thought, as she puffed away on her vape pen. She got up, looked in on the kids playing video games in the den, and then ran to her closet to find the hottest yet most professional outfit she owned. If she didn't have what she needed, she would have to go to the mall. *It's imperative that I look as good as humanly possible,* she thought as she looked in the mirror, holding up two dresses against her body.

CHAPTER THIRTEEN

2016
"Hypnotize"
by Notorious B.I.G.

The parents of the MDCCF were sitting on the football bleachers as the crisp morning air began to evolve into a warm day of late summer. The coaches had asked for an impromptu meeting before their last summer practice began. Coach Fitzpatrick walked to the front of the bleachers.

"Hello everyone! We have had a great three weeks of practice! Please make note of new practice times now that school has started. Now, there have been some executive decisions made concerning the younger girls' cheer team. Effective today, Jeni Wilcox will no longer be coaching. The girls will practice with Coach Sandy's group today, and the new coach will begin next week, after Labor Day weekend," informed Fitz as he gave a quick glance and smile in Lina's direction. He began talking again as the moms in the bleachers began whispering in shock that Jeni had suddenly been fired.

"Wow, she must have done something really *horrific*," commented Lina to no one in particular, in a loud whisper, to be sure others heard her.

Two of the other moms heard Lina and nodded in agreement with faces of deep concern. "That's so crazy," she continued, chewing her gum Chip-style and innocently looking off in Fitz's direction. She was resisting the urge to cheer and jump around the field in glee.

"All of the information is in the handout! If there are no further questions, we will see you in two hours, after practice," he gave Lina another confident, sincere smile before walking off to join his team.

###

Lina headed home quickly so she could spend the kids' practice time by the pool with Chip. His working as a private investigator resulted in odd working-hours which had benefited their affair. He was usually able to pop over during the day for a visit, even when her husband was in town. It had been a definite turn on for them both, knowing Luke could walk in from work at any time. He never came home during the day unexpectedly, but it *could* happen, which made sex extra-exciting.

Chip had actually fantasized about Luke walking in while he was pleasing Lina from behind. It annoyed and sometimes even angered Chip that this dork had actually managed to marry her. Chip wanted Luke Pratt to see the way that Lina cried out in ecstasy when he had his way with her. The whole affair with Nicolina Carlson had been an ego boost for Chip. Anytime he got a married woman to sleep with him, it gave him an extra rush, sexually. And anything that boosted Chip's ego tended to become an addiction for him.

Lina was in her new monokini, ready for her afternoon fun with Chip. He hadn't yet arrived, so she went out to grab the mail. She still hadn't heard anything about her dad's 401K and had been hoping something would arrive soon. She removed the curled-up stack of mail from her box when she noticed Seth Glickman's white Mercedes roll up and park at the curb beside her.

Crap, she thought. *Chip will be here any minute. I don't want Seth to see him here. Why now?*

"Well. hello, lovely old friend," said Glickman, eyeing Lina's figure in her skimpy swimsuit.

"Hello, Mr. Mayor," said Lina, smiling.

"Hey, if I haven't told you before, you look sensational!"

"Thanks. To what do I owe this pleasure?" asked Lina, hoping Chip wouldn't pull up yet.

"I'm heading up north to Crystalline Lake tonight for the holiday weekend and wanted to personally deliver my findings to you before I head up."

"Oh, I'm taking the twins up tomorrow morning, so we'll see you up there."

"Fantastic!" he said, sneaking another peek at her breasts. "So, it seems that the summer taxes on your dad's house haven't been paid."

Lina stood stunned for a moment. "Are you sure? The taxes definitely haven't been paid?"

"That's correct. As the Rochester Township mayor, I personally called the City treasurer and had him check to see if there were any unprocessed checks waiting. Nothing."

A prenuptial agreement requirement that Carol hasn't fulfilled, she thought as her body filled with hopeful glee. With that, she excitedly threw her arms around Seth's neck and gave him a kiss on the cheek.

"Thank you so much, Seth! I really appreciate it. Truly."

Seth Glickman wasn't sure why this would be good news for Lina but was feeling aroused nonetheless. He thought this might be a sign that he should ask his next question.

"So, Lina, I was wondering…"

"Yes?"

"There is a group of adventurous people our age who like to get together and have fun," he said, changing into a more seductive tone and looking at her to gauge her reaction so far.

"We take turns getting together for key parties. Do you know what a key party is?"

Lina started to laugh. "You mean like what people in the seventies did? Yes, I've heard of them."

"Well, I know if you were to show up at one, the other guests, both male and female, would be quite excited."

"As interesting as that sounds, I'll have to pass for now."

"If you change your mind, call me. It's nothing to be shy about, Lina. Sometimes, at our age, you just need a little extra *kink* to get you off harder," he whispered with a wink.

"I'll keep it in mind, Seth," she lied. "Thank you so much for your information. I really have to get going now though."

"No problem! See you up north!" he called before getting back into his car.

Lina hurriedly ran into the house and tossed the mail on the counter. She peeked through the window to see that Glickman was still there, messing with something inside his vehicle. *Shit! What is he doing? Go! Chip will be here any second!* she thought. Glickman's vehicle was finally beginning to turn around in the cul-de-sac, just as Chip's vehicle pulled up to the curb. She hoped that Seth wouldn't recognize Chip. She ran to her pool lounger, where she had instructed him to meet her. She wanted to look sexy and posed when Chip arrived. She would think about the information Glickman gave her after Chip left.

Lina's deep, dark tan was complemented by her skimpy white suit as she lounged poolside and waited for Chip. Her favorite summer playlist was streaming through the pool speakers, and it was a perfect eighty degrees outside. It was the last official weekend of summer, and soon she would be packing lunches and helping with homework. As she absorbed the sun's rays, she thought about what school supplies the kids needed. She suddenly smelled pot, and the sun became blocked. It was Chip.

"Hey, baby," said Chip as he bent down to kiss her. Lit joint in one hand, a beer in the other, and his briefcase flung across his shoulder with a strap. "Happy Labor Day weekend! Want some?" He offered her the joint.

"Chip!" she exclaimed, giggling. "No! What are you doing? We have to pick up our kids soon!" she said, scoping out the area for neighbors.

"My wife is picking up the kids. I am officially free to party!" said Chip as he took another hit off his joint. He smiled, then licked his fingers and extinguished it. He pulled his shirt off over his head, revealing the fruits of all his time spent at the gym, before taking a swig of his beer.

"Your wife? You mean ex-wife?" asked Lina.

"Yeah, sorry. I meant to say ex," explained Chip.

"Oh. Well, you know how much I love to party with you," said Lina seductively, as she smiled and rose to wrap her arms around Chip's irresistible neck. "But I can't today."

"Hey, I thought I saw Glickman in your cul-de-sac when I pulled up."

"Oh, yeah. He stopped by to give me some info about my dad's house…and invite me to a key party," she added, giggling.

This piqued Chip's interest. "A key party? Really?!"

"Yeah, apparently, people our age in town are doing this for an extra *kink*," she said, still chuckling.

Chip looked off into the distance, smiling pleasantly and considering the possibilities. *Remember to text Glickman the second you leave here*, he noted to himself.

He set his beer down on the side table and fully embraced Lina's succulent, shapely body. He kissed her gently at first, before passionately thrusting his tongue against hers. He lifted Lina's body in full embrace, and she wrapped her legs around his waist, fastening them around him with her ankles.

Chip's hands were firmly on Lina's derriere as he carried her to the tented pool gazebo. Once inside, he rested her bare feet on the pool cement. They continued to kiss before Lina broke away and began zipping the sides of the gazebo closed for privacy. Chip smiled and lowered himself onto the white, terrycloth lounging bed and smugly fastened his fingers around the back of his neck, elbows extended.

Lina finished zipping up the last side of the tented walls and walked over to stand next to where Chip was lying. The song "Level" by The Raconteurs played on the pool speakers as Lina stopped and looked into Chip's eyes. She reached behind her head to untie the top of her suit, allowing it to fall to her waist. Chip sat up and cupped her breasts in his hands. He put his face in her cleavage before running his tongue between her breasts until he reached her neck. Lina broke away and gently lowered Chip back down into position.

Lina pushed the rest of her suit down around her ankles and paused so Chip could admire her curves, before stepping up onto the lounger bed. She hovered above Chip's face before lowering herself down upon his mouth. She looked him in the eyes and stroked his hair as his tongue pleasured her. Lina threw her head back and released a moan as she reached back to soothe Chip's arousal with her hand.

She removed herself from Chip's lips and began sliding her body down his slowly, beginning with her bellybutton at his face, then her breasts. He kissed her nipples again before she continued to slide down, resting her breasts on his erection. She grabbed the top of his swim trunks and pulled them down with force before rubbing her curves all over Chip's excited body. She lifted herself and grabbed a ponytail holder from the side table to fasten her hair back, then she slid her naked body back down to inspect his manliness.

Lina tasted all of Chip. When he was deep in her throat, he let out a primal moan before pulling her up and resting her where her mouth had just been. He paused to look into her violet eyes, before poking himself into his favorite escape. Lina was Chip's addiction, and he couldn't get enough.

Sweat dripped from Chip's brow with each thrust, and Lina didn't mind as the tiny droplets landed on her breasts. Having Chip inside of her was the closest thing to heaven she could find, and watching his face as he enjoyed her brought her to ecstasy. They both forgot they were outside as they loudly succumbed to their pleasure. Lina rolled off him and into a naked embrace before reaching for her vape pen. She shared it with Chip, and then got up and put her suit back on. Chip watched her, thinking about how lovely she still was. Then he remembered that he had big news to share.

"Well, sexy. I have some information on your stepmother that I think you'll find very interesting," said Chip proudly. Lina turned very serious and rushed over to join Chip on the lounger.

"What? What did you find out?" asked Lina, feeling both excited and sick to her stomach all at once. Any mention of Carol tended to instantly nauseate Lina.

"Well, it seems Carol Lipshitz is actually Carolina Josephina Lipshitzenfeldt," reported Chip, reading her name from the paperwork he had just retrieved from his briefcase.

"What? She seriously chose to go by Lipshitz? I mean, if you're going to change it anyway…" asked Lina, astonished.

"*AND*, that's not even the kicker," said Chip.

"Well, what's the kicker?" asked Lina, holding her palms anxiously to the sky.

"It seems Miss Lipshitzenfeldt was born in Hungary to a German scientist and a Hungarian housewife. Her father brought their family over while he was here on a work visa. Carol's father died six months after their arrival, but it seems she and her mother stayed without ever becoming citizens. Looks like her four sisters became citizens, at least."

"Four sisters!? She said she had no family besides her recently departed mother!" cried Lina.

"She had better be careful too. If Trump gets elected in November, they are really going to crack down on illegal aliens."

Lina loved that Chip had referred to Carol as an illegal alien. She also loved that he was a Trump supporter, as they had previously discussed. Chip looked back down at his notes.

"Also, it looks like her last marriage didn't last very long. She married another guy just six months before she married your dad."

"What?! She told everyone that this was her first marriage! Are you sure?"

"Yep! Got married in Portland, then had it annulled once they moved to Michigan. Weird. I'll email all the information to you tomorrow. I'm meeting up with Fitz and Lawson tonight for drinks."

"I can't thank you enough. I mean, I knew she might have a past, but I was *not* expecting this!" exclaimed Lina, still processing this new information and wondering if it could benefit her. She glanced at her phone.

"Shit! I have to get going!" said Lina, suddenly flustered.

After the two emerged from the gazebo, Chip helped Lina tie her suit behind her neck.

"Wait. I'll miss you while you're up north. Let me take a couple quick pics of you," said Chip.

Lina smiled and kneeled by the pool, pulling her hair up in her hands, while Chip took some pictures of her with his phone.

He suddenly turned very serious and kneeled down before her. "Lina, this summer with you has been incredible. I love you and want to marry you."

Lina sat speechless. She hadn't even decided to get divorced yet, let alone get engaged.

"I love you too, Chip. But I have to go get the kids," she said, smiling into his eyes warmly. "This conversation will have to wait, sweetie."

"Of course!" he said, giving Lina a big kiss.

Chip picked up his beer, and the two lovers giggled as they entered the house. The neighbor, Mrs. Weiss, was outside watering her lawn. She had heard noises coming from the gazebo next door and watched as Lina walked inside with a man who wasn't her husband.

"Is that medicinal too?" asked Mrs. Weiss to herself with disapproval, as she continued to water the grass.

###

An hour later, the trio was home from practice. Lina casually began sifting through the mail while she drew a bath for Frankie. The twins had decided it was Frankie's turn to take a bath first that day.

Lina suddenly spotted an envelope from her father's 401K bank. She froze. *Either this is going to be horrible news, OR it's undecided and they're just asking for more documentation, OR it's fantastic news.* She prepared herself for the worst, as she had become accustomed to bad news. She took a deep breath and carefully opened the envelope along the top, using her thumb, and emptied its contents. There was a check made out to her for $858,000. She flipped it over to make sure it was real, and then flipped it over again. She counted the zeros to make sure she was reading it correctly. She read the letter that came with it. It was official. There had been no question who the beneficiary was. Bill getting married had no bearing on who he originally listed on his forms. This check was hers to do with as she pleased, and no one could refute it. Lina looked at the clock.

"KIDS! KIDS! Oh my God, we have to go! FRANKIE! TURN OFF THE WATER! Here, put your clothes back on!" she said, frantically trying to get Frankie dressed again.

"Mom, what is it?" asked Marty, confused.

"There's no time! The bank closes in twenty minutes, and it's a holiday weekend! We need to get a check deposited before they change their minds!" called Lina frantically as she struggled to find her other flip flop. There was still an element of fear in her that the bank was somehow going to change its mind if she didn't cash it right away. She was terrified of waiting to deposit it until after the holiday weekend, especially since she and the kids were headed up north the following morning.

"Come on! Go! Get in the car!" she coached. She motioned the kids into the car before hurriedly jumping into the driver's seat. "Everyone buckled!?"

Lina pulled out of her subdivision onto Rochester Road. She told her car system to call the café. She always called the land line at Motown Mood whenever she had extra exciting news for all three to hear. She heard Ricky's voice answer.

"Motown Mood! This is Rick!"

"Ricky! It's me. Guess what I'm 'straight up' right now?"

"Huh? Straight up…straight up a pole?" joked Ricky. He could tell this was playtime with Lina, and he naturally adjusted to her game. Whatever stressful situation might be going on at the time of a call, the two always switched gears to accommodate the other. Luckily, Ricky was already in a good mood and ready for fun.

"Nope," said Lina with a slight giggle. I'm straight up *gangsta*! That's what I'm straight up, baby! I'm on my *way* to the bank to deposit my dad's *401K*!" She laughed and glanced in her mirror to view the kids.

"She got the 401K!" yelled Ricky to Denise and Greta who were both standing near him, behind the counter. Lina heard

Denise's Long Island accent coming through the phone from across the counter.

"I knew it! I told you! That happened to Lorna Margolis! She was married thirty years, but Stanley never changed his old beneficiary forms. He dies, poof! First wife walks off with everything," called Denise before turning to continue the conversation with the customers at the counter who overheard.

"How much was it for?" called Greta from across the counter.

"How much was it for?" repeated Ricky, in case Lina didn't hear Greta.

"Eight hundred and fifty-eight thousand! I know it's not a whole lot, but I'm just glad he put something in there! That beneficiary form saved my ass!"

"Eight hundred fifty-eight thousand," relayed Ricky to Greta, Denise, and all the customers who were listening.

"Tell her to call my cousin Ari at the Investment Bank of Detroit! YOU REMEMBER ARI, RIGHT, LINA?" said Greta to Ricky, yelling louder so Lina could hear.

"Right, Ari! Okay, I gotta go. I need to focus on getting there before they close. I'm thirteen minutes out! Love you!" said Lina, ending the call with a happy smile. She then used one hand to shake some Nicorette lozenges out into her console. She needed nicotine but didn't want to vape with the kids in the car. She grabbed two without looking and shoved them into her mouth.

Lina and the twins were making good time traveling south down Rochester Road towards Downtown Rochester. It was a one-lane road that turned into Main Street once you hit town, then into a four-lane road as you traveled further south toward Detroit. A blue minivan pulled in front of her and began driving 35 MPH on the one-lane, 50 MPH road. As there was no way to pass this vehicle, she was stuck behind them.

"NOOOOO!" yelled Lina as she punched the top of her steering wheel. "Jesus Christ!" She held both hands in the air, hoping the driver ahead of her would see her dismay and change their ways. "We just passed the fucking speed limit sign! It says fifty! Are you blind?!"

Lina checked the mirror again. Both kids had their headphones on, playing with their tablets. She was glad they didn't seem to hear her angry rants.

"Move bitch," Lina sang in a whisper to herself, under her breath.

The slow driver turned right, and Lina was free to hit the gas, lightening her stress. *I can still make it*, she thought.

She turned up the radio to hear the intro of the song "*Hypnotize*" by Notorious B.I.G. She sang along with Biggie as he mentioned Detroit in his lyrics. Another glance to the backseat showed the kids were still in their own world with their headphones and tablets. She decided it was okay to blast her music. *It's a special occasion. I'm rich*, she thought as she cranked up the volume.

Lina was still absorbing the situation as she cruised down the road, bumping to her car's sound system. She began to giggle, then stopped herself, then sang along some more, before busting out in full laughter as she bounced giddily in her seat. It was then that she realized she was *literally* laughing all the way to the bank.

CHAPTER FOURTEEN

2016-Up north
"All Summer Long"
by Kid Rock

The morning had arrived, and Lina and the twins were packing for their three-hour trip up north to Crystalline Lake. She smiled to herself, and turned up the music on her radio, thinking about how Chip had professed his love for her and desire for marriage. She knew she could never actually marry Chip but loved the fact that he wanted to. There was just no way she could ever trust him, as she knew that past behavior is almost always the best predictor of future performance. Not to mention, if she were to get a divorce, it was Kirk she was truly in love with, and would always be. Lina knew full well she was in no mental condition to take any relationship seriously, regardless. But the thought of Chip LaBeau being in love with her still sent her to cloud nine as she moved to the music and closed her suitcase.

"Did you both go potty? If not, do it now and get in the car!" called Lina from her driveway, as she finished loading her Escalade for their trip up north. "We need to beat the traffic on I-75, and it's already ten!"

The twins ran to the car, each holding their tablets and headphones.

"My tablet isn't charged," whined Frankie.

"I told you guys fifty fuc-," Lina cut herself off, taking a deep breath, "I told you two repeatedly that you would need to charge your tablets *and* bring your chargers for them. Do you have the chargers?"

As the twins ran back inside to get their chargers, Lina counted to herself and concentrated on breathing. She knew she was stressed out and didn't want to take it out on her kids. *But I told them fifty fucking times. Nobody fucking listens. My dad would have killed me if I had never listened*, she thought, composing herself and getting the kids buckled into their booster seats.

After everyone was settled and equipped with snacks, Lina put on her playlist and headed to I-75 North. She and the twins would follow this expressway for three hours, making a stop at the Lumberjack Restaurant in West Branch along the way for dinner. She wasn't sure if there would be much to eat at the cottage and didn't want to risk it. She remembered grocery stores closed early up there and were few and far between. The Lumberjack was a popular place for travelers from downstate to stop and eat before reaching their cottages, and the twins were able to experience this for the first time. She was also feeling proud of herself for was making this trip with the kids on her own, and didn't need Luke.

The trio had finally made it to exit 244 to Crystalline Lake.

"We're here! We made it!"

The kids removed their headphones and cheered. They were so excited to visit this place that they had never been to, but had heard so much about. Some of their friends from school had cottages up there too.

The red Escalade drove a few miles before turning toward the state park. The Carlson family cottage was just down the beach from the park, with the Glickman cottage being one closer. The wealthy in Michigan always referred to their homes in Northern Michigan as "cottages," but the truth was that they were usually magnificent houses that stretched along the beautiful, glistening shores of the many lakes. The Carlson cottage was three thousand square feet, which was tiny compared to the

Glickman's six thousand square foot home next door, that also had an impressive stone staircase that led from the beach to their front door. Lina had always used this as her guide when out on the boat in her younger years, as Bill had taught her. "If you ever get lost, look for the Glickman's tall, wide front steps," she recalled her dad saying as she turned down their street and headed towards the water.

"Look! See the water? That is Crystalline Lake!" she called to the backseat. She smiled in the rearview mirror at the children's expressions, remembering how the sight of the lake had always filled her with excitement and still did. It had been over twenty years since she had laid eyes on the shore of Crystalline Lake, and she felt a flip of happiness in her belly, as she saw that her neighborhood was just as lively on the holiday weekends as it always had been.

Lina saw the Belmont's from Bloomfield Hills were already partying on their long, wide deck that stretched far out into the water, leading to their hoisted watercrafts. She lowered the car windows and heard the song "All Summer Long" by Kid Rock blasting through the air, as several people line-danced in their bathing suits along the Belmont's deck. She noticed Mr. Glickman, Seth's father, was in attendance too, drinking a beer with Mr. Belmont and waving in her direction. Lina was pleased to see that some things never changed as she pulled in her driveway.

"Mama, whose car is that? I thought we were going to be here alone," asked Marty, suddenly fearful that Aunt Isobel would be there. Fun never seemed to be allowed when Aunt Isobel was near.

"I don't...know," replied Lina, suddenly feeling panicked as she put the car into park. It was a white Range Rover just like Carol's car, but tons of people drove that same vehicle, so she hoped it was a home intruder instead. She knew Aunt Isobel wouldn't be there this weekend. Her anger began to boil as she and the kids exited the car. *That better not fucking be her*, she thought as she opened the side door to the cottage.

Much to Lina's dismay, there sat Carol at the kitchen counter with a cocktail. She was startled to see Lina.

"Oh, shit," said Carol with her thick, German accent as she looked at Lina and the twins standing before her.

"Wow, nice to see you too. What a nice way to speak in front of the grandchildren that you're suing me to have rights to. Yes, Kirk told me," said Lina with a cold stare.

"I'm not suing you! I was simply checking into zee options, since I promised my dear, late husband that I would look over *zose* children as they are my own."

"Well," said Lina, pretending to be moved. "That sure is a tearjerker of a story to gain sympathy from others, but we both know that is total bullshit, Carol."

The twins both stared in surprise at this exchange between their mom and Carol. Marty covered his dropped jaw with his hand.

"Now, why the fuck are you in my house? My other house got too boring for you? This is my family cottage, and you are not welcome."

"It is the *Carlson* family cottage, and I am Mrs. Carlson… Mrs. *Pratt*," snarled Carol firmly as she sipped her drink and pulled a cigarette from her pack. "Zis is as much my house as it is Isobel's."

As Carol spoke, Lina noticed a pair of men's brown leather shoes sitting by a closed bedroom door. Lina bit her lip to keep quiet, before quickly looking away, so Carol wouldn't notice she had seen them.

"Fine. Then we will stay on the boat!" suggested Lina, trying to make it sound positive and fun to the kids. "There is a small area in the front of the boat that goes under for sleeping," she told the kids.

"Das boot is mine," informed Carol.

The way Carol had said *Das Boot* instantly reminded Lina of a German movie by that title from her childhood. It was all Lina could do to keep from telling Carol that she knew she was an illegal alien, but she refrained. Lina had retained everything her Sicilian grandfather had taught her. *"Loose lips get fingers chopped to bits,"* she remembered her grandpa saying. She knew that the information that Chip had provided her could possibly be useful. She wasn't sure how yet, but she knew telling Carol that she had this information would be a mistake. Carol spoke again.

"The boat to which you are referring was inherited by me. You are welcome to stay on any of the other Carlson family boats though. All watercrafts that were specifically in his name went to me."

Lina knew full well that when Bill had said that in his will, he meant the Jet Ski that he had purchased for Carol as a wedding gift and maybe the small fishing boat he just purchased, but not that boat. She continued to hold in her rage, although she could feel the intense heat of anger and frustration begin to burn her skin. The Carlson family watercrafts consisted of a pontoon and the old boat that Aunt Isobel's third husband, Winston, had custom designed for the family years ago. Neither of those boats provided shelter of any kind, and Carol knew this, as she smiled kindly towards Lina and the kids.

"Come on kids. Carol doesn't want us here."

"Now, I didn't say zat! Zee children are welcome to stay here with me," she said with an evil smile as the alcohol made her accent more audible.

Lina grabbed each of the twins by their hands, as she contained her tears, and led them back to the car. She had driven three hours with them to escape the chaos, only to find that the puppet master of her despair had beaten her to the destination and had male company. If it had been possible for Lina's head to spin as smoke billowed from her ears, it would have happened at this moment as the two fingers of the snap met in the middle, almost making the noise, but not yet completing it. There was still a shred of sanity left in Lina, but that shred was getting smaller.

She said nothing to them as she buckled them in and drove down to the state park, where she silently sat in the parking lot, trying not to fly into a rage. She had to remain calm for her children. The twins seemed to sense this and remained silent as well. *What am I going to do?* she thought. *It's Labor day weekend. No hotel or rental cabins will be available*. She didn't want to ask the Glickman's, although she knew they would be welcoming to them. She pulled herself together and found Kirk's number on her phone. She knew he was even further north, in Traverse City at his in-laws, but needed to hear confirmation that what Carol was saying was true. Was she, in fact, the rightful owner of that boat? She heard the ringing tone.

"This is Kirk!"

Lina desperately blurted out to Kirk everything that had just occurred at the cottage. He confirmed that what Carol said about that particular boat was true.

"Look, you can stay at my place. It's on the opposite side of the lake. Let me give you the address."

"You have a cottage at Crystalline Lake?" asked Lina in surprise. Kirk's had been one of the few families growing up that didn't own a cottage.

"Yes. And I would give anything to be there enjoying myself than here with my wife and in-laws," said Kirk, obviously irritated.

"Are you sure? I mean, it won't be too weird? Would your wife be upset?"

Lina hated having to accept Kirk's kindness, but she had no choice. It was either that or drive her highly disappointed twins all the way back home.

"She won't know. I'll send the cleaning service over after you leave, and I'll just tell her I rented it out to a client for the weekend," he assured her.

Lina took down the address, and she and the kids were at Kirk's modest cottage on the opposite side of the lake within minutes. She found the spare key, where Kirk had advised her it would be, and entered the house.

The kids each claimed a bedroom as Lina slowly scoped out the second home of her lifelong crush. There were several framed family pictures, including one of Kirk and Kitty, standing together. It appeared to be an older photo. The two looked very happy, wearing formal clothes and smiling. His fingers were wrapped securely around her arm. More pictures showed their two children from the time they were babies until now, as teenagers. There weren't any recent pictures of Kirk and his wife, but there was one of his parents and brother. Lina couldn't believe how much older they looked.

Feeling slightly uncomfortable, she made her way to the master bedroom. She looked at the queen-sized bed and thought about Kirk having sex with Kitty there. How he had probably moaned with pleasure while thrusting himself inside of her. The same way he had done to Lina in her youth. *I had him before you*, she thought to herself as she flipped down his wife's picture that was sitting on the dresser.

It was getting late, and the sound of fireworks and laughter were easily heard inside the cottage. Even that far away from the state park, the ambiance and amusement of the northern air could be felt. Everyone was there to have a good time, no matter what their financial situation. Campers in tents and millionaires in mansions all shared their love of the lake.

After watching all the colorful bombs bursting in the summer air, Lina put the exhausted twins to bed. There was just something about the clean oxygen up north that had always had that effect on her as well. Also exhausted from emotion, Lina placed her head upon Kirk's pillow and quickly fell asleep.

At one thirty in the morning, Kirk's car pulled into his driveway at Crystalline Lake. He had had enough of his wife and her family and decided to make the one hour drive south from Traverse City. He felt like he just couldn't fake it with his wife anymore, and his in-laws just added to the tension. He figured an hour alone on the highway with some good music might save his sanity, and he just couldn't rest knowing the woman he actually loved was sleeping in his bed. He had told his wife he needed to help a client who had just been arrested for a DUI down in Crystalline Lake. This excuse was reasonable, as it was a holiday weekend, which enabled Kirk to leave the house easily and without incident.

The stereo in his black Land Rover was playing the song "Detroit Rock City" by Kiss as he rolled up. He noticed Lina's car and sat silently. He decided he hadn't thought this through before heading down, and he was beginning to question if he was being creepy. He didn't want to knock on the door and frighten her seven-year-old kids. After giving it some thought, he decided the best way to make contact with Lina was the old way. He exited the vehicle, being careful to shut his car door as quietly as possible. With no streetlights, he stumbled in the dark to find his bedroom window.

Lina was sound asleep when a tapping noise interrupted her dream. She opened her eyes, confused by her surroundings at first. Then she remembered that she was safe in Kirk's bed and closed her eyes. The tapping noise returned, and it was clear now that it wasn't just a tree branch in the wind. Someone was knocking. She froze in fear for a moment before hearing the faint sound of Kirk's voice through the closed window.

"Lina!"

Lina crawled out of bed as butterflies swirled within her upper stomach. Suspenseful adrenaline made her hands shake ever so slightly as she opened the bedroom window.

"What are you doing!?" she giggled.

"I had a client get arrested down here for a DUI," said Kirk

"You did?"

"No, but that's what I told Kitty," admitted Kirk with a smile.

Hearing Kirk say his wife's name made her stomach feel sick. Even the family pictures throughout the cottage didn't make Kitty as real as when he said her name. She managed a polite laugh. She was still elated that he was there. She looked into his brown eyes.

"I wanted to see you," admitted Kirk. "If you pull the screen at the top from the inside…"

"No! Are you kidding me?" she said, laughing again, "My kids are here! You cannot come in. Even if it is your house."

"Remember that last night? Right before I left for school?"

"Of course," she whispered, her voice catching slightly.

That night was something Lina had thought of, and held on to, her entire life. She would wake from dreams of that last night many times while living in San Diego. She remembered the way the cool June evening had felt, and how Kirk had kept her warm with his body on top of hers as they made love under the stars. The romance of the moment was overwhelming, and she wanted nothing more than to run outside, kiss him, and allow him to have his way with her. But those pesky Catholic morals kicked in, and she knew she just couldn't be the cause of someone's broken family. Lina was many things, but a homewrecker she was not.

She knew what it was like to be on the other end of that, and wanted no part of it, even if it meant she could never be with Kirk.

"Kirk, I want nothing more than to run into your arms. Kiss you. I want to feel you inside me so badly…"

"I know, so open the screen. Come on!" he said, giggling.

He was serious but thought the laughter might ease her worries and convince the girl to go all the way. He was still just a teen boy at heart. Especially when it came to Lina.

"Kirk, as romantic as this is, there are pictures of your wife all over this house. You said her name tonight. She is a real person, and I can't make love to you on her bed, or even in her yard. You can come in and sleep on your couch if you'd like, though. This *is* your cottage."

"No, you're right," he whispered sadly. "I'm glad you're okay, and I'm sorry about what happened with Carol. I'll call you when we return from Traverse City."

"Kirk, thank you. I don't know what I would have done."

"I'm just glad I could help. Now go get some sleep," said Kirk as he flashed an enamored smile in her direction and paused before walking off into the night.

The next morning, Lina awoke to the daylight kissing her face through Kirk's bedroom window. She sat up in bed, dreamily thinking about how Kirk sleeps in that bed, and how he had done the most romantic thing in the wee hours. She smiled, knowing it wasn't just a dream, and that Kirk must feel the same way for her as she did him, or he wouldn't have made that long trip in the night.

She was suddenly overwhelmed with endorphins as she recalled Kirk's kind gesture. She closed her eyes and dreamily pretended that her hands were his, as she thought about what *could* have happened, had she opened the screen. She heard the kids making commotion and was rudely brought back to reality. Lina forced herself up and called out to the kids.

"Brush your teeth and put on a swimsuit! You can put shorts and a shirt over top!" she called as she followed her own directions and put her hair in a ponytail. She applied some light make-up over her tan, and the three were off to find breakfast.

After leaving the small "mom and pop" restaurant in nearby Roscommon, Lina decided to swing by her family cottage. She had been thinking about the Carol situation all through breakfast, and while the coffee had helped, she was still fuming mad. *How dare that bitch show up at my family cottage after she is already living in my mother's house. What the fuck? Who does that? Is this seriously my life? And that bitch was going to sue for grandparents' rights after she gives away all of their toys, and people thank her for them on Facebook? Anything to make herself look good. I bet she can't even drive a boat,* she thought as she pulled into a secluded parking spot behind the trees and along the dirt road, behind the Carlson property.

"What are we doing, Mommy?" asked Marty.

"Oh, we're just paying a visit to Carol while we're in the neighborhood."

"But I thought you hated her guts," said Frankie.

"What? No! I don't hate anybody. Hate is a very strong word," she recited, just as Denise had when Lina was a child. "We don't say we hate people. That comes off as classless," she pulled from the Aunt Isobel lesson book. "And we always keep our opinions about people to ourselves because loose lips mean butchered finger tips." This final adage was added from the Grandpa Mancini playbook. She smiled, thinking about what a good parent she was, when she spotted Carol on a beach lounger with a book. "Kids, why don't you go say hello to Carol while I run inside and grab us some bottled water from the cottage? I forgot to bring ours, and I know Carol won't mind."

“But we have water already, Mama," said Marty, holding up his full water bottle.

“Well, this is special *boating* water that we keep in the cottage. For boating," informed Lina as the three unloaded from the car and began to walk toward the cottage and beach that was further down.

“Oh...and be sure to run around Grandma Carol in circles. She misses you guys and would really love to see your joy at the beach. Make sure to really kick up the sand with your toes when you run around her too. Okay? That makes it more fun.”

Lina quickly made her way into the unlocked cottage. She knew she had to act quickly before Carol suspected anything. The twins would only keep her distracted for a minute or two. At least by sending them down to annoy her, it would look less suspicious than if she were caught sneaking in. She ran into the storage room where bottled water was kept, knowing that this was also where the boat keys were. She did a quick survey of the room and spotted the keys hanging where they always had, each with the key to their hoist attached on the same ring for convenience. She grabbed a bottle of water and quickly flipped the desired keys off the wall and into her hand before concealing them with her beach towel. She noticed some snacks and decided to grab a bag of chips and some peanuts for good measure.

When she emerged from the cottage, she saw in the distance that Carol had lit a cigarette and was instructing the kids to stop running. The twins spotted their mother and quickly hurried to her as she continued towards Carol.

“Mom! Carol didn’t like the sand. She said a swear word about it," informed Frankie.

Lina said nothing as she took Frankie’s hand and gave the snacks to Marty to hold. She walked down to where Carol was sitting on her beach lounger.

"Hello, Carol. We were in the area and decided to grab some snacks from the house before we get set up on the beach."

"How kind of you to just help yourself. I will add that to your bill," spat Carol as she took a drag from her smoke - something that was strictly prohibited on the beach.

"Actually, I don't owe you anything. My Aunt Isobel's assistant, Olga, stocked the cottage the last time they visited, and she doesn't care if I eat the food. In fact, it is *expected.* Just as it was *expected* for me and the kids to be here. The person who *wasn't* expected is you," said Lina with a firm, cold stare.

"Well, I have had enough sun and surprises for today," said Carol, putting her cigarette out in the sand and standing. "I am going inside and *locking* the door. I need a bath after being kicked with sand."

"Have a nice day! Oh, and you *do* realize I have a key to *my* cottage, correct? Anyway…" Lina gathered the kids and headed back to the car.

As they left the Carlson property, Lina saw that Carol was brushing the sand off her capris and gathering her beach items. She also noticed that Carol hadn't bothered to remove her extinguished cigarettes from the sand that she had smoked earlier. As she walked closer to her vehicle, she saw a pair of police officers standing near.

"Excuse me, officers. How are you today?"

The officers both nodded.

"Hello, ma'am," said one.

"I hate to bother you guys, but there is a woman whom I've never seen before smoking cigarettes on the beach. And if that isn't awful enough, she is putting them out in the sand and just leaving them there! I said something to her, and she was very rude. Sounds foreign, too. Anyway, I normally would just mind my own business, but my children almost stepped on her burning cigarettes!"

"Don't worry, ma'am, we will handle this," said one of the officers with confidence as his eyes wandered up and down Lina's figure.

"Thank you so much. It's nice to know there are two *strong* men here to protect us. We are so grateful."

The police officers made their way down the beach to Carol, and Lina grabbed the children's hands and guided them to quickly walk out of view. She stood behind some trees and waited for Carol to go inside.

"What are we doing?" asked Marty, annoyed. He was anxious to get to this fun he had heard about.

"Nothing, come on. I have a surprise!" she said, thrilled that her little plan had worked.

She didn't know if Carol had been given a ticket, but at least she had been harassed. Lina led the twins to their private family dock where she and her father's favorite boat sat high up out of the water, on a hoist. Lina expertly unlocked the hoist and began to crank the boat down into the water. It was then that she realized that she hadn't thought this through. Getting the boat off and on the hoist had always been difficult, even when she was in the habit of doing it regularly. It had been over twenty years since she had last done this. She was now remembering that even just to bring the boat down, it took two people. Her father could have handled it alone and always did, but Lina was much tinier and less experienced. To her relief, she saw that Mr. Glickman and Seth were wading through the water towards her. Seth was dragging a six pack through the water, and each had a towel wrapped around their shoulders, heading out to their boat hoist.

"Hey, Lina!" called Seth from the water as the pair came closer.

"Well, look at these two handsome gentlemen! Hello there! Hi, Mr. Glickman! How are you?"

"Nicolina, you are looking most lovely, my dear. I'm okay, but Belmont and I sure are missing your dad this summer. We toasted him last night by the firepit."

Lina gave a polite nod and quickly changed the subject. "Do you think you two strapping young men could help a lady and her kids get their boat down?"

"But of course, madam!" said Mr. Glickman.

It was very clear that father and son had been drinking all day, which was usual for holidays up north. Mr. Glickman had been divorced a second time and was flirtier than ever. He had always been an extremely charming and witty man. Lina always thought it was so cool how Seth's dad would dance to the music downtown, just like she and Ricky always had. She often chuckled at the memory of him entertaining ladies with her dad that night during her senior year. She had begun to see that night differently, as she was now forty herself. He had always been a fun 'up north' neighbor, and he was just as attractive as ever with his tan skin and tall, lanky figure.

Lina continued to crank the hoist down before slightly stepping sideways on her two-inch-heeled sandal and stumbling. Mr. Glickman reached up from the water and grabbed her ankle for support, even though that action would not have saved her in any way.

"Whoa, I got you," he said. "Seth! Grab the boat when it comes off!"

Mr. Glickman was still holding her ankle as the boat came off and nearly ran over Seth in the process. He didn't seem to notice his son struggling, as he was still gripping and admiring her ankle and calf. He then noticed what he was doing and gave a small pat to the back of her calf and released her.

"Got it, son?" called Mr. Glickman, still smiling up at Lina.

Seth was trying to recover from being 'thrown under the boat' by his dad. He stood in the water, completely soaked and annoyed that his dad was cock-blocking him.

"I can't thank you gentlemen enough! I can take it from here," she said, jumping in to join Seth in the lake.

"Hey," Seth said quietly to Lina. "Let me know when you're free to hang out back home. I'll be here until tomorrow too, if you want to get together and party tonight." He spoke like a true childless man.

"Well, I have the kids, so…sometime when we're home."

Mr. Glickman was lifting both kids into the boat, and he helped Lina climb up the boat ladder and in. She put the key in the ignition and started it up.

"Thanks again! I can't thank you enough!" she said, idling towards the deeper water.

To her relief, boating was like riding a bike. She remembered to leave the stern up while in the shallow, brown waters. As she saw the lake color turn to a beautiful, clear sea-green, she knew the water was deep enough to lower the propeller. She moved the gas pedal with her arm and sped up. The twins cheered with joy! They were so excited just to be wearing orange life preservers, and now the suspense and mystery had become a reality. They were having the time of their lives. They couldn't believe their mom had such talents. They giggled with glee as they watched the water pass along the side of the boat.

"Marty!" called Frankie. "Look at the water from behind!"

The twins delighted in the sight of the water passing behind them as their souls seemed to soar through the air in weightless, windy wonder. The twenty-two-foot speedboat felt like nothing they had ever experienced. Lina would repeatedly turn the boat and do donuts over their own waves as the children playfully screamed. Marty watched his mom driving the boat, throwing her head back and laughing. *She looks different. She looks pretty and happy*, he thought.

Lina felt alive and was ecstatic to see that the twins were responding to the boat the same way she always had. She was thrilled to share with them something that had been a normal part of her own childhood. Something Lina had always taken for granted, until now. Boating had always had the ability to send her into a dream-like state. There was something about lake air and speed that seemed to deliver her to a place of zen, which always seemed unreal, but fantastic. Luke had never been interested in boating, but this day proved to Lina that it was truly part of who she was. She wanted to spend more time up north. The only problem was Carol, as usual. Carol was always holding her back, and she barely even knew the woman.

The mother and children anchored the boat near a sandbar where the old, sunken island was. She had been fascinated by stories of the former island in childhood, and the twins found this information just as intriguing as she always had. They snacked and listened to music on the boat stereo before jumping in with their life preservers on. This was the closest to paradise the twins had ever experienced in their short lives, and it was a memory they would each hold dear. Frankie decided that the mermaids definitely lived in the green water because that was the most beautiful color of the lake - just as young Lina had decided was the case many years before.

It was time to head in, and the twins protested. Lina reminded them that all good things must come to an end and pulled up the anchor. She continued the joyride through the deep, dark-blue waters and wondered if Carol had noticed that they took the boat. She hoped that the police wouldn't be waiting for them on shore. After not being able to locate the Glickman's grand stairway from the boat, she began to feel panicked. But that was quickly resolved as she finally spotted their glory in the distance. She pulled closer to land until she spotted Carol standing on the beach, using her hand as a visor. *Shit*, she thought.

When they reached three-feet-deep water, Lina threw in the anchor and jumped out of the boat. She lowered each child into the water with her before climbing back on to grab all their belongings and jumping back out. She instructed the kids to hold their towels on top of their heads as they walked into shore, just as she had been taught. The kids complained about the cold water, and she advised them that they would live. Lina giggled to herself thinking about how Denise and Greta probably wouldn't like it that she had them in the cold water either. They could be so overprotective.

As they came closer to where Carol was impatiently waiting, Lina was feeling bolder than ever. She was angry, plumb out of shits to give, and the current placement of the fingers in the snap were making her ruthless. Lina felt the earth below turn from slightly rocky to smooth sand as she came closer to shore. She glanced up at the Carlson cottage and saw a man's figure quickly disappear in the window.

"You want to tell me what za fuck you are doing!?" called Carol to Lina.

"Oh, Carol! I thought that was you! Thanks for lending us my boat! Here are the keys!" called Lina as she purposely tossed them deep into the sand. "I anchored it." She pointed to the boat in the distance. "You might want to get help putting it back on the hoist. It can be a real *bitch*!"

With that, she turned, grabbed her children's hands, and headed to the car.

CHAPTER FIFTEEN

2016-Luke
"Sail On"
by The Commodores

The new school year was back in full swing, and Lina had just seen the twins off at the bus stop. She was cleaning up the kitchen from breakfast and putting dirty dishes in the dishwasher. The whole Carol ordeal had been put on the backburner so Lina could focus on the new teachers, new routines, and schedules. The first two weeks and last two weeks of school were always the most hectic. She had to put Carol out of her mind so she wouldn't *lose* her mind.

Lina had known Kirk was going away for vacation with his wife over Labor Day weekend and into the following week. She hadn't even had a chance yet to tell him the information that Chip had produced for her. She began to think about Kirk as she washed a glass, wondering if she should call him or if he was planning to call her. *He must be back by now*, she thought.

Lina heard the garage door go up, then footsteps, and then the familiar thump of luggage hitting the floor. Her stomach turned. At this point, Lina wished he would just go away permanently. If she could just get her mother's house back and put that whole upsetting matter behind her, she might be able to gain the strength she needed to face a divorce with Luke.

"Hi," said Luke as he hurriedly approached Lina to give her an awkward kiss on the cheek and a loose hug.

“Hi," said Lina, feeling sickened by his touch and mildly guilty about her shenanigans in his absence. She dried her hands. “What would you like for dinner tonight?"

“Oh, um, didn’t I tell you? I have to leave for Memphis tonight," admitted Luke nervously while grabbing a cookie and taking a bite. Lina knew there would be no reason for his company to send him to Memphis. She *did* know that the co-worker she suspected him of sleeping with was originally from there though.

“What about the Art and Apples Festival?" asked Lina, annoyed. “You told the kids we would take them together. They have been talking about it!”

Both Lina and Luke were silent. Then Lina decided she wouldn’t hold back anymore. She *couldn’t* hold back anymore. Whether her life was already in ruins or not, she had no choice but to face her failing marriage head on.

“What are we doing here, Luke? I mean, what the fuck is this? Is this a marriage? I don’t know anymore.”

Lina waited for a response that never came, so she spoke again.

“I’ve suspected that you’ve been having affairs for years. Not necessarily with just one woman. I think there have been multiple," stated Lina.

Luke said nothing and looked to the ground.

After what seemed like an eternity of silence, Lina spoke again. “Okay, so I guess I have my answer.”

“Why would you pick a time like this to have this conversation, Lina? I just said I had to go.”

“Yes. You have to go," confirmed Lina as Luke went to the bedroom to drop off dirty clothes and pack fresh ones. She barely had time to think before her phone rang. It was a local number, so she answered, trying to sound like everything was normal. “Hello, this is Lina."

"FUCK OFF, BITCH!" said an unfamiliar, foreign accent through the phone.

"Um, excuse me?"

"YOU HAD YOUR FUCKING LAWYER EVICT ME? WHERE THE FUCK ARE ME AND MY FAMILY SUPPOSE TO GO?"

"You and your family!?" asked Lina, realizing it was her tenant. Excuse me, but you are the only one on the lease agreement! Not your twenty other family members from Iran! AND you haven't paid your rent!" There was silence on the phone, and she realized the disgruntled, soon to be ex-tenant had ended the call.

Lina put her phone down and crouched in the corner of her beautiful kitchen. The kitchen that she knew she may lose if she got divorced. She continued to squat below the counter, frozen, as she listened to the sound of her husband packing in the bedroom. She looked at the microwave clock. It was eight-thirty. She needed to get dressed and ready to visit Aunt Isobel before she and her driver, Fred, left for the airport at eleven.

Luke went into the kitchen to fix himself a sandwich as Lina went into the bedroom to shower and get ready. She pulled out a new dress she had just purchased online with the inheritance funds she received. It was a short, red, form-fitting dress she had found on sale.

Lina put the Moroccan oil in her hair and blew it out straight. She applied all the facial lotions and prepared her makeup table while she let her skin fully drink in the moisture. She had decided that today might also be the day she should visit Matt Munson at the bank. It was a task she wasn't looking forward to, but she really needed to get that account number. Lina could not properly manage a house that she owned without making sure payments and taxes were being made. Anger began to sweep over her again as she thought about how ridiculous it was that the bank wouldn't just tell her the mortgage account number, or at least mail the number to *her* primary address. They would only send it to the address of the mortgaged home, which Lina had no access to.

She finished applying her make-up and carefully pulled on her new dress, so she wouldn't accidentally get make-up or deodorant on it. She slipped her feet into her high heels and looked in the full-length mirror. Luke walked in to pack his toiletries and paused to admire her.

"Wow! You look *delicious*," said Luke as he came for her, trying to wrap his arms around her waist and seeming to forget the whole confrontation that had just occurred.

"I'm on my way to see Aunt Isobel off to England for the winter. She'll be staying with the cousins until spring," Lina informed, gently stepping away from his arms and grabbing an earring. "You know I like to look my best for Aunt Isobel. The last thing I need is criticism from her."

"Lina, you look great. You're so beautiful," he said with a tear beginning to form in one eye. "I…when I get back…can we ta-"

"I have to go," said Lina as she grabbed her new Dolce and Gabbana bag and headed out of the bedroom to the garage and into her car. She checked her phone. There was a text from Chip.

"I just woke up dreaming about you, baby. Please marry me. I love you."

Lina smiled as the warm fuzziness of Chip's text began to dissolve the awful morning she had been having. Although she was still legally taken and would never trust Chip enough to marry him, she loved that he wanted to. The fourteen-year-old girl in her was beyond elated that Chip LaBeau had said he loved her and wanted to be her husband. Since Chip had proposed, she had daydreamed about actually accepting and becoming his wife. The problem was that Lina just wasn't naïve enough at this point in her life to think that Chip would be a good husband or stepfather. *Reality can be so annoying*, she thought.

Lina started the car and headed to Fairview. She drove through town, then onto a small side road which led to her family's private driveway. As her car followed the long, secluded path to the house, she began to take inventory in her mind of all the important things she needed to ask Aunt Isobel before she left. Her elderly aunt didn't text to begin with and certainly wasn't going to use Facebook messenger to chat from England. Lina knew communication with Aunt Isobel would be difficult and sparse until next spring when Isobel would return. This was the very first time that Lina would be left with the full responsibility of Fairview's welfare. Her father, Bill, had handled everything since the passing of her grandfather, and now this was one more major thing that Lina had to manage.

Lina parked and knocked on the double front doors of Fairview. Olga, Isobel's housekeeper and caregiver, answered the door. She barely greeted Lina as she ran into the other room, frantically packing the last of their luggage and trying to remember if they were forgetting anything. Aunt Isobel emerged, holding her Louis Vuitton toiletry bag, and greeted Lina with a light air kiss.

"Where am I putting this?" called Aunt Isobel, looking around for Olga, who then came running down the stairs with another bag of her own.

"Mrs. Branigan! You can only have one carry on! You'll need to put that bag inside another!" said Olga, looking sweaty and exhausted in her casual travel clothes. Branigan had been the name of Isobel's fifth husband who had passed away some ten years before.

"Do you need some help?" asked Lina, wishing she wasn't there.

"We are all set," said Fred, Isobel's driver, as he entered the room with two heavy bags in each hand. He was trying to remain calm in all the chaos of two women preparing to leave the country for six months.

"Are you going with them, too?" Lina asked Fred.

"No, Fred is staying here at Fairview for the winter. He will run the water and make sure everything is shoveled and secure," said Aunt Isobel as she sat to dig for something in her handbag. "Thank heavens, because otherwise, we'd have to winterize the whole house! Lucky for us, Fred has nowhere to go."

Fred made a face indicating that he didn't share Isobel's enthusiasm at having nowhere to go.

Olga and Aunt Isobel were putting on their coats, as Fred was carrying out their baggage and wondering how he would fit it all in the vehicle. He put the larger ones in the trunk, then cursed under his breath as he tried to cram one in the passenger side. Once he was finished loading them up, his mood instantly softened. Fred was going to have a six-month break, and he couldn't wait.

Lina shut the rear door of the vehicle after saying her goodbyes to Aunt Isobel and Olga. Fred walked up with his coffee, beaming.

"Miss Carlson, if you need anything, please don't hesitate to call. Anything I can do to help, *really*. Just call. And by the way, you look lovely today," said Fred.

He gave her a jolly wink and smile before heading to the car to drive the women to the Detroit Metro airport.

Lina climbed into her red Escalade and took a puff from her vape pen. She flipped the mirror down to see how her cosmetics were holding up. She had received what seemed to be two very sincere compliments already, and she decided it was time to do it. She needed to stop putting it off and go see Matt Munson about the mortgage account number.

Lina's biggest worry about going to see Matt Munson was that he wouldn't remember her. It had been several years, and he had been three years ahead of her in school. She had only really known him from the Rochester Public Library, not to mention that she had been gone in California for twenty-two years.

Lina started her car and headed down to Main Street, where the local branch of her father's mortgager was located. She parked her car in the bank lot, then tried to adjust her clothing in advance, from her seated position, as best she could. She hated exiting her car and having to adjust her outfit in front of everyone. She sat and rehearsed what she might say to Matt, then took a nervous breath and got out of her car.

Matt Munson sat in his office at the bank, which had glass windows that overlooked the beautiful lobby of the old, historical building. He was working really hard at appearing to be busy, as he searched Match.com.

What Lina didn't know was that Matt Munson had been stalking her public Facebook page for the last six years after finding it. He never sent her a friend request, but he had saved all ten of the photos that she had set to public and often used them to pleasure himself.

Lina opened the heavy glass door to the bank. "Two Lovers" by Mary Wells was playing. A young employee was taking down the last of the bank's domino display in preparation to decorate for the Art and Apples Festival that coming weekend.

Matt saw the main door open from above. He saw a beautiful woman in a low-cut, red dress enter the lobby. He sucked in his breath. *Could that be*? he thought. He cleaned off his glasses and made another attempt at a positive identification. *That's her*! he thought as he suddenly became sick to his stomach with nervous excitement.

Lina looked around in awe at how wonderfully the building had been restored. She hadn't been inside that building in years, and just stepping inside began to bring back fond memories for her. She suddenly remembered going into that bank with her mother as a small child. The woman behind the counter had given little Lina a sucker, while her mother had chatted with other patrons and employees. Although she was very nervous, the memory put her somewhat at ease.

As she began to approach the teller, she decided she had better use the lobby bathroom first to collect herself. So she veered to the right and into the ladies' room.

After washing her hands, she used the bank's complimentary mouthwash before stopping to examine herself in the full-length mirror. She adjusted her dress and applied lipstick. She was beginning to chicken out.

Lina had thought long and hard about Matt Munson in preparation for this day. The few things she could remember about him was that he had worked at the library, had been a hall monitor, and had written and directed a school play that Ricky had acted in freshman year. It hadn't been *the* school play, but a play that the school had allowed him to put on in a classroom during school hours. He had been a senior, and all of his actors had been freshman, since nobody his own age had been interested. She remembered sitting in the back row after school, when Ricky was rehearsing with Matt, and giggling about how serious and Shakespearian Matt had been about everything. Besides that, she thought he used to play Dungeons and Dragons. Little did Lina know, he still did on Saturday nights with his friends.

As she continued to study herself in the mirror, she decided she had better add extra insurance, in case he was still the stickler for rules that she remembered him to be. She pulled a one-hundred-dollar bill from her small handbag and began to practice how she could have it in the palm of her hand as she shook his. Then she stopped and gave her reflection a devilish smile, as she took the money and stuffed it into her cleavage instead. She briefly practiced leaning over to reveal the bill, and the seductive way in which she would pull it from her breasts and hand it to him, if needed. *God helps those who help themselves. I have to use the gifts I was given,* she thought as she took a deep breath and pushed open the bathroom door. She headed directly to the bank counter where the two young, female employees were having a personal conversation. One of the girls glanced in Lina's direction as she reached the counter but quickly turned back to her discussion.

"She's an idiot if she takes him back," said teller 1.

"Amen, girl! Once a cheater, always a cheater," said teller 2.

"But didn't he cheat with you before too?" asked teller 1, suddenly accusatory.

"Hey, now! That ain't even part of this. That was two years ago," confessed teller 2, laughing.

Lina cleared her throat for attention, barely masking her annoyance. *A little less talky and a little more workie*, she thought with an eye roll and a loud sigh.

"Oh. How may I assist you?" asked teller 2, still laughing, without apology.

"Yes," said Lina, smiling through gritted teeth. "I was hoping to speak with your branch manager about an issue I'm having with a mortgage loan." *I hope Matt is working today*, she thought.

Matt was watching Lina's interaction with the teller closely when his office phone rang, causing him to jerk in his seat.

"Um, ah, yes. I'll be right down, Rebecca," said Matt as he felt the sudden urge to visit the bathroom. He composed himself and headed down to the lobby. *I wonder why she wants to see me?* he thought. *Perhaps her husband is dying, and she needs to remortgage her home*. Matt fantasized as he descended the stairs and met eyes with Nicolina for the first time in over twenty years.

"How are you, Matt?" asked Lina as she turned to meet his gaze. "Do you remember me?" She offered a small but sincere smile.

Matt was intensely aroused as he sat opposite Lina in his office. He was barely listening to the reason why she needed him to give her the account number. He was just daydreaming about kissing her moving lips and running his hands through her hair as he did it.

Matt quickly wrote the account number down on a sticky note for Lina and handed it to her like it was nothing. He figured if they got all the business out of the way, they could have a more personal conversation. Lina was mid-sentence as he handed her the note. *Wow, that was easy*, she thought.

She inconspicuously removed the money from her cleavage and placed it in her bag as Matt turned to look back at his computer screen. To his horror, Lina's inherited home, where her stepmother was residing, was in foreclosure. Matt froze. This was not the news that was going to make Nicolina fall in love with him. He silently cursed his luck, then interrupted Lina as she began to thank him. Lina could sense something was wrong as Matt's whole demeanor changed as he stared at his computer screen.

"Um. Ah, did you know the house was in foreclosure?" asked Matt, slowly, fearing that his long-lost love would shoot the proverbial messenger.

Lina felt her heart drop into her stomach. *This has to be a mistake. He's looking at the wrong account,* she thought.

"What? What do you mean it's in *foreclosure*?"

Matt continued to type on his PC before finally stopping to share further information.

"It looks like your stepmother hasn't paid the mortgage at all since your father's death. The last payment was back on June first," he said, reading from his screen.

Her gut did a somersault. She wasn't sure if she was about to lose her mother's house for good, or if this meant she could have her house back, since Carol obviously hadn't met the requirements for staying. Was it too late?

"Oh my God! Well, what do I do!?"

"So, it looks like you have until Tuesday to make the last three mortgage payments plus late fees. Otherwise, the bank owns the house," advised Matt, regretfully.

"Well, should I pay it all now?" asked Lina, frantically.

She had placed her newly-acquired inheritance money into an investment account and wasn't sure how quickly she would have access to the funds. Lina knew if she didn't put the money somewhere that was difficult to access, that Luke might spend it all or gamble it away. It was safely invested in her name only. She sat in disbelief, thinking she would need those funds immediately to save her mother's house. Then Lina quickly remembered Kirk telling her not to do *anything* without talking to him first.

"Could you send all the foreclosure and payment records to my lawyer? I'm working with Kirk Kavanaugh at Nelson Law."

"Of course, I can. I would be more than happy to. And yes, I would recommend speaking with your attorney before just paying it. You have four days to pay, and you will want the records that are sent to Kirk to reflect the current status," assured Matt with lust in his eyes. He suddenly reached for Lina's hand. "I would do *anything* for you. I mean, anything for *any* of my customers." He corrected himself as he blushed.

"I can't thank you enough," said Lina as she gave his hand a soft squeeze back before standing abruptly to leave. She grabbed her purse and headed to the door before turning to remind Matt to send the information to Kirk right away.

As Lina walked back to her car, her initial anger at Carol began to turn to hopefulness. *She didn't fulfill the requirements, as stated in the pre-nup. Does this mean I can toss her out?*

She tried to walk as quickly and elegantly as possible in her high heels before reaching her vehicle and jumping in. She immediately called Kirk on his cell phone.

"This is Kirk!"

Lina could hear in his voice that he was busy and probably stressed out. He sounded to be somewhere public by the background noise too.

"Hey, it's Lina. Are you back from Traverse City yet? I haven't heard from you."

"Yeah, just got in late the other night. Sorry, I'm completely swamped from being on my miserable fucking vacation with my wife."

"That good, eh?" asked Lina, secretly pleased he had an awful time with his wife.

"Yeah, so can I call you when I'm done with court tonight? I'm so backlogged. I'll be in court all day today and tomorrow," said Kirk, who was clearly distracted and slightly out of breath from walking.

"Kirk, hang on! I have info I need to give you really quick. It's important, just really quick," pleaded Lina.

"Okay, shoot!" said Kirk, giving Lina the green light to spit it out.

"Nutshell version. I got the mortgage account number."

"What!? That's grea-"

"The house is in foreclosure, Kirk! She hasn't made a mortgage payment since my dad passed!" exclaimed Lina.

"Okay. Can you have the evidence of this faxed or emailed to me right away?" asked Kirk, whose distraction had turned to full focus.

"It's already on its way! Bank is sending it to your office directly. Oh, and my Iranian tenants called me and told me to fuck off today, too," said Lina, remembering the unpleasant morning she had experienced.

"If they contact you again, you tell them to call me! Tell them any and all correspondence will be through me *only*," advised Kirk, firmly. "And do *not* say a word about any of this mortgage stuff to *anyone*! Lina, just keep quiet and calm until I can meet with you on Monday. I gotta go. I'll text you with a time for Monday. I will handle it!"

Lina's hands were still slightly trembling with adrenaline from the news as she began to drive home. *Kirk will "handle it,"* she thought, smiling. It was comforting to Lina to hear somebody say that to her.

###

Lina was at home now and had changed into her yoga pants and t-shirt, which she referred to as her stay-at-home mom "uniform." The lawn service, which was owned by Lawson Jones, was on location, finishing up. Luke had hired him for both lawn care and winter snow removal when they first moved to Michigan a year ago.

She sat on the couch and grabbed her new book from the public library. It appeared juicy, and she was looking forward to escaping into it a little, before the twins arrived home from school. There was a knock at the door. Lina let out an annoyed sigh, put down her book, and went to the front door.

There stood Lawson Jones at the door, looking more cleaned up than usual and holding a flower.

"Hi, Lina. I just wanted to let you know the crew is finishing up…and I wanted to give you this," said Lawson as he nervously handed her the flower.

"Oh, thanks. What's the occasion?" asked Lina, smiling politely. She really just wanted to get back to her book.

"Lina, I…" started Lawson as he took a breath and ran his fingers through his grey hair. "I find you very attractive. I know we have never been close, but I feel a connection to you. I've known you for so long, I mean."

Lina stared at Lawson with a blank expression. She had been dealing with this type of scenario for years now, and with everything else going on in her life, she wasn't in the mood. Not to mention, there was no way she would ever be interested in Lawson Jones. Even if she was already divorced, she still thought of him as the mean kid from the neighborhood. The attraction Lawson was feeling was definitely one-sided.

"Yes, we have known each other a long time…"

"Lina, I was thinking that maybe we could, yah know…have an affair? I would be completely discreet, I swear! Just a private little secret relationship," said Lawson, relieved to have gotten the words out, and now hoping for consent.

Lina stood in the doorway, looking down at her old classmate standing on the porch.

"You want to have sex with me," she said, letting out an exasperated laugh, "Do you think this is some fresh, new idea that only you have thought of? You really think that nobody else has ever had this cutting-edge idea of having an affair with me? It's insulting that so many of you think I'll do it, too! You all seem to think I'm THAT easy!"

Lawson hadn't been expecting that kind of rejection. His cheeks flushed and his demeanor changed. "Insulting!? I've got news for you, sweetheart. You're NOT all that! There are plenty of women who are hotter, Lina. You're NOT all that."

"I never said I was Lawson. I NEVER said I was!"

"You're the same stuck up little bitch you've always been! You're not friendly...I don't know why...I don't know what it is about you...you're like a pistol. It's shiny, but powerful...and you know approaching it can be dangerous." he softened. "but going to the shooting range is my favorite thing. It's never a bad day out with my pistol." he looked to the ground, feeling sorry for his words. "You've always been so mysterious. You're even pretty when you're mad. You get so riled up...I guess we all just want to shake the mystery box." He looked up to see Lina's reaction.

"I'll see you next week for lawn service," she stated, before shutting the door.

She let out a huge sigh. It actually felt good that she had just told Lawson off. She thought about what Lawson had just said, as she went to the kitchen to pour herself a glass of diet Faygo red pop, her favorite. After she headed back to her book on the couch, there was another knock at the door. She rolled her eyes and set her glass down. *Grand central*, she thought.

Lina opened the door, and this time it was Father Kowalski. Lina was shocked that not only did he know where she lived, but that he was at her house. She did not invite him in.

"Nicolina! Or should I call you Lina?" asked Fr. Kowalski with a big smile.

"Father Kowalski! What a surprise! What can I do for you?" asked Lina, annoyed but trying to stay polite.

"I'm a *deacon*, actually."

"Oh. So, what can I do for you, Father?" asked Lina as she frantically searched her memory banks for what a deacon was. It sounded really high up, like a cardinal or something. Her scattered thoughts were interrupted when he spoke again.

"My dear, you haven't been to church since…well, the last time I saw you there. I'm actually here about a personal matter. I've been having *complicated* thoughts since that day in church...impure thoughts...I was wondering if maybe you wanted to hang out, just the two of us...and pray about that together."

Lina had had enough that day. She couldn't even fake sanity at that point. She just wanted to read her book for a little while before the kids got home. Her facial expression changed from polite to crazy. The men in that city were relentless, and she was too stressed out to deal with it.

"You want to sin with me, Father?" she asked with a hint of laughter building in her voice. Her smile of insanity intensified. "You want to fuck me, Father? Get a little kinky?" She took a deep breath and let out a crazy giggle. "*YOU* and EVERYONE ELSE!" She waved her arm in the air for emphasis. "YOU… and EVERYONE ELSE!!!"

As she whipped the door shut, the deacon tried to get a word in. "I…I'm a deacon. You can call me Tom!"

Lina pressed her back to the closed door and looked up to the heavens. "Seriously!?" she asked the ceiling, before trying to see out the dining room window without being conspicuous.

She watched Father Kowalski reach his car and saw her neighbor, Mrs. Weiss, kneeling on the ground, gardening. The two exchanged a wave. *At least it looks good that a priest is leaving my home*, she thought. *I wonder if all women my age deal with this?* Her eyes then traveled to Mrs. Weiss' tacky, plastic gardening shoes. *Well, maybe not*, she thought.

CHAPTER SIXTEEN

2016-Art and Apples
"Nobody Knows"
by Tony Rich

The next day was the Downtown Rochester Art and Apples Festival. It had been an annual event in the city for over fifty years. Every September, the park was transformed into an outdoor art gallery where local musicians played, children made crafts, and everyone enjoyed apple pie for an entire weekend. This was also an event that had always pulled the middle-aged crowd back home to see friends and enjoy the night life in the city, after the daytime events ended each evening.

Lina brought the kids to the festival that day and delighted in watching them dip their feet into the Paint Creek, which ran through the Rochester Park. They watched the plastic ducks race through the creek for charity, and all the children rooted for theirs to win, the same way that she once had.

The event brought massive amounts of people in from all over Michigan. Shuttle busses from parking lots throughout the city dropped off people from all walks of life, just off Main Street. This always brought packed crowds into Motown Mood Café, which was great for business, but always hectic.

Ricky was working the day shifts for the busy weekend, but was free that night to hang with Lina. Greta had hurt her ankle and had requested the children's company while she sat out the festival and rested with her elevated leg upstairs. It drove her crazy that she had to just sit there while Denise, Ricky, and their other employees were bombarded. They had all decided it would be a good arrangement, as Ricky and Lina could hang out downstairs in the café and socialize with the town, while Greta felt useful tending to the children and giving Lina a break. The twins were to spend the night upstairs at the café, while Ricky and Lina enjoyed some BFF time. This would also allow Ricky to jump in at the café and help out if needed. He didn't mind, and it actually made him feel better, like he wasn't just abandoning ship on his mothers during his day off.

Once the kids were safely settled upstairs, watching Disney's *Frozen* with Greta, the two forty-year-old friends excitedly hurried downstairs and into the café. A few of the daytime musical acts from the park were scheduled to play the café in the evening. This drew in such large crowds, they had to do a headcount of how many were inside at a time, for fear of breaking fire safety codes. Luckily, the Goldmans owned the place and Ricky had reserved a small table for the two to share. Ricky had also been given a marijuana brownie by one of the young café employees, which he and Lina eagerly split, before slipping them into their mouths and taking their seats. Neither of them were big fans of alcohol, but it was a special occasion, and they could both use a drink. Ricky ordered two vodka and cranberries.

The two began to feel the effects as the opening Irish band performed their final number. The first intermission between performers was beginning, and Lina was relaxed and giggling, so Ricky knew it was time to relay the news that had been burdening him all day. He was building up the courage to speak, when Lina asked, "Hey, Ricky, what's a deacon in the Catholic Church?"

They both paused for a beat and looked at each other seriously, before Ricky responded. "Why are you asking a Jew?"

The pair burst out laughing, probably finding this funnier than normal due to the pot edible.

"Yeah, you're right," laughed Lina, barely able to speak.

"Let's ask Google," said Ricky, still chuckling, as he looked it up on his phone. "Hmm, apparently Catholic deacons can get married and everything. They do priest things, but they aren't priests."

"Oh," said Lina, suddenly feeling bad about the altercation with Tom Kowalski at her house. He *had* still propositioned a married woman, but it wasn't *as* bad, she decided in her high haze.

"Why do you ask, anyway? That was so random!"

"No reason," lied Lina, looking away to the side.

Ricky knew he had to bring up Chip now.

"So, how are things going with Chip?" asked Ricky, cautiously.

Lina took a sip of her drink. "*Well*, he says he wants to marry me!" proclaimed Lina as she sat up high, smiling, "I mean, Chip is *so* fine, but I'm just not sure I can see myself marrying him. I mean, I don't think so anyway. Besides, I'm still married."

"Lina… you're *both* still married," said Ricky, letting out a long exhale and taking Lina's hand from across the table. "Remember my ex, Mario, whose salon I hooked you up with? Well, Chip's wife is also his client. Mario was in here today, name dropping, and asking if I knew different clients of his. Anyway, her name came up, and they are definitely still married. Mario made a special house call for her the other day because her leg is broken. They are *very* married." Ricky looked down at the table. It pained him enormously to give Lina this news. She was already suffering enough.

Lina sat with her mouth hanging open in shock. *How could this be? That must be why he has never invited me over to his house,* she thought as her stomach turned.

Ricky sat patiently, allowing Lina to fully digest this scandalous information about herself.

“Wait," said Lina, raising her palm towards Ricky. “You mean to tell me that I have been sleeping with the *current* husband of one of the other moms from cheer and football!?”

Ricky nodded.

“Fuck!" said Lina, low enough that only Ricky could hear her.

“Okay, look. I didn’t want to be a total buzzkill with the news, but obviously I had to tell you. I couldn’t *not*," said Ricky, feeling awful for Lina. Then he quickly tried to change the subject, hoping she was high enough from the edible at this point to redirect her. “When do you meet with Kirk?”

“On Monday," Lina answered, then began to shake her head in disbelief over Chip again as she spoke. “Oh God, Ricky! What the fuck? Why does my life always have to be so fucked-up like this? Why can’t I ever just be like normal people?" she asked as she looked at what appeared to be some normal people, sitting near and sharing a laugh.

More customers were entering as the night grew older, and a long line was now forming at the door. Lina saw many familiar faces and greeted a few acquaintances. She noticed Kermit Karnes enter and sit with his two, much younger, gay friends who seemed to follow him everywhere. The young men couldn’t have been more than twenty-one years old and looked like perfect Abercrombie models. She had noticed previously that they tended to hang on his every word and laugh, as if he were Hugh Heffner and they were his playmates. She cringed when she saw Lawson Jones and Mitch Marquette enter. Mayor Glickman was making his rounds on the opposite side of the room. She figured Fitz wouldn’t be too far behind either.

Mrs. Hamilton, Mitzy’s mother who had been the librarian at the public library, was suddenly standing at their table. Lina was still angry about how Mrs. Hamilton had made Lina jump through hoops and sneak around just to check out a Judy Blume book. Anytime Lina had thought about how Mrs. Hamilton had wrongly imposed her beliefs and banned her from reading a youth section book, she became angry. Even though it had been over two decades, Lina still would complain about it over the years, which had always made Ricky laugh. He thought it was ridiculous that Lina still held a grudge, even though Mrs. Hamilton most likely had no recollection of such events at this point.

"Nicolina! How are you? I'm sorry again about your dad," said Mrs. Hamilton, giving a polite nod to Ricky.

"Yes, it's okay," said Lina, never quite sure what the appropriate response was to apologies about her father's passing. Lina spotted Mitzy already seated with some people across the crowded café.

"Mitzy says you have two children," said Mrs. Hamilton with a big smile. "I'm retired now, but I volunteer for the Rochester Junior Great Books Club held at the library. Are your children as enthusiastic about reading as you were?"

"Yes, they are. They love reading."

"Oh? What types of books do they enjoy?" she asked. "I can assign them to appropriate book groups, based on age and interests."

"They enjoy all kinds of books and have free access to them. I don't believe in censorship *at all*," said Lina, sounding more like a teenager than a forty-year-old, sophisticated woman.

Ricky looked up to the sky and ran his hand down his face until his mouth was covered, holding in his laughter and surprise.

Mrs. Hamilton was slightly taken aback. She smiled politely with confusion, and then excused herself.

"Give my regards to Mitzy!" called Lina, raising her hand to wave in Mitzy's direction as her mother worked her way through to the crowd to join her. Lina was relieved that at least she wouldn't need to go over and chat with Mitzy. The regards sent through Mitzy's mom and wave of acknowledgement would meet all social etiquette requirements, she decided.

The truth was, Marty was having some issues with reading and math, which had been adding to the pile of worry and stress for Lina. Having to wait to see Kirk about the foreclosure on Monday, and the news about Chip, was something even the edible couldn't soothe.

As Ricky chatted with some acquaintances, Lina was left alone with her thoughts. Chip had served as a distraction for Lina all summer, not only from her Carol issues and failing marriage, but she had been able to take out her sexual frustration with Kirk on him too. Keeping a strict schedule of Chip, pool, kids, repeat was how she had been managing to hold on. She had come to depend on Chip's texts throughout each day for little glints of happiness. Glints of feeling wanted, even loved. The realization that her whole relationship with Chip had been a lie, almost felt like a worse betrayal than her husband's philandering.

She had dreamily considered what it would be like to marry Chip. The sex, the eye candy, things to talk about. She always had fun with Chip and did enjoy her high school crush, even though she always knew deep down he was bad news and that she shouldn't trust him. Chip had been a coping method for Lina, and the thought of quitting him was worse than the thought of quitting her vape pen.

As Lina slowly scoped the room, she met eyes with Lawson Jones who was looking at her longingly. He winked, held up his beer as if to say 'cheers,' and then mouthed sorry. She quickly turned her head away to break the connection. She imagined he was probably having some kind of romantic, *they spotted each other from across the room* delusion and didn't care to entertain it. When she turned her head from his direction, she was met with the stare of Deacon Kowalski, from the other side of the room, looking at her apologetically. *Fuck. I didn't even notice him come in*, she thought.

Then the song "Nobody Knows" by Tony Rich began to play on the jukebox, as the bands were still on intermission. The lyrics resonated and began to mildly soothe her, when she saw Maxi and a group of lesbians take a table near the bathrooms. Lina was sure that Maxi was there to monitor her girlfriend, Sheila, while she worked her busy shift that evening. Full of emotions and immersed in her snap, the alcohol she had been sipping had given her liquid courage. She decided it was time to use the restroom and make a quick stop to set Maxi straight. She signaled to Ricky that she was heading to the bathroom, so as not to interrupt his conversation, then walked over to Maxi's group. She rested her elbows on the table and slid in close to Maxi's face.

"Oh, and Maxi. Just so you know…if I *wanted* your girl, I would *have* your girl."

With that, Lina pulled a cherry from Maxi's cocktail and put it in her mouth. She pulled the stem from her lips and chewed on the cherry seductively for a beat before placing the stem on Maxi's napkin. She made quick eye contact with all the ladies at the table, smiled smugly, and walked to the ladies' room.

The lesbian trio stared quietly with gaping mouths before Maxi's blonde friend spoke, "Is she gay? 'cause I get first dibs. You already have a girlfriend."

In the safety of the bathroom stall, Lina pulled her vape pen from her pocket and took a soothing hit. *I have got to quit these damn things*, she thought, angrily. She composed herself, cleaned up, and walked back to her table. As Ricky turned back to sit and face Lina, she glanced to the front of the café, and in walked Chip LaBeau. He spotted Lina and smiled lovingly as he made his way toward them.

"Oh, fuck," said Lina as Ricky turned his head, confused at what had caused the sudden upset.

"Oh, boy," said Ricky as he took a deep breath and released it. It sounded like air leaking from a deflated balloon, which caused his cheeks to ripple in the process. He raised his hand to get the attention of one of the employees and motioned for them to bring another round of drinks.

"Lina," said Chip, smiling at her with romantic eyes of love. "Hey Ricky, what's up? Long time, man." He offered his hand to Ricky for a shake.

"Hi, Chip," Ricky managed as he loosely accepted the handshake.

Lina rose from her chair and grabbed her purse as if to leave. Chip grabbed both of her arms and went in for a hug and kiss. Lina was high and began to forget she was in public. The anger and hurt had taken over her senses. She swung her arms down with force to free herself.

"Go hug and kiss your wife, Chip. I know you're married."

Chip's demeanor and facial expression were not changed at all by Lina's statement. His eyes remained full of adoration, and he continued to smile, as if his omission about his marriage status was just some silly hurdle they would need to get over.

"Lina, I wasn't divorced, but things have been *so* terrible in my marriage," Chip informed her as he moved back in to caress her arms.

Everyone in the café was now sneaking glances at them with suspicion. When the table of customers next to them got up to leave, Kermit and his buddies immediately took over their seats for a closer listen. Chip noticed Kermit and his crew and gave them his sexiest smile. Chip didn't have a gay bone in his body, but it still fed his ego to think that gay men wanted him or found him attractive. Chip didn't mind who his admirers were, as long as they were admiring. Lina began to break from Chip's grasp.

"Listen, I *wasn't* divorced," explained Chip, as the naïve smile remained on his face. "But my wife saw pictures of you on my phone, so now I really *AM* getting divorced. It all worked out!" He acted as if he had just delivered fantastic news.

"Suspicion confirmed!" exclaimed Kermit, proudly but quietly to his friends. He crossed his legs and sipped his drink with delight as he continued to watch the drama unfold.

"What!?" exclaimed Lina in disbelief at Chip's confession.

"No, don't worry," assured Chip, bending a bit at the knees, as if to beg briefly, while trying to get Lina to look at him.

"She didn't move to this area until after you were long gone in California! She doesn't know who you are, and she has a broken leg anyway! She won't be at any of the games! It's all good, really!"

Lina looked at Chip, incredulously. "All good? No, Chip. Lying to me is not *all good*."

"Lina, please."

"I can't deal with this right now," said Lina as she headed to the back of the café and up the stairs to join her kids and Greta.

One of Maxi's friends at her table looked confused before asking Maxi, "I thought she was gay?!"

###

Monday afternoon had rolled around and Lina was sitting across from Kirk Kavanaugh in his office. He was silently looking over paperwork, so Lina checked her phone. There was another text from Chip. He had been texting all weekend, and she had been ignoring him. Another text came in, and it was Fitz. Lina smiled to herself. *Fitz IS a good guy and the sex WAS actually better than with Chip*, she thought. But Lina couldn't possibly think about Fitz for long when she was sitting across from Kirk. She still felt butterflies anytime Kirk was near, but then her pesky commonsense and morals would take over and remind her that it wasn't meant to be. She had to stop thinking about him like that. *This is a business relationship*, she thought.

Kirk finally spoke, "I'm really surprised they gave you the account number after all that! Didn't you call a few times?"

Lina held her palms up to the air and shrugged innocently, as if she had no idea why suddenly it was fine for her to have the account number, when it hadn't been before.

"So, what does this mean? Does she have to get out now or what?" asked Lina, hopefully.

"Well, I met with Carol this morning. I showed her the documentation of foreclosure from the bank, showed her payment history, everything! That woman looked me in the eye and said she would never *not* pay. She said she had NEVER missed a payment! Even though I just showed her *all* of the evidence! I mean, in all my years practicing law…"

"See!" exclaimed Lina, vindicated. "I told you and everybody else who would listen! Everyone just thinks I'm a spoiled brat who is being mean to the poor widow who took until age fifty-five to find her true love." Lina stuck her finger in her throat and made a sound to emulate throwing up. "Do you believe me now that she's fuckin crazy? Master manipulator."

"Well, here's the thing. She's refusing to vacate the property! She said if the house is in foreclosure, then it is *your* responsibility as the owner to use your inheritance to pay off the house," informed Kirk, visibly irritated and stressed.

"Whoa, wait!" said Lina, holding up her palm like a stop sign. "She wants *me* to use *my* inheritance to pay off the mortgage on *my* house that I legally own, so she can live in it for free?! Are you *FUCKING* kidding me right now?"

"You can't make this shit up, Lina. Unfortunately, I am *not* fucking kidding."

"Well…she obviously broke the requirements of the pre-nup…so what do we do now?" asked Lina, desperately.

"Well, there's no question that she has no legal right to be in the house. I have officially advised her to retain her own legal counsel."

Lina could feel her temperature rise as she thought about how Carol didn't care if the house was lost, because it wasn't hers anyway. Lina thought about how her Mom used to bake cookies with her in that kitchen. She thought about her old bedroom, and the laughter that she and both of her parents had shared in the dining room. She remembered how proud her mother had been of her tomato garden. A tear welled in the corner of her eye when she thought of the tree that she and her grandfather had planted together in the yard, as a memorial to her mother. The tree had grown tall and strong. Carol had that tree chopped down almost as soon as she had moved in, and then apologized to Bill through tears that she hadn't known the tree was in honor of Fara. Lina had no doubt that bitch had known full well. She composed herself as Kirk interrupted her thoughts.

"The thing is, I have never encountered anything like this, ever. I've been trying to contact Jack, but he's in Bora Bora with his wife right now. Since she wasn't actually a tenant per se, I think this has now become a squatter situation!"

"Oh, great," said Lina, sarcastically.

"Don't worry. The law is on your side. I will handle this. But unfortunately, there is more we have to go over," he said as he moved the next stack of paperwork in front of him and let out a sigh before speaking again. "So, I arrived back from my *miserable* vacation to find several messages from contractors working on the Carlson project." Kirk's mood seemed to turn even worse.

"The city of Rochester has threatened to sue you. They paid Carlson's in full before your father's death, and because no work has been done, residents are complaining that the area is an eyesore. Basically, you have contractors who have been waiting around to get to work but are held up by ONE contractor who hasn't done their part. It's now October, and the ground is about to freeze. Once the ground freezes, it's too late. They'll have to wait to dig until the spring. You can't afford this bullshit, Lina!"

Lina was caught off guard by Kirk's anger, and it wasn't helping her to contain her own. His lack of sympathy and understanding was adding to hers. She had been doing the best she could under the circumstances. She had no clue what she was doing when it came to the final Carlson's project.

"Have you even *fucking* been down there??! Or have you been too busy fucking the whole town?!" yelled Kirk, whose face was now beet-red with anger as he flew into standing position from his chair.

"WHAT THE FUCK ARE YOU TALKING ABOUT?!" yelled Lina, her face stuck in a look of pure surprise and mortification.

"You know, I suspected maybe you had a thing with Fitz because you were acting so strange when I caught you leaving his office that day. But I never thought you'd fuck Chip LaBeau because he's *married*. I mean, that's the fucking excuse you give me!"

Lina was completely caught off guard and was sick to her stomach. Her heart was pounding in her chest.

"Where are you even getting this from?"

"That douchey, blond guy who graduated in your class! What's his name…fuckin'… Kermit the frog!" yelled Kirk as he extended his arm and pointed towards the newspaper office that Kermit Karnes owned.

Lina continued to sit with her mouth open, in shock.

Kirk continued. "After I had the pleasure of dealing with your crazy fucking stepmother this morning, I went to the Dairy Bar for lunch. I'm sitting there at the counter, trying to eat my *fucking* burger in peace, and that Kermit guy is talking away to some chicks around our age. I heard all about it, Lina."

"Who were the girls he was talking to?" asked Lina, feeling even more embarrassed.

"They looked familiar, but I don't know who they are."

Great, thought Lina. *They are probably people I know.*

"Maybe instead of spending your days shaking your tits all over town, you should be running your fucking business, Lina!"

"It's not *my* fucking business, Kirk! It's my father's fucking business!"

She was now enraged. All of her bottled-up emotions were coming to a head. She could no longer, and would no longer, keep her composure.

"Do you think my life is easy? Do you *really* think my life is fucking easy, Kirk? I have two seven-year-old children who have homework, projects, birthday parties, issues at school, sports. My husband is a cheater who won't even communicate with me! I'm basically a single mom, Kirk!" Lina's arms and legs were trembling with emotion as she continued. "And now, I'm supposed to just step into someone else's life, someone else's area of expertise, someone else's world that I know very little about, and just handle it perfectly!?"

Kirk looked down at the desk.

"I suddenly have deadbeat tenants who call me and tell me to fuck off," Lina said. "I have taxes and maintenance to deal with on those properties. I have a wicked stepmother from hell who won't even give me access to my mom's house or things…" She paused in an effort to hold back her tears. "I haven't even had a chance to grieve yet, Kirk! Did you know that just four months ago, I was lying in bed with my arms wrapped around my father's dead body? After begging Carol to let me in? I had to *beg* her to see my dad who just died, Kirk. His body was still warm." Lina choked back more tears as she said that statement out loud. She had never discussed any of this with anyone. "How the fuck am I supposed to take on the responsibility of someone else's life, when I'm barely treading water in my own?!"

"Lina, I'm..." started Kirk, now sitting calmly and feeling slightly ashamed.

"NO!" yelled Lina as she rose to a standing position. "And you have no right to judge me! I thought teenage guys were the horniest! Ha! Nope! The middle-aged men of this town are the horniest bastards I have *ever* encountered! They are relentless!" She grabbed her purse. "And you're no different!" She turned and left the office.

Lina bolted through the parking lot, reached her car, and climbed inside. She gripped the steering wheel with both hands as she stared blankly through the windshield. The humiliation was sinking in, and the only thought that came to her broken mind was a line from Emily Dickinson's poem "I'm Nobody! Who are you?" Without any thought, the words involuntarily trickled from her lips. "How public, like a frog," she whispered to herself, almost breathlessly with eyes that bore too much emotion to even cry. After a long pause, she pulled herself together enough to put the car in reverse and silently headed home.

<u>CHAPTER SEVENTEEN</u>

<u>2016-Snapping to it</u>
"Lose Yourself"
by Eminem

Lina was at home now. She removed her make-up and changed into comfortable clothes before crawling into bed. She still had an hour before she needed to collect the children from the bus stop, and she just wanted to hide. *The whole town probably knows by now*, she thought.

As she lay in bed, she decided her main focus needed to be the parking lot construction project. She briefly considered giving in and taking the Aunt Sophie route of suicide, then she quickly pushed that from her mind as she pictured her children's faces. She thought about how Aunt Isobel was far away from these troubles in England, and how her cousin Miles on Wall Street, was clearly not interested in assisting his estranged cousin. Miles had barely had any interest in his own mother over the years, it seemed. Lina had never felt so alone in life. She wished she had a supportive partner to help her maneuver her way through this. Her family had abandoned ship, and she knew it was entirely up to her. Lina was tired of being strong but knew she needed to complete this project as quickly as possible. One more hurdle she would have to jump over, in order to free herself.

She began to think about her grandfather and remembered that day, when she was eleven, that he had taken her to Bill's jobsite. Bill had been yelling at the Italian workers. She remembered Grandpa defending Bill to her, *"If you don't take control of your business, you won't have a business."*

Lina reluctantly called her father's secretary, Helen. She left a voice message.

###

The following morning, her cell phone buzzed. It was Helen calling from Carlson's Lumber. It was routine for all contractors to check-in with Helen for scheduling and other matters.

"Nicolina, hi. It's Helen. The contractors who are digging the initial hole are there at the jobsite."

Lina breathed a sigh of relief. They were actually there. It sounded positive.

"I went down there to take a look, since I know how upset you were on the voicemail. Anyway, they haven't done *anything.* And now they're saying they have to reschedule again because they have people out sick. This is the seventh time they've cancelled like this."

"You tell them I am coming right now and not to leave! Do *not* let them leave, Helen! I am coming down there *right now* to whip this bitch into shape!" said Lina as she hung up the phone and hurried to get dressed. She then realized she had used a phrase with Helen that her late father would have used.

Lina's Escalade pulled up to the jobsite. She spotted Joe Vicente, who she recognized as being the owner of the contracting company, Vicente's Digs. She knew most of the Italian contractors in the area, as most had shown up to her family funerals over the years, in order to keep a positive relationship with Carlson's Lumber and Building. She approached him hurriedly.

"Joe! Hey, what's going on? Helen said you guys were leaving. I need this job started two months ago!"

"Hey…Miss Carlson!" Joe said, surprised. "We were just getting ready to pack up. We have some guys feeling sick today."

Lina looked over at the workers, who all seemed to be having a good time. Nobody appeared to be ill. It then became clear to Lina that her suspicions about Joe and his company were true. Bill had already paid Joe to do the job before he became ill. It had been over a year now, and Joe had nothing but excuses. At this point, Lina knew without a doubt that Joe was just trying to wait her out. He hoped the entire deal would fall through. There was no way she would get back the money Bill had already paid. Lina turned back to face Joe Vicente.

"Your equipment is here," she said, pointing to the various construction vehicles that were parked on the site. "And the ground is about to freeze! You know as well as I do that would push the project into next spring. You are holding up all of the other contractors!"

"I can't do the job without enough men," said Joe, shrugging.

"You promised you would do it today, and I have a witnesses to this," stated Lina.

"I never promised such a thing, Miss Carlson. Who is this witness?" he said with a smug smile.

"It's Mrs. Pratt. And my witnesses are the Perillo family."

Joe stopped in his tracks and his facial expression turned serious. He knew who the Perillo family was. He knew Bill's late wife, Lina's mom, had been Sicilian, and Joe owed the Perillo Gambling House a lot of money. As Joe was still digesting what Lina had said, she turned and began walking towards the crew.

"Come on, guys!" she yelled as she carefully maneuvered each step over dirt and rocks in her designer heels and dress. "I need you to get to work. All of you look healthy! Please, I'm begging you!"

"Silenzio Puttana! (shut up, whore) Vaffanculo! (fuck you)." The crowd of Italian men broke out in laughter, and Joe froze.

Lina turned to face the men, the same way that her father had turned to face the crew all those years ago, when they began cursing at him in Italian. A different sort of boldness came over Lina, one she had never experienced before. A sense of courage that only comes with age and hardship. She was going to do everything in her power to take control of her business. Lina stood tall, took a deep breath, and then shouted confidently. "Sono Siciliana! (I'm Sicilian) Mia Madre! (my mother) and I know what you just said!" she stated in broken Ital-ish at best. She could only remember a few words from her grandparents, and they had spoken a Sicilian dialect, but she desperately needed to let these guys know who they were dealing with.

"Lavoro! (work)," yelled Lina as she waved her arms and clapped her hands together.

The men looked at Lina with surprise before chuckling with each other. They now found Lina more endearing and cute than anything.

"Get your teste (head) out of your culo (ass)!" she commanded in Ital-ish. "Or non ti pago! (I won't pay you)." This she remembered from hanging at the gambling house with Grandpa Mancini.

The men erupted into soft laughter, finding her even more adorable now. Joe made his way towards the men, so he could instruct them that they'd be completing the job that day.

Lina stopped him as he passed, "Tell them I will order lunch for everyone. This job begins *now*, Joe!"

"Yes, of course. We are starting the job right now! We have all the equipment here! We will have a beautiful hole dug for you today, Mrs. Pratt," said Joe, smiling as he nervously began to shout instructions at his crew in Sicilian.

Lina went and sat in her car the rest of the afternoon, watching them, to make sure they did the work. She ordered the crew lunch, as promised. As she sat in silence, watching the enormous hole being dug, she could feel tiny little weights being lifted from her shoulders.

The Perillo family didn't know anything about Lina's project for Carlson's or anything very personal about her. But Joe didn't know that. And she knew there was no way that Joe was going to call them and ask. Grandpa Mancini had taught her the importance of keeping a poker face. She was relieved that Joe Vicente hadn't called her bluff.

Lina made calls from her car to the other contractors, giving them a green light as soon as the city completed their first inspection.

The rest of the project went off without a hitch.

###

Lina had stayed up late scrubbing Frankie's cheer shoes with a magic eraser and laying out all the pieces of her uniform. It was the day of the annual "Monster Cheer" competition. This was the big event in which all cheer teams within the national organization competed for the winning title and trophy. The previous year, they had traveled to Chicago. Luckily, this year the MDCCF event was being hosted by Oakland University in Rochester, Michigan.

Lina sat on the bleachers at the local college with her son, Marty, and all the other exhausted parents. She looked at the brochure to find out when Frankie's team was scheduled to perform. She was disappointed to see they were second to last on the list. She let out a bored sigh as she put her arm around her son and looked at the clock on the wall. It was three o'clock. She checked her phone for texts. Nothing.

Lina looked to her left and was horrified to see Chip LaBeau with his son and wife, who was walking with crutches, enter the gymnasium. She saw Chip try to take his wife's arm to assist her as she angrily elbowed him and carried on by herself.

Shit! It hit Lina that the boys from the football team were required to attend to support the girls. This had slipped her mind as Marty would be attending with Lina, regardless. *What if she sees me and recognizes me from the pictures on Chip's phone*? Her stomach began to twist into a sick knot.

Chip spotted Lina and gave her a sad, desperate puppy dog look, as his wife struggled to get herself seated on the bottom bleacher. Lina pulled her hoodie up over her head and held onto it with her left hand, trying to keep her face hidden. She then crossed her legs and used her left thigh to support her left elbow as she made certain she didn't look to the left anymore. *I do not need this extra stress right now*, she thought.

As the Dallas team took to the mat to perform, she checked her phone again. There was a text from her young neighbor, Roy Weiss.

"All systems are go," it read.

"Excellent," she responded back.

Lina had a lot more on her mind than Frankie's team taking the Monster Cheer championship title. She noticed another text had come in. It was from Denise.

"I confirmed his schedule tonight with Sheila. He tried again to get her to come over to his house. Said he would be alone all night if she changed her mind."

Lina felt more weights lift from her shoulders. She had been meticulously crafting a plan for weeks. Denise didn't know why Lina was so interested in the schedule of Sheila's harasser, but she had been able to tell it was important. Sheila was a young lesbian at the café and one of the local police officers had been asking her out constantly. Lina had promised to tell Denise everything soon, and Denise didn't mind. She found it exciting, like she was an undercover spy.

A text came in from Mitzy. “I contacted your stepmother about needing renter’s insurance. She hung up on me. You may need to follow up with her.”

That won’t be necessary, Mitzy, she thought as she smiled to herself.

Lina’s eyes accidentally looked back to the left where she spotted Fitz chatting with Chip and his wife in the stands. Lina covered her face again and had a stiff neck by the time the competition ended.

CHAPTER EIGHTEEN

2016-The Takedown
"P. Funk"
by Parliament

Lina's red Escalade slowly pulled into the driveway of Walt Weimer. The lights in his house were on, as well as the porch light. *Good*, she thought. He was there as expected. She nervously pulled down her visor and checked herself in the mirror. "You've got this," she whispered to herself.

Walt's doorbell rang loud and long. She took a deep breath as she set her phone to record and waited in anticipation for him to answer the door. She slipped her phone into a shallow pocket in her handbag. She heard footsteps, followed by a pause. The blue door finally swung open.

"Lina!" exclaimed Walt with surprise and a big, horny smile.

Lina pushed her way in the door and shut it behind her. Walt, still thinking this was a social call, happily asked, "Can I get you a drink?"

Lina stared at Walt with a fake, seductive expression. She provocatively gazed into his eyes as she gently placed her hands on his chest. She slowly ran them down to his waist before turning his body and pinning his back to the closed front door.

"Remember that *special* day we shared together when I was sixteen?" she said in her sexiest, low, whisper-like voice.

"Yes," he said, now fully aroused and wrapping his arms around her. "I think that was your first time having sex." He used a sweet voice, as if speaking to a little girl. "I knew you wanted it, you were just too young and shy to ask." He smiled at her romantically as he leaned in for a kiss.

"I remember it really well too," she said, still speaking softly as she interrupted his impending kiss. Keeping her face close to his, her tone suddenly changed from sexy to stern. "And I can arrange for *you* to be taking it up the ass by noon tomorrow."

Walt's arousal turned to shock as she took a step back. She smiled at him, while holding her phone up and hitting the red button to end the recording, before placing it back in her purse. Without warning, Walt had his hand around Lina's neck, pinning her to the wall. Lina felt his grip tighten, as that all-too-familiar grimace came over his face. While she could still breathe to speak, she made up a lie. "That video was automatically sent to Ricky. It's on auto send."

Walt, being older and unsure if that was really possible, softened. He decided to err on the side of caution and released his grip. Lina was terrified but refused to let Walt see that.

"You will allow me to use your driveway tonight for as long as I wish," she commanded. "If I have *any* problems *whatsoever* at my dad's house, you will arrive immediately on scene. And the law will be on *my side*, no matter what. Do we have an understanding?"

"Ahh," uttered Walt as his mind raced.

"Good. Now give me all your cash," she said. That was not in her original script, but she was feeling empowered.

"Ah, um, o…okay," Walt managed to say nervously.

At that moment, Walt knew with certainty that he was fucked. In the past, he had been confident that nobody would believe a teenager over a police officer, but Lina was now an adult woman. Plus, this was a different time - not to mention his admission of guilt on video. He ran to grab his wallet, hurrying back to Lina. His hand shook as he produced a $5.00 bill from his wallet.

"That's it?" asked Lina with irritation.

"Well, I...I don't carry much cash."

"Listen to me," she said, leaning in, with her index finger pointed straight up, directly under his chin. "You will give me twenty thousand dollars in cash. I'll be nice and give you two weeks to come up with it. I don't care if you have to remortgage your house or take out a loan. I don't care what you do to get it. You have two weeks from today, or I'll drive straight to the cop shop!" As she paused for effect, it was as if decades of imprisoned pain bolted to the surface, desperate to escape through the wormhole that Lina's other detriments had been slowly sifting through, since her father's funeral. Her skin was suddenly crimson and her face shook as she released. "DO WE HAVE A FUCKING UNDERSTANDING???"

Walt's entire body vibrated as he stood, sweating, in the entryway of his home. He was only a year from retirement, and there was no doubt that Lina now had the upper hand. His mind raced to his credit score, and he briefly wondered if he would be able to come up with the cash.

"Oh, and leave Sheila the fuck alone too. Have you not met her girlfriend? Seriously, get a clue."

Lina paused to glare at Walt.

"You're my bitch!" she spat. "Don't even think of looking at or touching another kid. I'll be watching you." She stepped off Walt's porch. "Oh, and you were NOT my first. Thank GOD. Otherwise, I'd have thought your tiny dick was normal."

Full of adrenaline, but appearing calm, she slowly turned and walked back to her car. Walt watched her nervously for a moment before gently closing his door. *Part one of the plan was successful*, she thought, stepping up into her Escalade. *I will use Walt's money to pay for my divorce*, she thought. Walt's sins were going to pay for her mistake of marrying the wrong man, even though Lina could afford to pay for it herself now.

She put her Parliament playlist on the car stereo, adjusted herself for comfort, and then grabbed her vape pen from the console. She checked her phone for a text from her young neighbors, Roy and Tom.

"The cameras are disabled," read Roy's text.

She responded, "Excellent. You will find your reward in a cookie tin under the bushes outside your bedroom window. Delete this message."

Part two of the plan worked, she thought, feeling more relieved. She had left her college neighbor and his friend some pre-rolled joints as a token of appreciation. Then her stomach tightened, as the third part of her plan needed to materialize in order for her carefully-orchestrated takedown to be successful.

During one of her recent wakeful nights, Lina had decided that she would need a way to get Carol out of the house long enough for her to get inside. Lina had brainstormed how she might accomplish this. What was one thing that Carol would not decline an invitation to? What does Carol really want? Lina had remembered how important socializing with Bill's friends had been to Carol. She recalled how her stepmother would always act as if she were close with Bill's friends and their wives at other social events, even though they hardly knew her and didn't much care for her. She thought back to how Carol had shown up to the art gallery opening, even though she hardly knew the owner. Lina was certain that Carol's currency was social status. She would never dream of turning down an invitation to the annual "Club Members Social" at the country club. Lina had asked Mr. Glickman to have Carol invited, just long enough to receive an invitation. Mr. Glickman's son, Mayor Seth Glickman, then did Lina the favor of having her removed from the guest list. In order to buy Lina more time, Mitch Marquette had claimed and bragged to Lina that his job at the dealership somehow enabled him to disable cars remotely. She hoped this was true and was depending on Mitch to help add more time in her quest to infiltrate the house. Lina had to be ready as soon as Carol's car left for the event.

She continued to vape while listening to the long, six-minute masterpiece by Parliament. "P Funk" was the perfect song for this calm before the storm. The right amount of soft, groovy jazz mixed with a motivating burst of pure Detroit funk. George Clinton's voice was hypnotic, soothing, and motivating. She took a series of long puffs from her vape pen, exhaling each one slowly and methodically, as the little smoke figures danced into oblivion, honoring the music before descent.

Lina glanced at the dashboard and saw it was seven o'clock. If Carol was planning to attend, she would be leaving any second. Looking with her binoculars, she let out a sigh of relief when she saw the light from the bottom of her late parent's garage slowly appear. It gradually illuminated brighter from a small crack at the bottom until Carol's car was fully visible. Just as the song was shifting into the chorus, she took a long drag from her vape, set it in the console, and shifted the car into drive. Lina loved when songs just happened to coincide with what was happening.

"Give me strength, Mom. I'm about to exterminate that cockroach from our house," she whispered.

Lina continued to groove with Parliament, slowly gliding along the residential streets, taking her time to ensure she wouldn't be noticed by Carol. *Sucker*, she thought with a small, evil laugh.

After Carol's car had fully disappeared into the night, Lina pulled into her late mother's driveway. Using a garage door remote that had been left in the Corvette that Lina inherited, she hit the button and cruised inside. Lina's calm had now changed to adrenaline-fueled determination.

She jumped out of her car and quickly closed the garage behind her. She ran to lock down the garage door from the inside. As she made her way into the house, she took a breath. Lina's eyes surveyed the residence. As usual, Carol had left the kitchen piled with dirty dishes, and various clutter adorned the living room.

"Unbelievable," she whispered to herself.

Her thoughts and focus were saved with a loud pounding on the door. Lina was expecting Ricky.

Ricky was ready with a small toolbox and new doorknobs they had purchased days earlier at the hardware store.

"Change the locks, and I'll cut the wires," commanded Lina as she trembled with urgency. Ricky gave a quick nod as he went to the front door first.

Lina was prepared with new, sharp shears in her purse. She ran to the den and began cutting the surveillance wires. She imagined each wire being Carol's throat as she cut with precision and force. Like a pro, she walked quickly from room to room, cutting each wire with one clip. The college kids may have disabled them remotely, but she needed those cameras *killed* for good. Lina's phone began to ring from inside her purse. She set the scissors down on a desk and answered a call from Mitch.

"Hello?!" she answered. She heard what sounded like thumping noises and a chimp screaming in the jungle.

"Lina! Hey, sorry, but I couldn't disable Carol's car! Eight Mile Mary is here…and she's channeling. She's channeling HARD...SO HARD," he said, breathing heavily and sounding more intense. "Channel it good, baby, CHANNEL!"

The screeching animal noises became louder. Lina's jaw dropped in disgust as she held the phone away and hit the red button to end the call.

"SHIT!" yelled Lina, still shaking off the ick factor.

"WHAT?" called Ricky.

"Eight Mile Mary is channeling with Mitch, and he didn't disable her car! SHIT!" she rambled, frantically.

"Did you really think Mitch could do that, Lina? He just wants to get in your pants."

She ran into the bathroom and looked at the mirror. *Please still be there*, she thought.

"RICKY! COME HELP ME!" she called out.

Ricky ran in, prepared with his drill. The two struggled to get the mirror down. After finally getting all the screws out, Ricky put down the drill. The two friends maneuvered the heavy, old mirror to the ground and leaned it against a wall in the hallway. Lina was almost afraid to look.

Still shaking, she was ready for the moment of truth. *Had her father ever mentioned the hiding spot to Carol? Did he even remember it was there after all those years? Did he remove the gold and other possessions before his death?*

Lina walked back into the bathroom and looked at the shelves. There was the fireproof safe, along with other familiar items that she had forgotten about. She pulled the safe from the shelf and was relieved to find it unlocked. Her hands trembled as she peered inside to find some rare coins, Fara's jewelry that had been inherited from her own mother, and some old family pictures. Then she spotted the dark-blue, velvet bag the size of a deck of cards, just as she remembered. She reached for the bag and gently lifted it. It felt heavy. She slowly pulled back the velvet to reveal a golden color. She held her breath and smiled before rapidly removing the object to reveal the gold block. Laughing and crying at the same time, droplets of stress, grief, and betrayal escaped her body with each tear that fell.

"I take it that's the infamous gold bar!" exclaimed Ricky, kneeling beside her on the bathroom floor. He put his arm around her shoulder as they studied and ran their fingers down the shiny, smooth jackpot that Ricky had only heard about.

"What the hell are you doing in my house?" scowled an angry female voice. A male voice was then heard calling out from another room "Want me to call the cops, babe?"

Lina and Ricky froze. A shot of fear ran up and down each of their spines in unison. Lina had prepared for this moment and was ready for a fight.

Lina rose from her kneeling position, as Ricky remained on the floor, watching. She stood tall before looking Carol in the eye and slowly sauntering toward her. Once toe to toe with Carol, Lina presented a devious smile. "*Whose* house?" asked Lina.

Carol's demeanor quickly went from self-righteous to that of a frightened child.

"I am to stay here as long as I wish. The documents say zis," proclaimed Carol, looking at Ricky in hopes of manipulating his mind against Lina. They all paused when they heard the back door slam. Carol's male companion had decided not to stay.

"You *know* you let this house go into foreclosure, which breaks the contract you signed," stated Lina.

Carol was holding the garage door remote in her hand. She had brought it in with her, thinking it needed new batteries when the garage had refused to open.

Lina grinned sweetly, taking a step closer to Carol until they were nose to nose. She placed a light grip over Carol's hand, which clutched the garage remote, as she leaned in closer. "I'm…in control…now," Lina said as she tightened her grasp on the remote and ripped it from Carol's hand.

Lina walked to the kitchen and texted Walt Weimer as Ricky finally stood.

"You have twenty minutes to grab whatever belongs to YOU and get the fuck out of here!" called Lina from the kitchen.

Just then, Deacon Tom Kowalski peered in the front door and interrupted cheerfully. "Hi all! I was just visiting with some parishioners across the street and saw you all here with the door wide open! I thought I saw Lina in here," said Tom as he craned his neck to look towards the kitchen. "Anyway, thought I'd say hel-"

"Shove it up your ass, preacher!" scowled an angry Carol.

"I...I'm a deacon," stammered Tom, dumbfounded, as he realized this wasn't a good time. He quickly ducked out.

"She cannot do this! Bill would not allow me to be thrown into the street! I call the police, they come," shouted Carol to Ricky in desperation.

Lina entered the room again. "You won't be thrown into the street," said Lina, grinning pleasantly as she slipped on her other driving glove. "Fred is expecting you at Fairview. It shouldn't take you long to pack, since very little in this house actually *belongs* to you."

Carol knew it was over and began to feel slightly optimistic about moving into Fairview. *Living in Fairview would be much more impressive to everyone,* she thought. *I could say Bill left it to me, instead of his spoiled sister and daughter. It will prove to everyone what I say about Lina. My love and I could finally live in luxury. We just have to get rid of Isobel in the spring.*

Lina and Ricky both watched as Walt Weimer appeared in the main doorway, still wide open.

"Officer Weimer! What a lovely surprise!" chided Lina in her best 1950s persona. "Would you be a *darling* and stay to help us see Ms. Lipschitz out?"

"It's Mrs. *Carlson*," corrected Carol.

"Whatever you say, bitch," said Lina with a polite smile. She turned and walked toward the door, motioning for Ricky to finish the lock change.

As Carol went to her bedroom to pack, Lina approached Walt. "Remember our deal," she said firmly. "I trust you'll see Carol out?"

Walt nodded somberly. “Don’t worry. I’ll make sure she leaves and that the house is secure. I’ll…I’ll do everything, Lina.”

She was confident that Walt wouldn’t dare mess this up. She collected the treasures uncovered from behind the mirror. Then she and Ricky finished the locks, before sitting together on her childhood steps. They had shared so much laughter on those cement slabs over the years. Even tears when discussing break-ups or the time that Lina had tripped and skinned her knee on them. She thought about the boys who had nervously walked those steps before knocking on young Lina’s door. Kirk with his model good looks and Chip with his charm. The pair quietly walked back to their vehicles when they heard Carol was ready to depart.

CHAPTER NINETEEN

2016-Free to Be
"Because I'm Me"
by The Avalanches

It was Tuesday, November 8, 2016. Lina was lying on her bathroom floor, sicker than she had been in years. Ricky was on his way over to bring her soup, Vernors soda-pop, and 'any kind of flu drugs he could find,' as per Lina's request.

It was election day, and Ricky was secretly elated that Lina would be too sick to vote. He had decided he would vote for Hillary first, and then tend to Lina and make sure she didn't leave the house. He felt bad that she was sick, but he knew she would recover soon enough. And he did *not* feel bad that Trump would be getting one less vote in Michigan. As he prepared to leave his apartment, he caught himself giggling with delight as he passed a mirror.

Lina was too nauseated to care who won the election. Her internal anger had begun to cool after Lina had successfully taken back her mother's home. Carol had been arrested the first night at Fairview when Fred called the police for a domestic violence issue between Carol and the mysterious boyfriend. Lina had already reported her and given the address of Fairview to Homeland security, which Lina assumed had probably made matters worse for Carol.

Lina wasn't quite sure if she was sane enough to make life-altering decisions though. She doubted if she should be casting a vote that would affect the whole United States of America.

Happy to sit this election out, she wondered what was taking Ricky so long with the Vernors.

###

Almost Thanksgiving, the city of Rochester was trading in their apple cider and donuts for the winter holiday festivities. Each year, all the businesses along Main Street would be strung from ground to roof with lights that would illuminate the entire city. Horses pulling elegant white carriages filled the streets of this Detroit suburb. It was known to be the most photographed Main Street in history. The city's famous "Big Bright Light Show" had begun the evening before with the official lighting of the city hosted by a local radio DJ. The Detroit news stations were always there to capture the excitement. The city would light up at exactly five-o'clock every evening until January.

Lina had taken the kids to the official lighting ceremony the evening before, but tonight the twins were staying home with Luke. The confrontation with Lina a month prior had frightened Luke, and he was trying to be home more and spend time with the kids. He still wasn't communicating much, but Lina was grateful he was at least making an effort to be present for the children.

Lina was alone with her thoughts as she walked along Main Street, enjoying the rare, sunny November afternoon. She and Ricky had decided it was time to have their big talk with Greta and Denise, and Lina was rehearsing what she might say.

The "Big Bright Light Show" brought in droves of people and served as an unofficial, end-of-year 'bonus' for the small business owners downtown. This also meant that after the city lit up nightly at five o'clock, Motown Mood Café would be swamped. Lina knew if she and Ricky were going to find an opportunity to speak to the moms anytime soon, it would have to be during the day, before five.

She made her way down the street looking very casual in her white puffer and Fendi sneakers. Her brown knit cap with a brim matched the brown Fendi logo that adorned her shoes. She kept her car fob and her phone in her coat pockets and her vape pen in her car. She didn't like to carry a bag when the city was crowded with strangers. She was feeling extra free and comfortable as she walked to the beat of Aretha Franklin's "Rock Steady" and into the café.

Lina saw Ricky talking to the DJ at the booth. She knew they were most certainly going over the approved songs list from the city manager. Although Motown Mood was permitted to raise the music volume on the outdoor speakers for the holiday season and "Big Bright Light Show," all songs had to be pre-approved by the city. Every tune played had to be family friendly, and they were required to put holiday music in the mix. Ricky noticed Lina and gave her a nod of acknowledgement as he finished his brief meeting with the DJ.

Ricky left the booth, and the two met each other with looks of sheer terror.

"You ready for this?" asked Lina.

"As ready as I'll ever be," said Ricky as he took a deep, nervous breath.

The pair approached Denise, who was standing near the bar.

"Mom, can Lina and I talk to you guys about something?" asked Ricky as he placed an arm around Denise's shoulder. Her eyes grew wide as she turned to face him and realized this must be something serious. Greta noticed this exchange, and Denise motioned for her to join them.

"The kids want to talk!" called Denise to Greta.

Greta approached, holding the schedule for that night's live music lineup that she had been looking over. "They want to talk?" asked Greta as she eyed the two suspiciously, like they were teenagers about to confess to something they had done. “What did you do?"

“Nothing, Ma," assured Ricky as he guided his two mothers to the booth that was practically hidden in the back. After the four took their seats, Denise and Greta watched Ricky expectantly for an explanation.

Lina knew that Ricky’s problem would affect his mothers much more directly, so she decided to go first. “I want to get a divorce," blurted Lina.

The two matriarchs looked at each other for a moment before Greta spoke. “Is this something you’re sure about, honey?" asked Greta gently as she reached for Lina’s hand.

“Yes, he has been cheating on me, as you know.”

Both moms nodded.

“And I’m sure the rumor mill has already made its rounds to the café. I haven’t been perfect either," confessed Lina as tears began to flow. “I just don’t want to make a huge mistake! He is the father of my children…”

Denise scooted closer to Lina and wrapped her arms around her.

“Have you talked to a lawyer yet? You need to protect yourself. Maybe Jack Nelson or that Kirk you’ve been working with?" offered Denise.

“You could move into your parent’s house now," offered Greta.

“Do you think I’m making a huge mistake though?" Lina asked as she wiped her tears.

“Only you can answer that, sweetheart. But whatever you decide, we will support you one hundred percent," said Denise, rising slightly from her seat to give Lina a kiss of comfort on her head.

Greta gave Lina a long, serious look. A kind smile came over her face as she took Lina’s hand and spoke to her gently.

"If you're looking for permission to get divorced, *we* can't do that for you, Lina. Only *you* can give yourself permission to be happy. Once you give yourself permission to be happy, the answers you seek will appear. You have *our* permission, but it only matters if you give *yourself* permission," said Greta, ending with a firm, extra-loving squeeze to Lina's hand.

Lina could feel the burden of her decision begin to lift. Having the support from the moms was what she needed in order to move forward.

"Thank you," she whispered to them each as she continued to dry her eyes and blow her nose.

Denise was emotional too, watching Lina go through this, and was doing the same.

Greta looked at Ricky. "Well? What have you got?" asked Greta, turning the conversation to her son.

Ricky decided to go with the 'rip off the Band-Aid' approach, as Lina had.

"I'm in love!" exclaimed Ricky.

Lina watched as Greta and Denise looked at each other with surprise and smiled.

"Are you getting married?" asked Greta.

"Oh, oh. Did you get someone pregnant?" joked Denise.

Ricky took a deep breath and let it all out.

"I auditioned to be a back-up dancer for a Korean pop star. His name is Jihoon, and we've been seeing each other for a few months. Not only am I in love, I've been offered a back-up gig on the road with him. The tour begins right after the holidays," confessed Ricky with desperation in his voice.

His mothers exchanged a look. The reason Ricky wanted to speak with them was sinking in now. They had planned to leave for Miami right after the holidays, while Ricky took over the café. They were preparing to retire and slowly pass the torch on to Ricky.

"I'm forty years old. You know how incredible this is to even get an *offer* to tour at my age."

A thoughtful expression came over Greta's face as she looked at Ricky and Lina.

"You are both forty. I've been expecting this to happen," she said, smiling bigger now. "In the Jewish religion, forty represents transition, change…renewal, new beginnings. It would be morally wrong to stand in the way of your evolution, Ricky. You two should be studying the Kabbalah materials I ordered for you! Our rabbi said forty is the age you should start!"

Although Denise was silently conceding that Greta was right, she looked down at the table. She was happy for her son's new beginning, but she wasn't sure how to feel about it. It would affect her own evolution of spending winters in Miami.

Lina saw this and quickly offered a solution she had been planning to present. "I will run Motown Mood in Ricky's absence!"

The moms looked at each other, surprised by the offer.

"Seriously! I can do this! Your other employees have been here for years and know what they're doing. They can guide me. I can hold down the fort for you until spring, when you return," said Lina, watching their faces closely for a reaction, before adding, "I'm going to need to get back into the working thing anyway."

Greta and Denise gave each other another telepathic look before turning to her in unison.

"You're hired!" exclaimed Denise.

After she and Lina stood to hug each other, she turned her attention back to Ricky. She made her way to his side of the table. "I'm so happy for you!" she exclaimed. "So when do we meet him?"

Greta was still seated, watching Denise and Ricky hug.

"Is he Jewish?" asked Greta with a straight face, before laughing.

"Nope, as I said, he's Korean," said Ricky. He laughed at his mom's joke and wiped away a tear of relief.

The two exchanged a hug before Greta remembered they needed to be in work mode. "Okay, we have to get back to work! You two go take a walk!" commanded Greta, looking at the clock. "You both need some fresh air. It's almost five."

Five o'clock was when the city would light up. The crowds were about to leave work and invade the town. Greta was still motioning for them to go walk, so the two headed towards the front. Ricky stopped at the DJ booth and took a quick glance at the songs he had up on his screen.

"Play this one!" he quickly advised his young employee. Then he offered Lina his arm and escorted her towards the front of the café.

Ricky wanted something upbeat for their stroll, and he also wanted to take advantage of the fact that they could play music much louder than usual due to the holiday. The beginning vocals of the song "Because I'm Me" by The Avalanches began. It was a new mix using the music from the old Detroit hit "Want Ads" by Honey Cone. He and Lina had listened to this new mix before and really enjoyed it. The opening chorus of the song was playing as the two reached the glass door at the front of the café. They paused to give each other subtle smiles as they zipped up their jackets.

They exited the cafe door and entered Main Street, walking swiftly, before slowing down as the change in scenery and cool air produced a calming effect. The instrumental portion of the sampled Honey Cone song, recorded in Detroit, seemed to lift the moods of everyone walking the street in anticipation for five o'clock, when camera shutters would click and children would stare in wonder as the city would illuminate.

They continued to walk side by side, but each looked straight ahead, in deep thought, as the burden and fear of letting others down began to dissipate. As the music and vocal samples of Honey Cone filled the air, it was as if the poetry of Detroit's past, the emotions that the weather brought, and the air that they breathed, had been encapsulated and preserved forever by Detroit artists. The same mix of melancholy and sheer delight that former seasons had brought and taken, the sound that had inspired an industry of audio candy and eventually a café, thirty minutes north of Detroit, called Motown Mood.

Ricky and Lina's faces had independently softened, and each sneaked a peek at the other. Smiles began to form and stress dissolved into relief, producing tiny bubbles of elation within them. They were adults and didn't need permission to do anything, but the fact that Denise and Greta said it was okay for them to make life-changing decisions, had let the light of possibility shine. The two caught each other's eyes, as they stole another glance and grins emerged.

As Camp Lo began the rap portion of the Avalanche's remix, Ricky and Lina both instinctively jumped to the side, with one leg bent and the other leg extended. Ricky veered to the left, Lina to the right. The dancer in Ricky couldn't resist and his soul mate, Lina, was riding a telepathic vibe, her spirit synching with his, as they ignored the world and danced like the town was their stage.

The two came back together and placed one palm against the other's as they locked eyes and did a half circle with the music, in marching fashion, before stopping and switching sides to repeat. Ricky then grabbed Lina's hand and twirled her freely and wildly with the music.

Ricky began to show off his professional dance moves, while Lina tried her best to keep up and follow. Bill had never enrolled her in dance lessons, but Ricky had taught her over the years, and she had been a quick study. He unzipped his jacket as he did a sexy turn and grabbed Lina's hands. The two did a twirl before Ricky fist-bumped some children who were now grooving to the music with their parents. A group of young, corner DJs sat on two benches that were on either side of a tall, cement flowerbed, taking a break, as they slapped their knees in groove with the music.

Ricky used a bench to step up and onto the tall, barren flowerbed that three teens were sitting on the front side of. He swung an imaginary bat to go with the song lyrics he was lip-syncing to. Everyone turned to watch as Ricky rapped along with the song and extended his hand to Lina, still on the ground below. She took his hand and used the other bench as a step to join him on the flowerbed, as the singer rapped. She was with Ricky now, dancing along the edge and singing with the music, as the teens stepped away and grooved as they watched.

The little boy's voice from the mix could be heard again, singing the bluesy lyrics. Ricky then jumped down, offered his hand again, and helped Lina back to the sidewalk. The pair continued to take steps forward, bending their knees down low with each, almost like "Laverne and Shirley" in their show opening. They suddenly stopped and stood stationary on one leg, while using their other to turn them, pulsing three times, before clapping and doing the same with the opposite leg in place, like they used to do at the clubs in the nineties.

As the two began to dance forward again, skipping in unison, an angelic vocal note from the original song boomed through the downtown speakers, as if the goddesses of Detroit's past had summoned the deities to let there be light.

"Ohhhh…"

Just then, the clock struck five and the city lit up like magic. The two gleefully continued dancing as they walked, throwing out their best moves, as they made their way.

The colored lights and the shiny spotlights cast upon the two best friends, as they lived out their own personal musical. This was their awakening, the lifting of their burdens as their souls shifted to a new chapter through dance. At age forty, their season was changing, just as the city transformed to a winter wonderland from a crisp, sunny autumn. It was their town, their turf, and they gave life to the land, just as the city gave life to them. It had made them what they were, molded them, and tonight was their performance for the heavens.

The upbeat melody shifted again, and the two automatically went into an old dance routine from their youth that Ricky had choreographed. It had been a long time, but the moves seemed to flow without effort, like riding a bike.

Ricky ran up the steps of an old shop and took Lina's hand to follow as they danced up and down the historical stairs. Once both were back at ground level, they began to skip to the beat, as they danced their way down the busy street. Witnesses called out things like *yeah* and *right on*, since it appeared to be a professionally choreographed dance routine.

As the last lyrics from the song rang over the downtown speakers, Mr. O'Malley was outside his store, "CUT OUT THAT CRAP!"

Ricky and Lina ignored him. They laughed and put their arms around each, other before turning the corner.

"That was near perfect choreography," bragged Ricky.

"Yeah, and I think I pulled a calf muscle," admitted Lina as the two threw their heads back and laughed.

CHAPTER TWENTY

2016-On to new greats
"Good as Hell"
by Lizzo

A week had passed, and Lina was in Downtown Rochester, Christmas and Hanukkah shopping, while the children were in school. She had always found it best to shop during the day, while most people were still at work. She noticed Mr. O'Malley, aka "Fuck Face," standing in the doorway of his store as she turned to enter the coffee shop.

Five minutes later, she emerged, holding two cups of coffee. She made her way down to O'Malley's and stopped in the doorway. She lightly tapped on the glass to get his attention. She took a step back, so he could open his door.

"Coffee?" asked Lina as she held it up and offered it to him.

Mr. O'Malley's expression instantly softened before quickly changing back to accusatory. "What do you want for it? I didn't ask you for no damn coffee! WHAT ARE YOU TRYING TO PULL?"

Lina simply gave him a loving, warm smile. The same type of smile that Denise would have given when killing someone with kindness.

"I don't want anything, sir. Merry Christmas," she said, still smiling, before turning in the doorway back onto Main Street.

Kirk Kavanaugh had been watching Lina from his office window. He wondered why on earth she had been talking to Mr. O'Malley and seemed to have bought him a coffee.

As Lina slowly made her way down the street, she suddenly heard Kirk's voice.

"Hey! Lina!" he called to her, slightly out of breath. He half-jogged to catch up to her. "What are you doing?"

Lina turned to face Kirk, and the two stopped walking.

"Hey, Kirk," said Lina with a shy smile. "Just doing some shopping." She felt really bad about their last exchange when she had stormed out of his office.

"Did I just see you bring coffee to Mr. O'Malley?" he asked in a teasing manner.

"Yes," she said. She took a deep breath, feeling grateful that Kirk didn't seem to be angry anymore. "This past year, I have realized that everyone has their own private battles going on, and the best thing to do is to just be kind." She gave herself a confident smile of approval.

"Isn't that in a Facebook meme?" he teased.

"Yes, but it's true," she admitted, slightly embarrassed. "Besides, something could have happened to him, to make him the way he is."

"Yes, being an alcoholic can make you that way," said Kirk with sarcasm.

Lina smiled and the two shared a brief, awkward moment before Kirk spoke again. "Look, I'm sorry. You were right. What you do is none of my business, and I feel so bad about our last meeting. I'm just…" Kirk took a deep breath before continuing. "I'm just so in love with you, Lina."

Surprised by Kirk's sudden confession, Lina broke eye contact and looked quickly to the ground. She felt her stomach flutter as a lightning bolt of excitement shot through her body. Her enthusiasm ended almost as quickly, though, when she remembered that he was married with two teenagers.

"You know how incredible those words would have been, if you had said them to me when we were teenagers?" she asked with a pained smile. "Or if you were actually available?"

The exchange was abruptly interrupted with the distant sound of Mr. O'Malley's hard voice. "There's no cream in this coffee!" complained Mr. O'Malley from his doorway.

"Beggars can't be choosers!" Kirk called back at him without even turning his body in Mr. O'Malley's direction.

"Who's beggin'?" he called back, before waving his arm dismissively and going back inside.

"Have you ever heard of 'no good deed goes unpunished'?" teased Kirk softly with a smile.

Lina and Kirk looked into each other's eyes. She focused on Kirk's masculine, sculpted jawline, and the sunlight revealed that he still had his childhood freckles.

Their moment was interrupted by the sudden presence of Mr. O'Malley. "Sweetheart, I'm sorry. I want to thank you for the coffee. That was kind of you, honey," he said as he gave a shy nod and turned to walk away. Before Lina and Kirk had a chance to digest what had just occurred, Mr. O'Malley called back to them, "And if you need anything from my store, you are welcome to come in. You gotta buy the stuff from me on eBay, but I got chips and pop to sell too."

Lina and Kirk looked at each other with wide eyes. When Mr. O'Malley was safely back inside, the two began to laugh.

"See!" exclaimed Lina as she gently tapped Kirk's chest with the back of her hand. "A little kindness can go a long way."

Kirk's mood became serious again as he continued to take in Lina's beauty. He longed to kiss her right on the street, in front of everyone, but he knew he couldn't. "So, what are your plans now? I'm going to miss seeing you all the time," asked Kirk, sadly.

“Well, I’ve decided to get a divorce. And now that Carol is out of my parent’s house, I’m going to move into it.”

“Have you heard anything about Carol? What ended up happening?”

“All I know is that she has legal issues to deal with. A couple of arrests. My Aunt Isobel’s driver, Fred, told me. He was there at the time. I’m not sure what will happen to her, but she is no longer my problem and it feels amazing! I’m free to move forward with my life now!" proclaimed Lina.

“You got everything you wanted," said Kirk, softly.

Lina *had* gotten everything she wanted. Carol was out of her life and she had her mother’s house back. She had successfully handled the final construction project, the tenants she had been in the process of evicting were gone, and she had all the money she was going to get out of her father’s estate. She had accepted the loss of funds that were left to Carol by Bill, but she was so grateful she had been the sole beneficiary of her father’s 401K. She was now able to free herself from her unhappy marriage and let go of her anger towards Carol. Things had worked out for her, but she was still in love with a married man.

“Yes, I did. Well, almost everything," she said as she looked back up into Kirk’s golden-brown eyes.

“Lina, I want to see you. I want to take you out somewhere. I want to be with you.”

Lina wanted nothing more, but she refused to be a homewrecker. She had her faults and was far from perfect, but she was not about to be the cause of someone’s failed marriage.

“Kirk, you have to make decisions about your own life before I can be a part of it. I would love nothing more than to be with you, but you and your wife need to figure things out first. If you become available, I’d like to be the first to know. But I can’t be a factor in your decision, okay?”

"Okay," he agreed, drinking in her violet eyes and holding back tears. "Fair enough. I should get back to the office now."

The Christmas song that had been playing over the speakers ended, and the opening notes of Lizzo's "Good as Hell" began to play. Kirk put his hands on the shoulders of Lina's pink puffer jacket before giving a little tap to the visor of her white, knit cap. She watched Kirk as he headed back in the direction of his office. Lina turned slowly to walk in her original direction when she heard Kirk's voice again.

"Hey! Don't you need a lawyer for your divorce?! I'm available!"

Lina spun around, walking slowly backwards and called back, "I don't know! I would need to read your reviews first!"

She giggled and spun forward, continuing her stroll down Main Street. She glanced back playfully to see Kirk standing with his palms to the sky laughing.

"Um, okay, call me!" called Kirk, his smile softening now. He knew he had important decisions to make in his own life.

Lina felt at peace as she took in all the holiday excitement that rippled through her hometown. Shoppers with merchant bags filled the sidewalks and laughed with friends, as they headed into the various restaurants for lunch.

She didn't know if she and Kirk would ever be together. Just like Scarlet O'Hara with Ashley at the end of the movie, Lina wondered if it had really been Kirk she longed for, or if she was just missing something within herself. Perhaps it wasn't meant to be, and she was also in no hurry to start any kind of relationship. Chip had finally stopped texting, football and cheer season was over for their league, and Fitz had invited her to his upcoming Japanese fencing match. Deacon Kowalski apologized, and was not only being supportive of Lina studying Kabbalah, he had also joined an online class with she and Ricky.

The deacon also smiled each Sunday when Lina would arrive to mass with her children.

Lina smiled, remembering how Grandpa Mancini would always remind her to 'Tell people who you are. Use that Carlson name!' Her connections in that suburban city had meant everything. Chip finding out Carol's citizenship status and past, Mayor Seth Glickman giving her tax details, and Matt Munson from her library days giving her crucial mortgage information. She felt comfort, knowing Grandpa and his wisdom still lived on through her. *What a gift*, she thought.

She looked at the mannequins in the various shop windows. She needed something to wear to Mr. Glickman's annual Hanukkah party. She giggled, hoping that Seth wouldn't try to turn his dad's party into a key one. She made a mental note of gifts she needed to buy and was grateful that she would be able to afford presents this year.

The only thing that Lina was certain of was that she was feeling happier and more hopeful than she had in years. She thought about the various phases and people in her life that had resulted in who she was so far. She smiled, thinking that she liked who she had become, and felt a jolt of excitement for the future.

A chilly breeze swooped in and caressed her face, as her feet retraced the concrete path of her childhood. She zipped her jacket up to her chin and wondered what her next "Great" would be.

CPSIA information can be obtained
at www.ICGtesting.com
Printed in the USA
LVHW031107020322
712194LV00004B/81

9 781647 199463

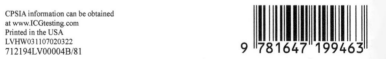